The Thin Blue Line Series

JUSTICE
for Loretta

Cindy -
Thank you for your support,
but especially your
friendship.
LeeAnne James

LeeAnne James

Black Rose Writing | Texas

ISBN: 978-1-68433-997-6
PUBLISHED BY BLACK ROSE WRITING
www.blackrosewriting.com

Printed in the United States of America
Suggested Retail Price (SRP) $21.95

Justice for Loretta is printed in Calluna

"*Justice For Loretta* is a skillfully crafted mystery that will leave readers anxious to turn the page as the story winds through the demise of a marriage and the legal process that follows. Author LeeAnne James schools her readers on the legal process from investigation to final justice and brings those readers to a conclusion no one could have imagined. I couldn't put it down and can't wait to read more of James' *The Thin Blue Line Series*."
– Barbara A. Luker, author of *I Carry Your Heart*

"A youthful courtship in college grows into a family lost in selfishness. James takes you on a journey from innocence and youthful pleasures, where love and understanding is replaced by control and lies, ending in the nightmare of a marriage gone horribly wrong."
– Stephen W Briggs, author of *Lies Leads to Death*

"Part domestic drama, part courtroom thriller, *Justice for Loretta* packs a punch as it traces the anatomy of a crime from the victim's early years until the aftermath of the trial. Peopled by fully drawn characters and a deep understanding of procedure in police stations and in the justice system, this suspenseful page-turner kept me reading late into the night on the way to its shocking final chapter that I'm still thinking about. A stellar debut from LeeAnne James."
– Steven Rigolosi, author of *The Outsmarting of Criminals*, an Oprah selection

"Things aren't always what they seem. I have an interest in stories that feature a hero who acts on his or her instincts that challenge a hasty or unjust conclusion *Justice for Loretta* is about just such a hero: Sergeant MacIntosh. Eager to find out what unfolded next, I read this book in two days. I found LeeAnne James' writing relaxing, consuming, and invigorating. I recommend this book for fans of crime solving, police procedure and the quest for justice against dissent."
– Sasha Lauren, author of *The Paris Predicament*

"Justice for Loretta is highly recommended to readers who enjoy surprise-ending mysteries filled with real-life police procedure and courtroom drama. Even those who read closely might not see it coming."
–John Marks, author of *Rail Against Injustice*

"A love gone sour, a murder, a dramatic court case. *Justice for Loretta* is an enthralling window into the evolution and resolution of a heinous crime. Or is it?"
– Jean M. Roberts, author of *The Frowning Madonna*

"Interesting crime novel that reads like a true-crime drama."
– Michael Veletsky, author of *The Guest List or Chatting with Saul*

Acknowledgements

I'd like to dedicate this book to my co-workers, who have given me endless supplies of material. A special thank you goes out to Luke for reading the manuscript and guiding me on the technical side of collecting evidence and presenting that material at trial. Always stay safe, my friends in blue.

A huge thank you goes out to my family, who never stopped supporting me. Without you, this wouldn't be possible.

*"You should never, never doubt
what nobody is sure about."*
—Willie Wonka

List of Characters

Carter Mills—Investment adviser
Loretta Sampson Mills—wife of Carter Mills
Steven Mills—Carter and Loretta's oldest child
Danny Mills—Carter and Loretta's middle child
Margaret Mills—Carter and Loretta's youngest child
Kim Sampson—Loretta's sister
Michael Mills—Carter's father
Suzanne Mills—Carter's mother
Tommy Gleason—family attorney
Bernie Lehrman—Loretta's lover
Irene Stapleton—Mills' family housekeeper
Sgt. Steve "Mac" MacIntosh—detective
Inv. James "Coop" Cooper—detective
Ofc. Brandon Powers—officer and evidence technician
Ofc. Patrick O'Malley—officer and evidence technician
Anita—civilian clerk
Dennis Wozniak—District Attorney
Kimberly Coville—Assistant District Attorney
Julie Fletcher—defense counsel
Bruce Keegan—defense counsel
Hon. Evelyn Johannsen—judge
Dr. George Schmidt—coroner
Dr. Anthony Santangelo—pathologist

John Foote—blood spatter expert
Kevin Porter—paramedic
Sarah Whitman—medic
Tony Anderson—broker at Mills, Hanover and Mills
    Financial Advisers
Dorothy Beckman—office manager at MH&M
Catherine Dumont—financial adviser at MH&M
Martin Haggerty—financial adviser at MH&M

JUSTICE
for Loretta

Prologue

After twenty-seven years of marriage, three kids and more grief than any man should have to put up with, she was dead. The ambulance, the cops, rescue squad, and the medical examiner just left. Now it was up to him to tell the kids what had happened, that she had fallen in the shower, hit her head, and died.

Margaret was the youngest. She had been home when Carter discovered his wife's body. Margaret and her mom were very close, almost inseparable. They were always shopping together, getting manicures and pedicures or going to the movies. They even volunteered together for every ridiculous event that came down the pike. School, church or a local charity, it didn't matter. They volunteered every chance they got.

The boys, however, were more stoic. Steven, the oldest, had left home for college four years before. Danny, the middle child, had followed two years after that. They would be heartbroken, but they were tough. He had taught them to hold their heads high. After all, a lot of responsibility came from being born into the

Mills family. Carter believed they were better than most people and needed to maintain a higher standard.

His family would get through this crisis the way they had through any of the others. As their father, he would see to it.

Chapter 1
1976

Loretta Sampson, at only thirteen years old, had her first experience with death. Timmy Rafferty had fallen from the top of the playground slide and hit his head on a rock when he landed. He was only nine years old.

Loretta was the only other person at the playground when Timmy fell. He wasn't moving after he landed on the ground, so she poked his shoulder with her finger and kept calling to him, but he didn't answer.

It scared Loretta that she might get into trouble. She ran the three blocks home as fast as she could to tell her parents. She would ask them what to do. They would know.

Loretta was crying and sobbing, but she took a deep breath and, in between hiccups, told them what had happened. She thought for sure she'd get in trouble, but her parents didn't scold her at all. Her mother, Adelaide, called 911 while Loretta and her father, Frank, jumped in the family station wagon and hightailed it back to the playground. Frank pulled up to the curb in front of the playground, just as a police car came around the corner and screeched to a halt in front of them.

It looked like Timmy hadn't moved at all. Loretta stood back and watched as the officer put his hand on Timmy's wrist, then on his neck. He put his ear next to Timmy's mouth for a few moments. He said something into the walkie-talkie radio he pulled from his waistband, then started pushing on Timmy's chest.

The ambulance arrived only a few moments later. Loretta and her father watched as two men in white uniforms picked Timmy up and put him on a stretcher. They pushed him into the back of the ambulance and sped off with the lights blazing and the siren wailing.

The officer asked Loretta what had happened. She told him what she had seen, that Timmy had been standing on the small platform at the very top of the slide when suddenly he tumbled over the side. No, she didn't know why he was standing up instead of sitting down on the platform. No, she didn't know what caused him to fall sideways. All she knew was that one minute he had climbed the ladder and was standing at the top of the slide, and the next thing she knew, he was on the ground, not moving and not answering her when she called his name.

Loretta and Frank drove back home after giving the officer directions to Timmy's house.

When Loretta was seventeen, her grandmother came to live with them after she'd gotten sick with cancer. Their house was small, with only three bedrooms, one for Loretta, one for Kim, and one for their parents. The grandmother would need a room of her own, so Loretta and her sister Kim doubled up in Kim's room. The grandmother used Loretta's room as her own. Loretta loved Kim and didn't mind sharing a room with her. That wasn't the issue. It's just that she needed the quiet and solitude her own room offered. Things could get noisy when everyone, meaning her mother, father, sister and two dogs, were all home. Loretta always had to work especially hard on her schoolwork because learning didn't come easily to her. Once she learned something, she could retain it, but while she was studying, her mind wandered, making it difficult to concentrate on her homework. It was even more of a struggle to keep her mind focused on her studies now that she didn't have her own familiar room with her own familiar desk.

As the illness progressed, the grandmother—her mother's mother—would just lay in bed. She could no longer come to the table for meals or even go to the bathroom without help. The family took turns staying with the grandmother in Loretta's old room, with Loretta's turn coming right after she got home from school. If she was lucky, the grandmother would sleep, which would allow her to do her homework in peace and quiet. Most times, however, the grandmother would moan even in her sleep, which made studying almost impossible. The doctor had prescribed morphine, but by then, even that wasn't enough to help control the grandmother's pain.

One terrible afternoon, the grandmother was very restless, shifting her legs and softly moaning from the pain. With that much distraction, Loretta knew she would never get her calculus homework done.

"Loretta, please ... come ... here," her grandmother said. It seemed to take all of her energy to get the words out.

Loretta slapped the cover closed on her math book with a sigh and turned towards the grandmother. "What?" Her tone was sharper than it should have been, but Loretta didn't care. Calculus was her hardest subject, and she needed quiet time in order to concentrate.

"You ... need ... to help ... me."

"Yes, I know. What do you need this time?" Loretta asked. She knew she was being rude. Snapping at her grandmother in other circumstances would have gotten her a reprimand from her mother, but she couldn't help it. She was getting frustrated. She needed to get her homework done, and it didn't look like that was going to happen.

"Please. I can't ... stand ... the pain. Give me ... the ... morphine."

"Grandma, you've already had it and you're not supposed to get any more medicine for another hour yet," Loretta said.

"Please, Loretta. You ... don't ... understand. I ... can't go ... on ... like this. Please. Give ... me enough ... morphine to ... end my ... suffering. It ... will be ... a blessing. Please."

Loretta was stunned. The grandmother was asking Loretta to give her an overdose of the pain meds. "You can't be serious, Grandma."

"I am ... very ... serious. I'm ... begging ... you, Loretta." With all of her energy spent from the conversation, the grandmother fell asleep. Loretta sat at the desk and stared at her grandmother. She wasn't sure she'd correctly understood what her grandmother was asking her to do.

An hour later, Loretta sensed a change in her grandmother's breathing. She didn't seem to take as many breaths as she normally did. Loretta ran to the top of the stairs and called to her mother.

"Come quick! Grandma's not breathing right!"

Her mother, father, Kim and Loretta all crowded together in the room with the grandmother. Her father sat on the bed next to the grandmother and put his hand on her chest.

"I'll call the doctor." Her father went back downstairs to make the call.

By the time the doctor arrived twenty minutes later, the grandmother had stopped breathing. Loretta didn't know who, but someone must have called the funeral home because a while later, men in dark suits came to pick up the grandmother's body. It was too much to bear, so the family stayed in the kitchen so they didn't have to watch as the grandmother left the home for the very last time.

Loretta stood off to the side and watched her family. Her mother was sobbing as she clung to her father. Her father had his arms wrapped around her mother and was rubbing her mother's back. He kept saying things like, "she's at peace now. She's with your dad, and I'm sure they're both happy."

Kim sat at the kitchen table and cried, her hands clutching a wad of tissues that she used to cover her eyes.

Loretta went back upstairs to change the sheets on the bed. Now that it was her bed again, she wanted her favorite sheets and comforter. She opened the window to air the room and get the stale odor of sickness and the grandmother out of the bedroom. With a heavy sigh, she sat down at her desk and picked up the calculus book, knowing that it was a wasted effort. After all, it's not like she'd be able to concentrate after everything that had happened today. Then again, it didn't really matter. She figured she wouldn't be going to school until after the funeral, anyway. Loretta was staring out the window with her chin in her hand, thinking about how much harder it will be to catch up after missing those few days at school. *Thanks a lot, Grandma.*

Chapter 2
1984

Twenty-one-year-old Carter Mills walked across the lush lawn of the campus with a bounce in his step, paying no attention to the sidewalks. He gave a nod of his head or a wave hello to those he passed on this brisk autumn afternoon, sometimes adding a wink if that person just happened to be a cute girl. Carter was in his third year of college studying financial investment at Johns Hopkins; he had decent grades, was captain of the soccer team, and he thought of himself as very handsome. A true lady's man. At 5'10", he was shorter than he would have liked, and yet, with his piercing dark eyes, wavy brown hair and wide, muscular shoulders, he had convinced himself he could have any woman he wanted. His father referred to him as the big man on campus because of his cockiness, but Carter didn't care. It was thanks to the old man's money that he had a new Buick Riviera convertible sitting in the student parking lot and a wardrobe of expensive designer labels. The old man could say whatever he wanted as long as he kept throwing the cash Carter's way.

There was, however, one flaw to his theory that he could have any woman he wanted. One woman, Loretta Sampson, was beautiful, and he wanted to get to know her, but she seemed immune to his flirtations no matter how many smiles and winks he threw her way. That was definitely not acceptable to Carter. Winning her over had become a challenge, and he hated to lose once he accepted a challenge, even one he brought on by himself. He wanted—no, he needed—to win her over, so he found his attention going more and more in Loretta's direction these days. In fact, at that very moment, he was on his way to class, and it was a class he shared with her. That thought brought a smile to Carter's face.

Carter walked into Legg Mason Tower for his Statistical Analysis class and took his usual seat to the left of Loretta. He looked at her and smiled, but she glanced away, choosing instead to watch Dr. Bower as he entered at the front of the classroom.

"Hey, Loretta. How are you today?" Carter asked. Whenever he looked at her, she got that deer in the headlights look and her cheeks took on a pretty pink blush.

"I'm fine, thank you." She glanced at him for a millisecond and then found a hangnail that needed her immediate attention.

Of course, Dr. Bower chose that moment to begin class, so Carter's conversation with Loretta would have to wait. Finally, class ended and the students all stood in unison in their rush to head out. But before she could gather her things, Carter put his hand on her elbow.

"Would you like to get a soda?" he asked. "I know of a quiet little place not too far from here."

Loretta looked at him wide-eyed, and her mouth dropped open a bit, before she turned her attention to the notebook she was trying to stuff into her backpack.

"Um ..." was all she could manage.

"I promise I won't bite." Carter gave her a warm smile.

Loretta glanced back at Carter. "Okay. Sure. Yeah, that would be nice." He watched as her face got red, but he thought her blush made her look even prettier.

"Yeah? That's great!" When Dr. Bower raised his head to look at them, Carter realized he'd said it a little louder than he should have. Carter, always trying to play the part of a gentleman, helped Loretta into her coat and offered to carry her backpack. She politely declined his offer and tossed it over her shoulders. They headed outdoors together and turned towards East Pratt Street, taking a shortcut by walking across the lawn. Carter didn't care for sidewalks when he had some place to go and could get to his destination quicker by walking on the lawn.

Once they got closer to the marina, they had to work their way single-file through the thick afternoon crowd, making conversation all but impossible. They walked into the soda shop and placed their orders at the counter. As the server made their root beer floats, Carter paid the bill and headed towards a table for two in a quiet corner of the room, with Loretta following. He helped her shed her backpack and coat.

They sat at the small cafe table opposite each other. "So ... here we are." Carter gave her one of those smiles that he believed to be irresistible to women. "So, tell me about yourself. Where are you from?"

"I'm, uh, I'm from Rockville. How about you? Where are you from?" Loretta asked. Carter noticed she had an annoying habit of looking down, rather than at him. Carter would have preferred that she kept her head up. She had gorgeous blue eyes, and he enjoyed looking at them.

"Rockville, huh? That's not too far from my home. I'm from Alexandria. So, what do you think of Dr. Bower's class? He's an excellent instructor, but he puts me to sleep," Carter said with a chuckle.

"Yeah, me too. It's a hard class so I have to struggle to stay awake and pay attention." She finally looked at him for longer than a second and gave him a smile.

"I could help you if you'd like. My dad's an investment adviser, so I've kind of grown up with this stuff. I used to help in his office whenever I was on break from school, so I learned a lot by working there."

"Really?" He watched as her eyes grew wide. "That would be great! Right now I've got a C in his class but I'd like to get at least a B."

He thought she might be warming up to him because she wasn't playing with the plastic straw in her root beer float as much.

"Sure. Actually, I'm not doing anything tonight. How about we get started right away?" he asked. "There's no time like the present, right?"

"Well, okay. Yeah, we could start tonight. I can meet you in the library. What time?" Loretta said, as she looked at her watch.

He was disappointed she didn't ask him to meet at her place. "It's my night to cook dinner for my roommates. I told them I'd make tacos, but that's quick. It shouldn't take long at all. How about we meet at 7:30?" Carter suggested.

"Sure. That works for me." Loretta got up to leave, pulling on her coat. Carter jumped up to help her with her coat and backpack. His father had always told him to act like a gentleman around the ladies.

"Thanks for the soda, Carter. I'll see you later," Loretta said with a smile.

"Can I walk you to your apartment?" He didn't want the afternoon to end, but if she invited him in, it wouldn't have to.

"No, thanks. I have to meet my roommate. I'll see you at the library tonight." She gave him a slight wave as she turned to leave.

Carter watched her as she headed out the door. *She definitely has a nice ass,* he thought.

That night, Carter was a few minutes late getting to the library. He found Loretta already sitting at a table near the door, surrounded by books and papers. She was looking at her text book with a frown creasing her brow. He noticed she was chewing on her bottom lip, deep in concentration. He wondered what it would be like to taste those lips.

As he got closer, Carter cleared his throat. He wanted to warn her he was there, and he needed to break the spell to get his own mind out of the gutter.

"Hey. How are you doing? You look like you're deep in thought with whatever you're reading in your book."

"Oh, hey. Yeah, I started working on Bower's assignment but I have such a hard time with this stuff." Loretta shook her head and gave a deep sigh of frustration. Carter put his books on the table, took off his coat, and settled into the chair next to Loretta. He moved his chair close enough to hers that their elbows and knees were almost touching. Carter opened his textbook and turned to the correct page. If it was his choice, he would have preferred to just sit and talk for a while, but he could tell from her frown she was focused on the homework.

They killed the assignment in just a couple of hours. Thanks to his know-how, he was able to show her the best way to work with the figures.

"Thanks, Carter. I appreciate your help. I think I'm understanding it a lot better now." She looked at him out of the corner of her eyes, and then said, rather sheepishly, "You're a good teacher."

He saw she was blushing again. "That's great. I'm glad I could help." Carter reached out and gave her hand a quick squeeze. "Say, my roommates and I are having a small get-together Saturday night. I'd like it if you came."

She hesitated. "I don't know. I usually go home on the weekends to help my folks."

"Can't you miss a weekend?" he asked. Carter was hoping he could talk her into staying.

She paused for a few seconds, as if she was mulling it over in her mind. "I suppose I could. I wanted to study for the test I have on Monday and it's hard to do that at home. Alright. Sure. I'll stay here this weekend." He liked the way her eyes lit up when she smiled at him.

"Sweet! Why don't you give me your phone number and I'll give you mine and my address." Carter was already opening up his notebook to write her number.

Over the next few days, Loretta had an especially hard time concentrating on her school work because her thoughts kept wandering to Carter. One of the most popular guys on campus, and he had asked her out. Unbelievable! At 5'6" and 135 pounds, Loretta always felt that she was average. Not ugly, not beautiful, but somewhere in-between. She'd had a crush on him since their first day of Statistical Analysis class back in August, but she never dreamed that he would ask her out. Having a date with Carter was exciting and nerve-wracking at the same time.

It was only Thursday afternoon, but she was pulling everything out of her closet trying to decide what she should wear on Saturday. She should have checked with Carter to see if this was a casual gathering or something a bit dressier. Finally, she decided on her favorite pair of jeans, paired with a sky-blue blouse and a waist-length denim jacket. Her sister, Kim, said that the color of the blouse accentuated the blue of her eyes. Her hair was a mass of tight blonde curls, so she would have to spend some time on Saturday afternoon getting it tamed.

Saturday night arrived, and Loretta walked to Carter's apartment. It was only a few blocks from her place, and even though it was late September, it wasn't chilly yet. The denim jacket had been a good choice.

Loretta found Carter's apartment building with no trouble and waited only a few moments for him to buzz her in. She climbed the stairs and found apartment 3B easily. It was the one with the open door and the music playing loudly enough that she could hear it from the hallway. Before she could knock, Carter met her at the door. He reached for her hand and gave her a kiss on the cheek. She could feel the heat rising on her face, sure that she was blushing, but hoped Carter wouldn't notice.

"Hey, you look great! Come on in. I'll introduce you to everyone," Carter said as he pulled her into the apartment. He still held her hand, knitting his fingers into hers. She met his three roommates and their dates, Tony and Courtney, Dennis and Bonnie, Devonte and Aliyah. There were a few other people at the party he introduced her to as well.

Carter offered her wine or beer, but she asked for a soda instead. She was already nervous and wasn't much of a drinker to begin with. She didn't want to add drunk to the mix.

⚖

The night passed by in a blink, and it surprised Loretta at how comfortable she felt with Carter and his friends. She was not normally an outgoing person, especially with people she didn't know. Her mother, always trying to soften her words, would refer to Loretta as shy, but she considered herself more socially awkward. None of that seemed to matter as Loretta found herself drawn into the conversations as if she'd known them for ages. They had talked and laughed about so many things. Loretta's head was spinning, but in a good way.

At the end of the night, Carter walked Loretta to her apartment. He asked if he could come in, but Loretta said no. It wasn't the answer he wanted to hear, but he understood. He gave her a kiss on the cheek and a warm smile before he turned to walk back to his own apartment.

She laid in bed, unable to sleep, as she played the night over and over in her mind. She would have liked to ask him in, but it was too early in the relationship ... if this was the start of a relationship. Only time would tell, but she certainly hoped it would continue. She liked Carter a lot.

The next morning, Carter called and asked her to brunch. They spent the rest of the afternoon together at his apartment, talking, laughing, and playing a few rounds of the latest popular board game, Balderdash. Sometimes his roommates would even sit with them for a few minutes before they ran off to whatever they were doing. Carter made a point of sitting very close to her on the couch. He held her hand, and every once in a while, he kissed her.

This time, when he walked her home, she invited him in. He stayed until the next morning, only leaving because they both had to get ready for class. It was the first time a boy had ever spent the night with Loretta.

From that day on, Carter and Loretta were together as often as possible. She no longer went home on the weekends, telling her mother she had too much work to do at school.

"But, Loretta, honey. You know I look forward to seeing you on the weekends." Her mother missed her and was pleading for Loretta to come home.

"I know, mom, but things are getting tougher. I need the time at school to study and do my homework. I'm sorry, mom, but it's a lot quieter here than it is at home and I can concentrate better. You know how I struggle with studying. It helps me to study at the college library where I'm not being disturbed."

Loretta promised to come home soon. She'd be home for Christmas break, which was right around the corner, anyway.

She was not looking forward to being away from Carter for so long. The four weeks of break would seem like an eternity. On the other hand, they lived close enough to each other that they might be able to get together at least a couple of times. At least, she hoped so.

⚖

Loretta had only been home on Christmas break for two days when Carter called.

"Hey! I miss you already, so I had to call. How are you?" Carter asked.

Loretta was almost breathless when she heard his voice on the phone. "I'm good, but I miss you, too. How are you doing?"

"Going crazy," Carter said with a growl. "I need to see you. Can we get together soon?"

"Yes, I'd like that, Carter. Would you like to come meet my parents?" Loretta began bouncing on her tip toes. She had been wanting to introduce Carter to her family for a while. This could be the perfect opportunity. Her family could finally meet the man she'd been talking about for the last few months.

"Yeah, well, I was thinking more like meeting someplace where we can have some fun, if you know what I mean." Loretta understood his suggestion. She could picture Carter as he spoke with a cheesy grin, his eyebrows fluttering up and down suggestively.

"Oh, I don't know, Carter." Loretta lowered her voice. "I mean, it's weird talking about that when my mother is in the other room." Loretta looked over her shoulder to see if her mother was listening. "My sister has my car, but if you want to come pick me up, maybe we can sneak away somewhere. I don't know where, though."

"Seriously, Loretta? You never went to a motel to get laid before?" Carter asked, even though he knew she hadn't. "If I drive all the way to Rockville, there had better be someplace where we can go. I'm going crazy here. But if you're not interested, I'm sure I can find someone else who is."

"Wait, Carter. Don't do that. I'm sure we can find a place where we can … well … you know." Loretta hoped she didn't sound as desperate to Carter as she sounded to her own ears.

"Great. I'll be there in an hour. Wear something sexy, okay?" Carter disconnected the call.

Loretta looked at the phone in her hand and blinked back the tears. She enjoyed being with Carter. He had been her first, and she enjoyed the physical part of their relationship, but sometimes he made her feel used and dirty. The idea of going to a cheap motel in the middle of the day made her feel sleazy.

I guess people go to motels all the time, she thought. Maybe if I change into something nice, like Carter suggested, I'll feel better about this. She slowly placed the handset on the cradle of the wall phone and went upstairs to get dressed.

One thing that Loretta found troubling about her relationship with Carter was the difference in their family dynamics. As an only child, he was part of a small family that didn't appear to be that close. From what Carter had said, his father was always working while his mother was always busy with social functions and charity events. Neither one seemed to have much time for Carter, so they left him to fend for himself. Usually, he told her, he hung out with his friends. His father had once told Carter that as long as he didn't get into trouble and embarrass the family name, he didn't care what Carter did.

Loretta, on the other hand, came from a close-knit family. She grew up in a household where her mother, father and sister Kim would eat dinner together every night and share the day's events. Sometimes dinner would last over an hour before they finished talking and eating. Then, three or four times a week, they would play cards or a board game after dinner, rather than sit in front of the television.

They went to church every Sunday morning, but Sunday afternoons were the best times. They had a big dinner after the church services with their family and friends. The families would take turns hosting the dinners in their respective backyards, with the traditional red checkerboard tablecloths covering the picnic tables. Each family would bring dishes to pass, ensuring that there was always more than enough to eat. Throughout the school years, her parents never missed a sporting event, concert, or play that she or her sister had been in. Loretta couldn't imagine having it any other way.

Chapter 3
1987

Carter and Loretta had been dating for a year and a half. It was all set up that after graduation, they would move in together in an apartment that Carter had already picked out in Old Town, Virginia. It was a red brick townhome with a large kitchen, dining room and living room, three large bedrooms, and fireplaces in the living room and master bedroom. The kitchen featured Formica counter tops and all new appliances. Loretta had to agree that it was beautiful. Still, she was a little put out Carter hadn't consulted her before he signed the lease.

They both had their jobs lined up as well. Carter, of course, would go to work as an investment adviser at his father's firm in Alexandria, while Loretta, thanks to Carter's family connections, would also work in Alexandria but at the Bank of America as a financial broker.

The night of graduation, both families went to a celebratory dinner hosted by Carter's parents, Mike and Suzanne, at Arturo's, the most upscale restaurant in Gaithersburg. After the server cleared away the dinner dishes, Carter stood up and raised his hand in the air.

"If I could have your attention, please." All eyes were on Carter as he pulled a small velvet box from his jacket pocket. Loretta's eyes grew wide and her chin dropped as Carter turned to face her. He reached for her left hand, slid a gorgeous diamond ring on her finger and said, "Loretta, I have loved you since we first met in Dr. Bower's class almost two years ago. Would you do me the honor of becoming my wife?"

The words stuck in her throat. All she could do was nod her head yes, yes, yes, as the tears of happiness flowed down her cheeks. She stood up, wrapped her hands around his neck, and kissed him while their families clapped and congratulated them. Even some of the other patrons at nearby tables realized they were witnessing a wedding proposal and joined in by clapping and offering their congratulations.

Rather than wait, they hosted the wedding at the end of October. It took place on a beautiful autumn Friday evening at Alexandria's elegant Carlyle Club. In true Mills' fashion, there were three hundred guests at the formal reception, followed by a two-week honeymoon in Belize. Loretta was on top of the world. She'd married the love of her life, they were doing well at their new jobs and the future looked bright.

⚖

Over the next several months, things went well for the young couple. They'd had their difficulties, but for the most part, it was an auspicious time. They both continued to work hard and excelled at their jobs, enough that they were building a good-sized nest egg in the bank.

But they were eager to start a family. After two years of marriage, Carter and Loretta welcomed their first child, Steven, followed two years later by Danny and three years after that came Margaret.

Loretta had been working from home since before Steven was born, so that she could spend most of her time with the children. She very much wanted to raise them in the kind of close-knit family background that she had, rather than the distant familial setting that was Carter's. The problem was that Carter seemed to spend more and more time away from the family. He blamed it on his job.

Carter had come home early from work one afternoon, not long after their second son, Danny, was born. He was excited to tell Loretta his good news. They had made him a partner at the firm, which would now be called Mills, Hanover and Mills Financial Advisers. There was no partner named Hanover anymore—Philip had passed away a few years before, but his legacy continued to live on in the company's name. It was a natural progression for Carter that he be made a partner to take Philip's place. He explained to Loretta that, now that he was a partner, it meant more meetings, more time spent with clients, and less time spent at home. It was as simple as that, he said, but the money he'd be making in the process would more than make up for his absence.

One morning while Carter was at work, the boys were at school and eighteen-month-old Margaret was napping, Loretta sorted the laundry, getting it ready to take to the dry cleaners.

She searched the pockets as she always did, discarding gum wrappers and parking lot receipts. To her shock and dismay, Loretta found a receipt from the Sunset Motel in Carter's suit coat. The date on the receipt was from the previous Thursday afternoon ... a day when he'd told her he couldn't attend Steven's parent-teacher conference because he had an important meeting. Meeting, hell. She knew there was only one reason for a receipt from a no-tell motel.

Her first reaction was to cry, and she did plenty of that. Eventually, the tears gave way to anger, and she got angrier with every passing hour. She spent the rest of the day lost in thought and staring off into space while drifting from chore to chore. After the boys got home from school, it was a struggle, but she helped them with their homework, fed them all dinner, got them bathed and tucked them into bed. The hardest part was trying to hide her emotions from the children. She didn't want to have a meltdown in front of them, or worse, take her anger out on them. It wasn't their fault that their father was a lying, cheating bastard.

Loretta spent a lot of time that night thinking about Carter and what made him the man he was. There was no question. Carter was extremely self-centered. He always felt that because he was privileged, he could do whatever he wanted. But deep down, there was a kindness about Carter that he rarely showed. He could be a thoughtful husband and father when he wanted to be. Unfortunately, that side of him rarely bubbled to the surface.

His father, Mike, seemed to be the exact opposite of Carter's selfish ways. Mike believed in being honest and ethical. He worked hard in the investment world so that he could provide for his family. And yet, it never seemed quite right to Loretta that he worked his fingers to the bone for his family, but never had time for them. Most people knew him as a serious individual who rarely let his hair down, but Mike was kindhearted and compassionate. Over the years, Loretta learned to respect and care a great deal for her father-in-law.

Mike had tried in vain to pass on that work ethic to his only son. He had raised Carter with a firm hand, often applying that firm hand to a young Carter's backside when he felt it was necessary. However, his mother, Suzanne—not Susan, or worse, Sue—had a much different outlook on raising their son than Mike had. She enjoyed her wealth and played the part of the lady of the manor well, looking down her nose at those she considered beneath her—including Loretta. Suzanne believed the family wealth was to be shown off at every available opportunity, from the designer clothes and garish jewelry to the expensive cars and lavish parties she hosted. She would coddle Carter, her mini-me, and let him get away with anything. If Mike said no, Suzanne would secretly say yes and give in to Carter behind Mike's back. As a result, Carter grew up only having to care about himself, his wants and his wishes. He knew that, one way or another, he would always get what he wanted. He never got into any serious trouble, but what few scrapes he'd had when he was younger, his mother was there to rescue him and pick up the pieces he'd left behind.

By the time Carter got home at nine o'clock that night, Loretta was fuming. He was met with her icy glare as soon as he walked into their bedroom and found her sitting up in bed.

"Where the hell have you been?" she asked him, her voice louder than it normally was. She had her arms crossed in front of her, in an obvious display of anger and defiance. Loretta tried not to be a confrontational person and rarely raised her voice, but this situation was more than she knew how to handle.

"I told you. I had a dinner meeting with a client. What's your problem?" He looked at her with a frown.

"Really? Is it the same client you took to the Sunset Motel last Thursday?" She watched him closely for a reaction, sure she saw a flicker in his eyes. He hesitated for a split second before continuing to loosen his tie from around his neck. How she would have liked to tighten it instead.

"How did you find out?" He didn't look at her, choosing instead to concentrate on folding and refolding his tie.

Loretta looked at Carter wide-eyed. He wasn't even going to bother denying it! "What difference does it make how I found out? So it's true? You're not even going to deny it happened? You bastard!"

Loretta flew off the bed in a rage and let out a loud, guttural sound that was a cross between a wail and a growl. She charged at Carter, raising her hands over her head as if she was going to pummel him with her fists.

He grabbed her wrists just before she connected with the side of his head. "What in hell do you think you're doing? Loretta, stop! Enough! You need to calm down!"

Loretta struggled against Carter's firm grasp on her wrists, but she was no match for his tight grip. After a few moments, she stopped trying to punch Carter, but she was still furious. He slowly and cautiously let go of her, letting her arms drop to her sides. Loretta stomped back towards the bed. She stood there, keeping her back turned to him as she swiped at the tears streaming down her cheeks.

Carter looked at her in shock, surprised at her physical outburst. "Listen. I'm sorry. It was the only time I've ever done anything like that and I've been feeling like shit ever since. It'll never happen again. I promise you that. It was a mistake," Carter said.

"I wish I could believe you," Loretta said. She kept her eyes on her hands and played with a hang nail, the way she still did when she was uncomfortable with a situation. She climbed back into bed but still wouldn't look at him.

Carter sat on the edge of the bed next to her. "You can believe me. I promise." He leaned over to give her a hug, but she kept her arms crossed in front of her, clearly not budging.

"Aw, c'mon, Loretta. You know you can trust me." At least she was looking into his eyes, but she remained stiff as he held her shoulders at arm's length. Slowly, he drew her into his chest. She began crying into his shoulder, although she tried hard not to. After several moments, she gave in and wrapped her arms around him.

"See?" Carter pulled away so he could see her face. He gave her a smile and said, "Isn't that better? Now, I don't want to hear any more about this nonsense. It's late and I have to get up in the morning. Let's just forget about this and go to bed."

He walked into the bathroom and turned on the shower. Loretta watched him go, wondering if that was a touch of perfume she thought she had smelled on his collar.

The next few weeks were difficult ones for Loretta. Carter swore nothing was going on with the other woman, that it had been a one-night stand and there was nothing more to it than that. But she was having trouble trusting him and every time he was late or busy or couldn't make a family function, she found herself still doubting him. He still seemed to have a lot of late-night dinner meetings, and that only added to her feelings of doubt and insecurity. She hadn't asked who the other woman was, so for all she knew, he could still be in contact with her. But when he was home, he seemed to be overly attentive to her. Twice he had brought her flowers, something he hadn't done since their third wedding anniversary. She had accepted them with grace, but hadn't been able to completely forgive him yet. She wanted to forget all about it and forgive him, but the hurt was too much. It would take time to move forward.

It was a very confusing time for Loretta and she didn't know what to do about it. She felt like her heart was being torn in two. Usually, she would talk to Kim about her troubles as sisters do, but Loretta was too embarrassed. Cheating was something that just didn't happen in her circle of family and close friends. How could she admit to someone else that her husband had cheated on her when she had enough trouble admitting it to herself? Sure, he was a bit of a flirt, but that's the way he'd always been. Was it her fault? Did she lead him to it? Maybe she wasn't woman enough for him and that's why he looked for comfort elsewhere. The questions kept circling in her mind, stirred on by her sense of uncertainty.

Carter knew he had dodged a bullet. He still didn't know how Loretta had found out about Amy, but he knew he was going to have to cool it for a while. He had no choice. He also knew he didn't want to give Amy up. Sex with her was just too good to give up.

Carter had been seeing Amy for a few weeks by the time Loretta had found out about it. She was drop-dead gorgeous and was great in bed. She did things to him he hadn't experienced with a woman since before he married Loretta. But he would have to play it safe for a bit and let the wife cool down and then he'd pick up with Amy where he left off. Just thinking about her made him want to pick up the phone and call her, but he needed to bide his time. It was safer to let Loretta believe it was over. All he had to do was wait and then, when he could finally see Amy, she'd be in for the ride of her life. He was driving himself crazy just thinking about her.

By the time Carter figured enough time had passed and it was safe to give Amy a call, it had been three months since they'd last talked.

"Amy, hey, this is Carter. How are you doing?" Carter asked.

"Carter? Seriously? What happened to you? I haven't heard from you in months. I thought you fell off the face of the earth." He could hear the surprise and then the anger in her voice.

"Yeah, well, Loretta found out about us, so I had to behave myself for a while. I can't stand this. I need to see you again. When can we get together?"

"Forget it, Carter. I'm seeing someone else now." She then disconnected the call without waiting for a reply from Carter.

With an irritated "pffffftttt," Carter hung up the phone. He was disappointed, but not surprised. *That's the problem with women like Amy. They aren't happy unless they have a man hanging off their sleeve all the time. God forbid they should be single for more than five minutes.* Amy had told him she wasn't in it for the commitment, so dating married men wasn't an issue, but she enjoyed knowing that she always had a man around, preferably one with money. She reminded Carter of the character named Blanche on the television show, *The Golden Girls.*

Carter would miss her ... not her, per se, but he would miss the sex with her. Ah, well. If he ever wanted to go down that road again, he was sure he'd be able to, as long as he was more careful. Besides, sex with Loretta wasn't bad. It's just that she wasn't nearly as adventurous as he was. For now, it would have to do.

Margaret's second birthday was approaching, so Carter and Loretta made plans to host a small family party for their little girl. Loretta's parents and her sister, Kim, would come, but Mike and Suzanne wouldn't be able to make it that Thursday night, the day of Margaret's birthday. Suzanne informed Carter that they would come on Saturday afternoon instead. Loretta was irritated, but not surprised, when Carter shared that information with her. Suzanne and Carter always seemed to make their own set of plans, with no regard for Loretta or anyone else.

The original plan for the birthday dinner was to serve filet mignon for the adults, and hamburgers for the children, but since it was only Loretta's family that would be attending, Loretta opted for grilled hamburgers for everyone. As much as her family liked filet mignon, she knew they would be just as happy, if not more so, to relax on the back deck with plates piled high with burgers, macaroni salad, fresh greens, and watermelon.

Loretta even bought balloons for the party, along with streamers, party hats, and those silly horns with the fringe at the end. Everyone donned a hat, tooted the horns and joined in the fun. Everyone except Carter, that is. He called it foolishness. For Loretta, her family and the children, it turned out to be a wonderful evening with lots of laughter and fun that stretched well beyond the children's bedtimes.

The festivities with Carter's parents, however, would require a different type of gathering. The emphasis would be on Suzanne and Mike, even though it was their child's birthday party. Since it was scheduled for midday, as decided by Suzanne and Carter, Loretta would make finger foods rather than a meal. She made several kinds of elegant hors d'oeuvres, and put together a charcuterie board with a variety of cheeses, crackers, olives, grapes and smoked salmon. Instead of the beer and soda that her family enjoyed, Carter's parents preferred top-shelf wine and whiskey.

After Mike and Suzanne arrived, Loretta tried to make herself scarce. She got along well with Mike, but she had never been comfortable around Suzanne, always feeling inferior, like she could never measure up to Suzanne and her high standards. Things with Carter had continued to be tense since his affair. That, coupled with the stress of having to put on airs around her mother-in-law, only made the day more uncomfortable for Loretta.

The children were in the backyard playing out of sight, as Suzanne had requested, so they didn't disturb the adult conversations that were taking place indoors. Loretta was taking her time in the kitchen as a way to avoid her mother-in-law for as long as possible. She had already washed the dishes, brought the fancy hors d'oeuvres into the sitting room, and was now adding colorful edible flowers to decorate the charcuterie board. Knowing she couldn't put it off any longer, Loretta took a deep breath, wrapped her fingers around the handles of the wooden tray and headed towards the sitting room. She was only a few feet from the doorway when she heard their conversation. She stopped to listen.

"Darling," Suzanne was saying, "she's a pleasant woman and pretty enough, but she will never fit in with the likes of us. She doesn't seem to know how to carry herself among the elite. Lord knows, you've tried to teach her, but either one is adept at mingling among the upper class or one is not. Frankly, I don't believe she is, nor will she ever be."

"Mother, I appreciate your candor, but she's my wife, and it's none of your business. I knew when I married her what she was like and yes, she's a bit socially awkward, but I don't see it as a hindrance. Besides, she doesn't come to most of the functions anyway, so it really doesn't matter."

"Suzanne, Carter. Please, that's enough." Mike said, pleading for them to stop.

It was as if someone had pulled the rug out from beneath her feet. Loretta felt her heart pounding in her chest. The drumming in her ears drowned out any other conversation. The tears burned at the back of her eyes, but she blinked them away. She would never let them see her cry. She took a few moments, trying to steady her breathing. It took all of her energy, but Loretta lifted her chin and walked into the room. As she did, the conversation stopped. Without looking at any of them, she placed the wooden serving board on the coffee table, turned on her heel, and left the room.

The last thing she heard from the hallway was Mike saying, "Oh, shit."

Loretta went to their bedroom, climbed onto the bed, and let the tears come. She had always known deep down that Suzanne did not approve of her, but actually hearing it was another story altogether. And to hear her own husband agree with Suzanne was just heartbreaking.

A few minutes later, there was a soft knock on the door. "Loretta. It's me. Can I come in?" Loretta didn't need Carter to state the obvious. She knew who was knocking. He walked in without waiting for her answer and stood next to the bed. "Come on, Loretta. Don't do this. You know how my mother is. Just let it go."

"Go away, Carter. Just leave me alone." Loretta's voice was soft, barely above a whisper, but firm.

"Are you seriously going to act like a spoiled child?" When she didn't answer, he said, "Fine, have it your way, but don't blame me because Margaret's party is ruined now." He poked her shoulder as he spoke, as if he was driving his point home. "This is on you."

Within the hour, Loretta could hear the front door open and close as Mike and Suzanne left, with Carter following suit a few minutes later. Knowing the kids were alone downstairs, Loretta got up, splashed some water on her face, and went to find her children. She knew Carter would be gone for the rest of the day, so she decided she would make the best of it for the sake of the children, as she always did. Their father may be an ass, but it wasn't their fault.

Chapter 4
1998

Time had flown by, as it does when young people were in the home. The days were busy with the kid's school activities, sporting events, and play dates with other children. Before they knew it, two more years had passed and to the outside world, life seemed good for the Mills family. However, behind closed doors and within the privacy of the family, they continued to have their issues.

Carter still had his long meetings and was away from home most of the time. Loretta would tell him as often as she could that his absence from the family was upsetting to her and to the children.

Then something changed. Loretta no longer asked him where he was going and when he was going to be home. It was almost as if she accepted that there was nothing she could do about Carter's absences, and that this was the way things were going to be.

Carter didn't care what changed or why. He was just glad that she wasn't reading him the riot act every time he went out.

Steven was now nine years old, Danny was seven, and the baby, Margaret, was four. Loretta was no longer working at the bank, preferring instead to immerse herself into being a stay-at-home mom. She kept busy by volunteering at the boys' school whenever a parent was needed for a function or a committee. She also found solace in volunteering at the church for things like the occasional craft fair or the chicken and biscuit dinners. As long as she could stay busy and be near the children, she was content. It's not like the family needed the money her paycheck would have brought in anyway, since the Mills' firm had been doing exceptionally well.

Their three-bedroom townhouse in Old Town was nice, and Loretta loved the neighborhood. She was especially fond of the quaint shops around the harbor and loved to go window shopping, with Margaret in the stroller while the boys were in school. The problem was that as the family grew, they found they needed more space. Carter felt it was time to move up in the world and live within their ample means. He felt they had financially outgrown Old Town.

With no input from Loretta, he'd bought a large home on the west side of Gaithersburg, Maryland, that reflected his idea of where they belonged on the local social registry. The house was a stately brick McMansion with a large master suite, five additional bedrooms, a spacious kitchen complete with high-end appliances, and a sun room that overlooked the in-ground pool in the backyard. There was even an office with its own entrance on the ground floor for when he preferred to consult with clients at home.

Next to the pool was a beautifully landscaped area, filled with rose bushes, hydrangea bushes, all kinds of flowers, cobblestone paths, and marble benches. It would be an added expense to hire a landscaper who could tend to the gardens, but it was worth it. Carter could easily picture himself and Loretta entertaining both clients and their friends here. The house had been built to impress.

Carter also decided that he would hire an interior decorator to furnish the home. Loretta had decorated the townhome, and it was okay, but had never been up to Carter's high standards. However, he felt that a home like this one required a professional touch, especially if he would entertain not only friends but also clients. Loretta seemed hurt by this, but she'd get over it. To appease her and to make amends, he let her decorate the family's bedrooms. Not the guest bedrooms. The decorator would be in charge of them. Instead, he allowed her to pick out the wallpaper, paint, and furnishings for the master bedroom and the children's bedrooms. It was a minor consolation, but Loretta seemed to like that idea.

Until now, Steven and Danny had spent their whole lives in the same room, sleeping in bunk beds, but both were excited to have their own rooms. They were best friends, but as Steven said, having their own rooms was "way cool!" Danny didn't seem as confident about being alone at night as Steven did, so Loretta made sure that their rooms were right next to each other. Margaret, however, would take the room next to Carter and Loretta, since she still had the occasional child's nightmare and would call out for her mother.

Loretta decorated both of the boy's rooms with matching sports themes and basketball hoops hung over the doors. She decorated Margaret's room with a beautiful pink and white princess theme, including a bed covered with a lace canopy. When Carter saw the completed rooms, he had to smile. Loretta outdid herself, and he was impressed.

Gaithersburg was proving to be an up-and-coming area made up of wealthy young people, so that was the place where Carter felt they belonged. Carter especially liked the fact that this housing tract was expanding as more and more couples like themselves moved to the area. Located right in the middle of their development were tennis courts, a swimming pool, and a large community building that could host anything from small birthday parties to a good-sized wedding reception. He especially liked the large swan pond that had a trail around it for walking and running, and Carter thought that if he was lucky, he might even do some networking while he was out on his morning runs.

The only downside was that it was now at least a forty-five minute drive to work at the firm in

Alexandria. For years, he'd been trying to convince his father to open a satellite office somewhere, and Carter thought this might be the perfect time and place. All he had to do was convince the old man that Gaithersburg would be a lucrative town in which to set up an office, and he wouldn't have to worry about spending almost two hours out of every day driving back and forth to Old Town. He was much too busy to waste that much time day in and day out.

Besides, with a new location and a lot of new people to meet, there would be fresh blood he could tap into. The investment business was doing very well with their current list of clients, but it's always a good idea to keep a steady line of new clients and their money coming through the door.

"Look, father," Carter said. He was standing in front of his father, Mike, in the Alexandria office. He was trying hard to stay level-headed and not blow up at the old man. "If we open an office in Gaithersburg, we could reach out to a whole new clientele. The people in Gaithersburg need us. We need them. Just think of the money that would flow through our fingers if we set up an office in that area. There was no one else established there other than a few rinky dink wanna-be's and the population is mostly made up of professional people— doctors, lawyers, engineers, and politicians. We could make a killing!"

Carter was holding his hands out like he was pleading with his father. Actually, he *was* pleading with his father. He was sure the old man just could not understand how important this could be for the firm, but especially for Carter.

Michael Mills sat behind his heavy mahogany desk, tapping his Mont Blanc pen on the top of a manila folder. After a few moments, he cleared his throat and spoke to Carter. "I know you've wanted this for a while, so I've been thinking about it, anyway," he said. "You've brought up some interesting points in your argument. If I have my secretary reach out to a realtor, and the realtor finds an office that's agreeable to both you and I, I have no objection to opening an office for MH&M in Gaithersburg."

Carter's heart was racing, and he felt like pounding the air with his fist, but he'd learned long ago not to show that much excitement in front of his father. He let out a breath he hadn't even realized he'd been holding. "Excellent!" he said. "I think you'll be pleasantly surprised, father. We have an excellent reputation, and when people hear we're in the area, I'm positive they'll be knocking down our new door to meet with us."

"I certainly hope so," Mike said. The old man pulled a handkerchief out of his shirt pocket and cleaned the lenses of his glasses. "Besides yourself, I recommend we have two more financial advisers to start. We'll see if anyone in the Old Town office would like to transfer there. If not, we'll hire two advisers for the new office and the necessary support staff as well." He had stopped polishing his glasses but used them to point at Carter. "And I expect the office to be showing a respectable profit inside a year. I want a detailed report once a month, starting thirty days from its opening. I want the report to reflect expenditures, including rent and salaries, as well as the number of new clients and the amount they are investing. If, within a year, the office is not showing a profit, I will shut it down. Do you understand me, Carter?"

"I understand, father, but I'm sure you have nothing to worry about. I'm confident that this will work," Carter said. He slapped his hand on the top of the heavy mahogany desk for emphasis, ignoring the annoyed look from his father.

Carter left his father's office much happier than he'd been when he went in. He'd finally be able to open his own branch of the firm without being under his father's constant scrutiny. He'd be able to manage the business the way he wanted it managed. At least, his part of it.

Later that afternoon, Marjorie, his father's long-time secretary, placed a call to a local realtor she knew. Within a week, Carter and the realtor had visited several locations before agreeing on an ideal office space on the more historic east side of Gaithersburg. A large Victorian home, it had been renovated about eight years before into upscale office space. Almost all the other homes on the street had also been converted into commercial office space and part of the curb appeal for this area was that they still maintained the lush green grass, the mulched beds of azaleas and the beautiful magnolia trees of the era in which the homes had been built.

On the main floor was a spacious waiting room, a large conference room and what they would use as a receptionist/secretary's office. In the back was a fully equipped kitchen complete with appliances, although they were a bit too low-end for Carter's tastes and would need to be replaced. An airy sun room off the kitchen overlooked a paved lot in the back where their clients would park. On the second floor were four large offices, each with their own private bathroom, in each of the four corners of the building. Carter had already picked out the largest office of the four for himself. It was located towards the front, overlooking the quiet street. It was, given his status, preferable to one towards the back that offered a rather dismal view of the roof of the sun room and the parking lot below. No, he would need an office befitting his new station, and an office tucked away in the back would not cut it.

Later that afternoon, Carter met his father at the Alexandria office. He was showing his father the photos of the office building from the postings on the realtor's website.

"So, father," Carter asked, "what do you think? The location is perfect, there's off-street parking, lots of space inside, and it has an elegant yet hometown feel to it. I'm sure our clients will feel welcomed and quite comfortable doing business there."

"Carter, I don't have a problem with the building, but the rent is very high." He leaned back in his chair, tapping the desk with his pen, while holding Carter's glare with one of his own in a stare-down contest of sorts.

The old man had a way of making Carter very angry in a very short amount of time. All he ever did was find things to bitch about. Couldn't he see how perfect this place would be?

Carter would not back down. He said, "Father, you know as well as I do, you have to spend money to make money. Besides, I'd like to talk to the realtor about the possibility of a 'rent to own' agreement. At least then we don't have to invest a lot of cash up front, but if we end up buying it, we'll already have some equity in it. On the other hand, if for some reason it doesn't work out, we can go somewhere else, because we haven't committed to this place."

"You know the deal. You need to show that you're making a profit within a year, so if you can bring in enough new clients to cover the expenditures and still make money, I have no objections." The old man put on his glasses to read the portfolio that was on his desk. Carter knew there would be no further discussion on the matter and his father had dismissed him. But at least he gave Carter the approval to open up the new office at the location he wanted. He'd worry about the client list, the profits, and expenditures once the new branch was up and running.

Three weeks later, they had the "rent to own" agreement that Carter wanted. And the best part was that, because of the amount of money Carter planned to spend on the improvements, he had even talked the owner down on the price of the rent. The old man would be happy to hear that. It was a win-win situation all the way around.

Only one adviser from Old Town, Tony, wanted to transfer to Gaithersburg, but Carter was fine with that. He and Tony had been roommates back in their college days, and Tony was the only one who had known about Carter's fling with Amy, and maybe two or three others that he'd had. Tony was not in any position to judge, however, because despite being married, he also liked to have a little something on the side. He and Tony had had each other's backs on more than one occasion over the years.

The first thing on the list was to hire another adviser for the Gaithersburg office. To Carter's relief, his father would find the replacement for Tony in the Alexandria office. Carter was not fond of going through the hiring and interview process, but after he'd had to suffer through only a few of them, he hired Catherine Dumont. She was young, only twenty-nine years old, and pretty. And because she was so young, she didn't command as high a salary as someone with more years of experience. The old man would be happy with that, too.

Carter also needed to hire a secretary-slash-office manager. He wanted someone who could answer the phone, set up appointments, take care of the office bookkeeping and run the whole shebang without bothering him with the minor details. He was pleased to hire Dorothy Beckman, a middle-aged, African-American woman who came with excellent credentials. She had been working at an architectural firm when Carter had convinced her to come work for him. She had answered Carter's ad on Indeed because she was looking for a place that was closer to home, and the idea of working for a smaller firm for a bit more money was even more enticing to her.

Dorothy had told Carter that she enjoyed baking and offered to bring in freshly baked goodies to serve to the clients every day. It was her idea, but Carter agreed that having a tray of cookies, brownies, or whatever she'd like to bake was a clever treat that his clients would remember. He took it one step further and asked her to bake the goodies right there at the office. What would be better than having his clients walk into a picturesque Victorian building that smelled like freshly baked cookies?

Carter had expensive taste and spared no expense in decorating the new office building. He had the entire interior repainted, all the carpeting removed and new hardwood floors installed throughout the first floor. The kitchen and the upstairs offices, however, had beautiful hardwood floors that were in great shape, so they would remain. The next step was to order the furniture and supplies for each of the offices, the kitchen, conference room, and waiting room. *I'll have to bury these bills so the old man doesn't see them,* Carter thought with a smirk. *He would be angry if he saw these receipts. He'd probably have a stroke!*

Carter was on cloud nine. He was happiest when he was making money, and with the opening of the new office, he was well on his way towards making a lot of it. In an unusual act for him, there was one day when he told Loretta to bundle up the kids so they could take a ride to Baltimore. The kids had always loved going to the National Aquarium that was at the Inner Harbor, and Carter thought it was a perfect day for an outing. The sun was shining, the day was warm, and he was in a good mood.

On the highway, Carter was driving well-above the speed limit, zipping between the lanes and passing cars that got in his way a bit too closely for Loretta's comfort.

Loretta was getting nervous. "Carter, will you slow down?"

"What's the matter with you? Where's your sense of adventure?" he asked.

"Carter, I'm serious. Don't be crazy like this with the kids in the car."

Carter looked in the rearview mirror. "What's the difference? They're asleep."

Loretta looked over her shoulder and saw that Danny and Margaret were asleep, but Steven was awake. He looked at his mother with eyes that were wide open in alarm.

"Carter, please. Please slow down." She gripped the handle of the door so tightly that her knuckles were white.

"Fine. I'll drive like a freaking little old lady." He abruptly stepped on the brake and slid into the right-hand lane, narrowly missing the front bumper of a car as he cut them off. That car beeped at Carter, who then displayed his middle finger in return. Loretta looked back at Steven and tried to give him a reassuring smile, but he was looking out the side window with his lips tightly clenched.

Loretta tried very hard, for the sake of the kids, to make the rest of the day a pleasant one. Carter, however, was still angry with her. He lagged behind the family as they walked throughout the facility and refused to join in their excited conversations. The kids, sensing the shift in his mood, gave him a wide berth. Before too long, they were engrossed in the fun of watching the fish and seemed to forget that he was even there.

Later that night, after she had tucked the kids into bed, Loretta found Carter in his office, nursing a bourbon. She confronted him, saying, "What is wrong with you? Going to the aquarium today was your idea and the whole time we were there, you wouldn't even talk to me or the kids. I made sure they had a good time, but you made it very difficult for me to do. Why did you have to act like that?"

"I didn't appreciate you yelling at me in front of the kids, and I don't need you telling me how to drive. I was doing fine until you opened your big mouth."

"That's why you're mad? Because I asked you to slow down? That's ridiculous, Carter."

"You might think it's ridiculous, but I don't. How dare you?" Carter was raising his voice, pointing his finger at Loretta. "How dare you correct me in front of my children? I'm their father, damn it, and I deserve to be treated with respect."

Loretta stood in front of Carter, soaking in his words for a moment before she answered him. "You're right. You are their father, but if it's respect you want, you need to earn it. That's not something I can teach them."

With that, Loretta walked out of the office and went to bed.

⚖

After three rushed weeks of renovations—he paid dearly for the rush job—Carter hosted a grand opening on a warm Tuesday night at the Gaithersburg office of Mills, Hanover and Mills Financial Advisers. The wait staff, dressed in tuxedos, wandered through the crowd while carrying silver platters with an endless supply of food. There was bruschetta, goat cheese canapes, smoked salmon with dilled cream cheese on puff pastry, crab-stuffed mushroom caps, and beef tenderloin on toasted focaccia squares. Bubbling champagne in crystal flutes was served by more tuxedoed servers, although for those who preferred something stronger, an open bar in the conference room was available.

It was an elegant affair, designed to attract a crowd of wealthy prospective clients, and from what Carter could see, it seemed to have worked. He didn't stop to count, but if he had to guess, Carter would say there were close to a hundred people that had come to the event. If he could get as many as a third of these people to sign up with him, he'd be in great shape and would consider the evening a success.

Carter tried to mingle with as many people as he could. He knew many of them already, but he made a special point of introducing himself to those he didn't know. Carter poured on the charm and shook as many hands as he could, making sure everyone had a beverage and something to eat. He was careful—he didn't give them a sales pitch. Instead, he had strategically placed brochures and business cards throughout the building, and invited his guests to take them if they were interested.

Loretta had come with him to the grand opening and she looked beautiful in a burgundy cocktail dress. That's one thing he liked about her ... she cleaned up nicely and made a great trophy wife. He introduced her to Catherine and noticed that she seemed to scrutinize his new adviser with a strange look in her eyes. *What's up with that? It's not like he was sleeping with Catherine. At least, not yet,* he thought with a slight smile on his lips.

It was after ten o'clock before Carter and Loretta got in the car to head home. It was a quiet ride. Carter was thinking about how successful he thought the grand opening had been, while Loretta looked out the passenger side window for the entire trip. But once they were home and getting ready for bed, she found her voice.

"You didn't tell me that your new adviser was so young and so pretty." Loretta sat at the vanity, aggressively brushing her hair while she stared at his reflection in the mirror.

"Is she? I guess I hadn't noticed." Carter loosened his cuff links, trying to show indifference to his wife's questions.

"Really, Carter? You hadn't noticed how pretty she is? I find that hard to believe." Her tone was icy.

Carter turned on his heel and glared at his wife. "What do you want from me? So, she's pretty. Big deal. She also happens to be a good adviser that came highly recommended. I need someone that will make money for the firm. If that adviser is a pretty, young female, that's not my fault."

"Are you sleeping with her?" Loretta stood up from the vanity bench to face Carter, clenching the brush in her hand.

"Oh, c'mon, Loretta! Give me a break. Why do you always do this? Why?" He was shouting, suddenly furious. He was struggling with shaking fingers to unbutton his shirt. He finally just pulled the shirt hard enough to pop the last button, sending it flying across the room. "It was a great night. Lots of people showed up at the opening, and you just have to ruin it for me, don't you?"

Carter back-handed Loretta across the face. She hadn't seen it coming and had no time to react. She fell to the floor in a heap, stunned. Loretta brought her fingers to her lips, and when she drew them back, she saw blood on the tips. She could taste the blood on her tongue from her split lip.

Carter grabbed his robe and stalked off to the bathroom, slamming the door behind him. He let the water from the shower wash over him, but it did nothing to settle the anger that brewed inside him. *Who in hell does she think she is? I can hire whoever the hell I want to hire, and she has no say in the matter. She's not the person in charge. I am. I shouldn't have hit her, but she deserved it. She's constantly bitching at me. She needs to learn her place and to shut the hell up.*

When Carter finished his shower, he walked back into the bedroom to find Loretta in bed, facing the wall and hidden under the sheets. He didn't see the washcloth filled with ice that she held to her lip. Carter slept in a spare bedroom that night, but if the truth be told, he spent very little time sleeping. He spent some of the time fuming over Loretta's comments, but he spent the majority of the time with thoughts of Catherine running through his mind. He had lied to Loretta when he said he hadn't noticed how pretty she was. Of course, he'd noticed. She had that 'girl next door' look, and he liked that about her. The only problem was that he didn't want to make a move on someone that worked for him. That presented way too many problems, but it didn't mean he couldn't enjoy looking at her all day. Carter estimated she was about 5'10", maybe 130 pounds, and with all the curves in the right places. She had gorgeous blue eyes, shoulder-length blonde hair and long, perfect legs that seemed to go all the way to her shoulders. No doubt about it, she was mighty sweet to look at.

It turned out that Gaithersburg was the perfect location for the new office. Within the first three months, they had brought in almost forty new clients. A few of them had followed Carter and Tony from the Old Town office, so the old man hadn't wanted to count them since, in his eyes, they were not considered "new" clients. He only wanted to see the facts and figures on those that were new to the firm, but to Carter, money was money, so he added them to the totals, anyway. After all, they could have gone to another investment firm, but they stayed with him and Tony. So what if it inflated the totals a bit? Their investments could be just as profitable to MH&M as anyone else's.

Things at home were not going as well for Carter. Since the night he'd hit Loretta, he had moved out of the bedroom he shared with her, preferring to stay in a separate en suite bedroom down the hall. It seemed like he was constantly under Loretta's scrutiny and he was tiring of it. If they saw each other at all, she was cold to him, and he was cold to her. Each did their best to avoid the other, and that suited both of them just fine.

There had been quite a few late-night dinner meetings, he had to admit, but it was all in the name of introducing their investment firm to prospective clients. He needed to wine and dine with people if he was going to get his name out there. In the beginning and before their huge fight, Loretta had gone with him a few times, but it got to where it just wasn't worth it. He couldn't even talk to another woman without getting the stink eye from her while they were still at the function or the third degree from her when they got home. She just didn't understand that socializing was an important part of the game. Besides, he had asked Catherine to be there with him at a few of these functions, strictly as an employee, of course, but it would be best if Loretta didn't know about that. Why rub salt in the wound? What Loretta didn't know wouldn't keep her awake at night wondering, as the old saying went.

Catherine was already proving to be a tremendous asset to the firm. As the daughter of wealthy parents, she had grown up among the upper crust, so she knew the nuances of moving among the elite. Unlike his wife, Catherine understood image was everything in the financial world. Most of their clients were men, and Carter noticed that she very much appealed to several of them when she poured on her flirtatious Southern charm. There were a couple of men that had specifically asked that she represent them as their advisor. Carter was more than happy to oblige them and assigned Catherine to their portfolios. He didn't care if they got a little eye candy as long as he raked in the money. Besides, she seemed willing and even flattered by the attention, anyway.

One morning, Carter picked up his phone and called Catherine on the intercom. "Catherine, do you have a minute?"

"Certainly." Carter watched as she walked toward him, floating across the room like a ballet dancer. He shouldn't stare, especially when she could see him doing it, but he was finding it harder and harder to resist watching those long, shapely legs.

She sat down in one of the leather chairs in front of his desk, leaning slightly to the side, and crossing her legs at the ankles. Her short skirt rode up her thigh just enough to make him want to reach over, push it up even more, and see what was hidden underneath that skirt. He cleared his throat and took a sip of coffee, trying to regain his focus.

"Catherine, you've come with me to a few business dinners, and I'd like to thank you again. I hope I'm not keeping you from anything at home when I ask you to go to these dinners." Carter was fishing, but even though she wasn't wearing a ring, he wanted to know if she had a boyfriend or husband. Up to this point, most of their conversations were work-related, but he felt the need to get to know her on a more personal level.

"It just so happens, Carter, my boyfriend and I broke up about four months ago, just before I came to work here. So, no, you're not keeping me from anything. And I certainly don't mind going out with you." She gazed into his eyes and lifted an eyebrow suggestively.

Was she flirting with me? She didn't say "go with me," she said "go out with me." And I'd swear, with that coy look she just gave me, she is flirting! Damn!

Carter cleared his throat. "Okay, that's good. Not that you and your boyfriend broke up, I mean, it's good that I'm not keeping you from anything ... or anyone." He could hear himself stumbling over his words like a teenager with a high-school crush and took a deep breath to calm his nerves. "I was just wondering ... do you have any lunch plans today?"

"No, I don't. I was just going to grab a salad at the café next door, is all." She lowered her head, looking at him through her long eyelashes.

Carter felt his heart pounding in his chest. "Well, there's a great Thai restaurant a few blocks from here, and I'm not fond of eating alone. Would you like to join me?"

"I'd love to. Let me freshen up and I'll be right back." She slowly stood up, smoothing her short skirt with perfectly manicured fingers. Carter's eyes were glued to her thighs and the hands that seemed to caress them as she turned and walked away, ever so slowly, her hips swishing from side to side.

They sat at the restaurant for over two hours, sharing a spicy beef salad, Pad Thai with shrimp and a couple of glasses of wine each. The conversation was light and enjoyable, the time passing quickly. When they got into Carter's BMW to leave, he started the ignition, but didn't put it in gear. He turned to look at her and said, "It's a shame we have to go back to the office. I've enjoyed spending time with you and I don't want it to end."

"It doesn't have to end. My apartment is not too far from here. Would you like to have a drink at my place?" She reached over and put her hand on his leg, her fingers gently caressing the inside of his thigh.

By the time he got home much later that night, Carter was grateful that he had moved into his own suite of rooms and Loretta wouldn't hear him come in. It had been a great day and the last thing he needed was to have her bitching at him. He got undressed and slipped under the covers of the bed, the light smell of Catherine's perfume still in his nose. He was asleep almost as soon as his head hit the pillow, a smile on his face.

⚖

Carter didn't realize that Loretta could hear him when he came home so late at night. Because her bedroom suite was near the garage, she could hear the car coming up the driveway, and then, after he came through the kitchen door from the garage, she could hear the familiar beeps as he set the security alarm on the keypad. That night she'd been lying in bed with a magazine on her lap, not even bothering to turn the pages. She'd forgotten it was there, her thoughts consumed by Carter, their marriage, and the many infidelities she'd suspected him of having over the years. He always said that nothing was going on, that he's been working so many hours to drum up the business he needs to keep the office afloat. If that's true, then why does she have such a sick feeling in her stomach? She had no solid proof he was cheating on her, at least, not since she found the receipt from when he took that whore to the motel. But it was a gut feeling and a strong one that she just couldn't shake. The new adviser, Catherine, was lovely, and the kind of girl that Carter always liked. Would he be foolish enough to have an affair with someone in the office? She just didn't know anymore.

There was a part of Loretta that still cared about their marriage, about making it work for the sake of the children. But there was another part of her that didn't care anymore. It seems like they had drifted apart over the twelve years of their marriage and no longer had much in common. He had become obsessed with money and the prestige it provided to his ego. Money and a high social standing were never that important to her, and even though they were well off, thanks to the business and their own personal investments, he was always hungry for more. She, on the other hand, was grateful for what they already had—three beautiful children, a pleasant home, nice cars and enough money to take the kids on vacations to exciting places and have fun. That was more than she had ever thought possible, and she needed no more than that.

Loretta knew she was partly responsible for the marriage falling apart because she had such a volatile temper. It was one of her worst faults. It didn't help, either, that she immersed herself in the children and the church, rarely taking time for her and Carter as a couple. But she couldn't help the way she felt. As someone who was socially awkward, as Carter used to call her, she especially didn't enjoy schmoozing at those events that were supposed to boost his business. She felt like she was on display and had to put on airs, that she couldn't be herself. At one of those dinners after he'd had too much to drink, he told her she made a good trophy wife, that all she had to do was stand there and look pretty. He said that *her* image helped make *his* image. He might have thought it was a compliment, but she didn't take it as one. In fact, she was so hurt by his comments that she made sure that it was the last time she'd gone to any of his business functions. Her days of being on display like a dog at the Westminster Kennel Club show were over.

Danny's eighth birthday was approaching, and he'd been hinting to Loretta that he'd like a puppy. She told him she didn't mind, but he would have to ask his father. One night, with his birthday about a month away, he came right out and asked for the puppy while they were all seated around the dinner table.

"I promise I'll take care of it and walk it and play with it and make sure it has water and food and everything," he said. Loretta looked from Danny to Carter, with a hint of a smile on her lips.

It seemed like minutes passed with no one uttering a word. They were all waiting anxiously for Carter to answer. Danny looked from his father to his mother, back to his father. Carter finally finished chewing, and while keeping his eyes on his plate of food, said, "Absolutely not. Your mother has enough work to do without having to deal with a dog."

"But father, I promise I'll take care of it. Mother won't have to do a thing." It broke Loretta's heart as she watched Danny trying so hard not to cry. His bottom lip quivered and his eyes filled up with unshed tears.

"I said no and I mean no," Carter said. "Now that's the end of it. I don't want to hear any more talk about getting a damned dog."

Danny looked up at his mother, a tear rolling down his cheek as he ran from the room.

Later that night, Loretta lay in bed and replayed the conversation in her mind. It brought back a memory that she had long forgotten from the early days of when she and Carter had been dating. She had invited Carter to her family's home to meet her parents and her sister Kim for the first time, a couple of months into their relationship. As Carter came through the doorway, the family dogs ran up to greet him. Sarge was a nine-year-old black lab, and Oreo was a three-year-old Shih Tzu mix. Sarge gave one bark, his tail wagging furiously back and forth. Oreo, being the more rambunctious of the two, was yapping non-stop, and stood up to put his front paws on Carter's leg, looking for a pat on the head. Carter had reached down and pushed Oreo away, sending him skidding across the floor. Oreo had gotten up and gone back to Carter, but this time, Carter kicked at the dog, sending Oreo rolling across the floor with a yip. From that day on, Oreo would growl at Carter and give him a wide berth whenever he'd come to the house.

Chapter 5
1999

Even though he and Loretta weren't getting along like they used to, Carter was pleased with the way his life was going. He had a pretty wife at home who took care of all those mundane domestic things so that he didn't have to; they had three great kids, a gorgeous house, two high-end vehicles, and a job where he could set his own hours because he was the boss. But the best part was that he enjoyed his job of advising people on what to do with their big bucks, so that in the process, he could earn big bucks. And when he had the opportunity, he took advantage of having a little something on the side to keep things interesting. Life was good.

He and Catherine had been sleeping together for about two months, and the sex was fantastic. They had fallen into a pattern where they would meet a couple of afternoons a week and slip away to her apartment to spend a few hours living out their wildest fantasies.

One particular Thursday, Catherine had been out all day seeing clients. It was getting towards the end of the workday, and Carter knew Catherine would probably head home rather than drive all the way back to the office. He decided to surprise her, so he stopped and bought a bouquet of fresh flowers and set off through the rush-hour traffic towards her apartment. She lived in a secure building, but he had seen her punch in the code enough times that he knew what it was. He had seen her car in the parking lot, so he knew she was home. He let himself into the building and rode the elevator to the third floor, thinking about the passion they would share when she saw him. They hadn't had sex in almost a week, and he was definitely feeling the need. He rang the doorbell and within a few moments, she opened the door halfway, wearing a slinky lace robe tied loosely at the waist with a shiny satin ribbon. As she looked at Carter standing at the door, her face went pale, her eyes opened wide and her mouth formed an O.

"Carter! What are you doing here?" Catherine asked. Her voice was abnormally high-pitched, even though she spoke barely above a whisper.

"I thought I would surprise you. Damn, you look great," Carter said, as his eyes roamed over her sexy outfit. When he glanced back at her face, his smile quickly faded. "Catherine, is there something wrong? You look like you've seen a ghost!"

"Oh, Carter. You shouldn't be here right now," Catherine attempted to close the door on him. Carter put his arm on the door to stop her.

"Catherine, what's wrong? What is it?" Carter asked. It was then that Carter looked over her shoulder and saw a man standing in the living room with a small crystal tumbler in his hand that was filled with an amber-colored liquid. He was wearing nothing but a pair of silk boxers.

Carter's eyes locked on Catherine's, neither one saying a word as the realization dawned on Carter. He knew instantly the mistake he'd made by stopping by her apartment uninvited and unannounced. He dropped the flowers to the floor, turned on his heel and walked back towards the elevator.

The surprise of finding Catherine with another man irritated Carter. He'd never thought about it, but he'd assumed that she wasn't seeing anyone else. That night, he tossed and turned in his bed all night long, but hadn't been able to get any sleep, so early the next morning as the sun was rising, he went for a run to help clear his mind. Even that didn't seem to help. In fact, every time his feet met the pavement, it seemed to intensify the pounding of his headache. He cut the run short and turned towards home.

After he showered, Carter decided he might as well head to the office. At least he'd be able to sit and think before anyone else came in. As he sat at his desk, one hand gripped a coffee mug, the coffee now cold, while his other hand mindlessly tapped the arm of his chair like a nervous twitch. He thought about what to do next. He couldn't fire Catherine. That's all he would need, is a sexual abuse lawsuit. Even if she couldn't prove anything, the allegation alone would ruin him. Besides that, there were too many clients that she represented and if she left, they might also leave and take their money with them. But he also knew how chilly things were bound to get between Catherine and himself. *Who was that guy? Why didn't she tell me about him? Judging from the sexy robe she had on, I'd say they were quite close.*

Catherine finally came in about ten o'clock that morning and headed straight for his office. She looked beautiful as always, but her eyes seemed darker, more piercing than normal, her lips pressed together in a thin line, and there seemed to be an air of tension about her that Carter hadn't ever sensed before.

"I need to talk to you." Catherine said. She closed the door before he could respond. As she stood looking at him, she clasped her hands together and was rubbing the top of her hand with the opposite thumb in a nervous tic.

"Sure. Have a seat," he flicked his wrist towards the leather chair in front of his desk. She sat down, perched on the edge. He waited for her to begin, but she just sat in the chair, looking at her hands resting in her lap.

What is it with these women that they can't look a man in the eye? Carter shook his head at his own thoughts.

"That man at my apartment yesterday was my boyfriend. If you remember, I had told you we'd broken up just before I started working here." As she looked at him, Carter noticed how tired she looked. She had dark circles under her eyes her makeup didn't quite cover.

"Yes," Carter said. He was getting irritated. "I remember."

"Yes, well, we got back together again. I wanted to tell you, but I couldn't find the right time." She lifted her head to look at him, and Carter could see the tears welling in her eyes.

"Really, Catherine? You couldn't find the right time? How long have you been back together with him?" Carter was unaware that he was quickly tapping his fingers on the side of his mug in agitation.

"About two weeks. I'm sorry, Carter." She spoke softly enough that Carter had trouble hearing her. "What we had was nice, but it could never go anywhere. You know that. You're married."

"I'm well aware of the fact that I'm married. I don't need you to remind me of that." He knew he was being snarky, but he didn't care.

"Working together will be difficult, won't it?" She lifted her chin and sat up straighter in the chair.

"Not at all. We had our fun, but it was just a casual fling and now it's over." Carter knew that was a cheap shot and judging by the hurt look on Catherine's face, it had hit home.

Without another word, Catherine got up and walked back to her office. Carter decided he needed air, so he left the office, got in his car and drove, seemingly on remote control, as he wound his way through the Maryland countryside. He just needed to clear his head.

Catherine was fun, and he enjoyed her company more than he realized, but he was going to have to move on. She was right ... he was married. From now on, he would need to keep that in mind, so his liaisons became nothing more than a casual thing.

A month later, Catherine gave her notice. She and her boyfriend were getting married and would be moving to Virginia. Surprisingly enough, when the letter went out to her clients that she was leaving the firm, only two went elsewhere with their investments. *Hmm ... I guess the eye candy wasn't as sweet as I thought,* mused Carter.

Steven, now in the fifth grade, came home from school one day, his clothes torn and muddy, with scratches on his face and arms. He had a fat lip and the bruising around his left cheek would develop into a black eye within a few hours. Loretta had been trying to clean him up at the kitchen sink with a washcloth when Carter got home.

He took one look at his son, who was squirming under Loretta's care. "What happened to you, Steven?"

"Nothing, father." He jerked his head to the side while his mother dabbed painfully at his lip.

"What do you mean 'nothing'? It sure looks like something to me. It looks like you were involved in a fist fight. Am I correct, Steven?" Carter was angry.

Steven sighed and said, "Yes, father. I was in a fight at school." He wouldn't look at Carter, choosing instead to keep his eyes tightly closed as his mother, gripping him by the chin, continued to dab at his wounds.

"What does the other boy look like? Who won?" Carter asked.

Loretta spun around and stared open-mouthed at Carter. "Seriously, Carter? I can't believe you just asked him that." Carter ignored the icy glare coming from his wife.

"I don't know, father. I don't know who won." Steven's bottom lip trembled, like he was ready to cry.

"Steven, you are a Mills. You are better than the rest of those snot-nosed kids, and I want you to always remember that. And the next time you get in a fight, you damned-well better make sure you win. Nobody should beat you at anything, especially not at some ridiculous playground tussle."

As Carter walked out of the kitchen, he stopped to face his younger son, Danny, who had been sitting quietly at the kitchen table. Carter pointed his finger at Danny and said, "You need to remember that as well. You're never too young to understand what the Mills name means. We are better than most people, so we're held to a higher standard and we have a reputation to uphold because of it."

Both boys watched as their father left the kitchen, then turned to look at each other, as if trying to comprehend what had just happened. Loretta returned to dabbing at her son's wounds, a scowl on her face.

A few days later, Carter was enjoying a quiet drink in his home office when Steven poked his head through the opened door. He knocked on the heavy, carved door frame to get his father's attention. "Hello, father. May I come in?"

Carter looked over the top of his newspaper at Steven. "Certainly, son. Come on in."

"Father, I just wanted you to know that I won," Steven said. "The boy that I got into the fight with at school? Well, I got into another fight with him after school today and I won. I made sure of it this time."

As Carter looked at his elder son, he thought Steven was standing a bit straighter, a bit taller. Carter raised his glass to his son and said, "Well done, Steven." A corner of his mouth turned up in a slight smile.

⚖

At the end of the first year, Carter was pleased to show his father that the Gaithersburg office of MH&M was indeed showing a profit. It wasn't a huge profit, but they were operating within the black, nonetheless. A deal was a deal, so his old man relinquished full control over to Carter and would no longer be asking for the monthly report. Carter was now on his own in running the satellite office, and he couldn't be happier.

Carter had replaced Catherine's position by hiring Martin Haggerty, a man about five years older than Carter, with movie-star good looks and a charismatic personality. Martin came with excellent credentials, and although he demanded a higher salary than Carter wanted to pay, he was worth the extra money. He even brought in some of his own clients, which was a bonus for the firm. Martin was quite the salesperson and could talk a cloistered monk into buying tickets to a heavy metal rock concert. That's exactly the kind of person the firm needed.

Carter celebrated his success at the one-year mark by buying himself a present. That day, he came home from work early and asked Loretta and the kids to step outside. "I want to show you something," he said with a grin on his face.

Without waiting for them, he turned and went back outside. His family followed with excited questions of "What is it?" and "What's going on?" hanging in the air, unanswered. Loretta stopped dead in her tracks as she saw Carter standing in the driveway next to a brand new Lincoln Town Car. The kids ran up to the car and asked to get in, but Carter said, "No, I don't want you getting in it. This is my new car. Sorry, children, you can look but I don't want you touching it. It's very expensive." He looked towards Loretta with a sneer, just in time to see her turn on her heel and walk back inside.

Chapter 6
2005

Over the next several years, the boys had grown taller, Margaret had grown prettier, and Carter and Loretta had adapted to simply existing together. It seemed like they spoke to each other only when they needed to, but even that was to be avoided, if at all possible.

Carter still had the occasional short-lived fling, but they were nothing more than passing fancies. He had learned his lesson years before and didn't get too attached to the women that he slept with. Carter discovered that there were a lot of married women out there who liked to fool around as much as he did, and they had just as much to lose if their spouses found out, so there was little chance that they would get caught. He would have sex with them four, maybe five times, then kick them to the curb. If they were especially good in bed, they might last longer, but that was a rarity.

He could tell from the stone-cold glares that Loretta gave him, she still had her suspicions and continued to believe that he was being unfaithful. She must have found it easier to simply look the other way because she wasn't confronting him with the accusations anymore. As long as she wasn't asking, he wasn't telling. It was as simple as that.

In the meantime, Loretta immersed herself in various church functions and school activities with the kids in order to keep busy. Carter didn't seem to care what she did with her time. As long as she didn't climb all over his back, he couldn't care less and told her as much.

To help with the chores around the house, they'd hired a live-in housekeeper named Irene Stapleton, who loved the kids, took great care of the house and was a fabulous cook. Recently widowed, Irene had no children of her own, but she had worked as a housekeeper most of her adult life. Now, at sixty-seven years old, she had come to them with high praise from several other families in the Gaithersburg area. Best of all, Irene did not pry into the family drama, opting instead to finish her chores and go to her bedroom, especially when the fur was about to fly between Carter and Loretta.

The Mills still went on family vacations and had even invested in a condo in Punta Cana, one of their favorite places to visit. Being on the beach didn't change the feelings—or rather, the lack of feelings— that Carter and Loretta felt towards each other, but they seemed to come to an unspoken understanding, that the animosity they felt for each other was to be left behind at home. The kids enjoyed the ocean, and no matter what, it was always good to get away. They would go as often as they could, sometimes as many as four or five times a year, planning their time away to coincide with the children's school breaks.

Carter had been planning a getaway with his latest mistress for a few weeks. It would be the first time he brought anyone to the condo without someone from the family going along. The problem was going to be in pulling it off. He decided to tell Loretta that he would be entertaining clients at their condo and he would be going alone without her or the children.

Carter picked a night to tell Loretta while Margaret was going to be with them at dinner. Since their daughter would be present, he thought his wife would keep her temper in check. He couldn't have been more wrong.

"I'll be leaving on Monday for Punta Cana. I'm going to meet a couple of clients there on Tuesday and they'll be staying at the condo with me for the week. If I get their investment portfolios, it could be quite lucrative for the firm."

Loretta dropped her fork onto the plate with a sharp clang. She looked at him with an expression that Carter couldn't read. He didn't know if it was surprise, anger, jealousy, disbelief or all of the above.

"Clients, Carter? And who are these clients?" she asked him.

"You wouldn't know them. They're actually from DC. They're not local," Carter said.

"Yeah, right. What's her name, Carter?"

Margaret, meanwhile, had been watching the argument unfold, looking first at her father, then her mother, and back again, with tears forming in her eyes.

"It isn't a 'she,' Loretta. Cool your jets and calm down. I'm telling you, it's a couple of clients—male clients, if you must know—that I'm hoping to bring into the firm. Now stop this nonsense. You're scaring Margaret."

"You are so full of shit," Loretta said. Carter brought his head up in surprise because Loretta rarely cursed in front of the children. "How stupid do you think I am? You've been cheating on me for years. After I caught you the first time, you promised me you wouldn't do it again. You promised me, Carter."

Loretta stood up so fast, her chair fell over backwards, landing with a loud bang on the hardwood floor. She picked up her water glass, flung the ice cold liquid in Carter's face, and stormed out of the room.

Margaret hated seeing her parents argue. She ran from the table to find Irene, who was cleaning up in the kitchen.

"What's the matter, child? What's wrong?" Irene let go of the dishcloth she'd been wiping off the counter with and wrapped her arms around Margaret.

"Mom and dad are fighting again. Why are they always fighting? This time, mom threw her water at dad. He's soaked."

Irene took a tissue from her apron pocket and wiped the tears from Margaret's cheeks.

"There, there, child. It's okay. Sometimes that's what grownups do. I'll tell you what ... you can sit with me while I finish washing these dishes. Why don't you tell me what you did at school today and when I'm done washing these couple of pots, I'll get you a nice glass of milk. I made a chocolate cream pie today. Would you like a piece? With whipped cream? How does that sound?"

Loretta had always tried hard to control her temper when the children were within hearing range. She hung her head, very upset with herself and how she blew up at Carter when Margaret was there to witness their fight. She knew better than to believe Carter's excuse that he would be entertaining prospective clients, but deep down, she wanted to believe him. Loretta had found no proof he was cheating on her, except for that one time, but still the doubt kept eating away at her. Her feelings were all mixed up, and it was getting harder and harder to control her temper. After a lot of soul searching, she decided she would ask him to go to marriage counseling with her.

Not long after he got back from Punta Cana, Loretta found him in his home office one evening. She gathered up her courage and said to him, "I think you'll agree that there are some things we need to work on in the marriage, and for the sake of the kids, I think we should try counseling."

"You can't be serious. I'm not going to some cockamamie therapist, so she can tell me what I'm doing wrong. If I want to know what I'm doing wrong, all I have to do is ask you." Carter grinned, like it was all a big joke.

Loretta closed her eyes, took a deep breath, and said, "That's not what a therapist does. He or she could help us communicate better so we don't have as many arguments. He or she will tell us how to express our feelings and to listen to each other in such a way that we don't end up in a fight."

"I'll tell you what, Loretta. You go. You go and get all the answers so we can gather around the dinner table every night and sing 'Kumbaya'."

"Never mind, Carter. I knew better than to think you would listen, but I wanted to try." She slammed the office door on her way out.

Chapter 7
2009

Now that the boys had headed off to college and Margaret was in high school, there weren't as many school-related activities to occupy Loretta's time as there had been when the kids were younger. Instead, she found other things to do. She discovered a healthy escape in yoga classes that she would go to three or four times a week, and she continued to stay active in the church. She especially liked to go to lunch as often as she could with some of the women from the church. On the weekends, she and Margaret would get their nails done together or go shopping and out to lunch. But the bulk of her time was her own, and she understood that there had to be more to life than pedicures and lunch dates.

She had never had a lot of friends, but over the years, she found there were fewer and fewer women she could refer to as friends. She classified most as acquaintances. Was that one more thing that Carter had manipulated without her even noticing? Looking back on it, Loretta realized that yes, this was his doing, although she carried part of the blame. After all, she had allowed it to happen, even if it had been unknowingly. Maybe if she had known sooner how lonely she would become, she could have handled things differently. But what could she have done?

Somehow, Carter had pulled her into his clutches so that her life revolved around him, their children and only the things that he approved of. She used to enjoy it when they went to parties with other couples. Now, it was only Carter that went out at night while she stayed home, and she recognized it had been that way for years. When the kids were young, she had asked many times if they could hire a sitter for the evening, but he was always quick to say no. He said he didn't trust anyone else to be with his kids, that it was her job to stay with them. Even asking to go out to dinner for a few hours with a couple of her girlfriends became more trouble than it was worth. He claimed he was too busy to stay home and watch the kids while she was out having a good time and that she was being selfish for even asking. Eventually, the hurtful words became too much for her, so she'd stopped asking.

Loretta tried to turn a blind eye to the loneliness and depression that she felt. She decided that if she didn't think about it, she wouldn't feel it. When the kids were at school during the day, or on the rare occasion when all three were involved in some kind of after-school activities or out with their friends, she would do a few things with the ladies from church or with Kim. But no matter how hard she tried to ignore it, she couldn't hide the feeling that there was still something missing in her life.

What she wanted was to just spend some quality time with someone. She wanted to talk with someone who would actually listen while she told them about her day, the kids, current events, or the latest book she was reading. She wanted to enjoy a conversation that involved talking and listening back and forth. The church ladies were okay to talk with, but some of them always turned the conversation to themselves. And Loretta still wasn't very good with conversations in a crowd, so that always presented a problem, too. She realized with a sigh how lonely and depressing her life had become. It was an awful feeling to know that she could feel alone in a crowded room.

And then it came to her. What she really wanted—no, what she really needed—was to enjoy the company of a man. She was almost embarrassed and felt guilty for thinking it, especially after all the years of thinking that Carter was being unfaithful. But she could truthfully say that it wasn't about the sex. That was the least of it. She wanted to be with someone who would pay attention to her, enjoy spending time with her, and make her laugh. Maybe even pamper her and make her feel young and beautiful. Someone who would not put her on display as a "trophy." Someone who would appreciate her for being the woman that she was.

She wanted to talk to Kim about it, since they were sisters and best friends, but that meant admitting things about her marriage that she didn't want to admit even to herself, let alone to Kim. And there wasn't anyone else that she felt comfortable confiding in. She supposed she could talk to Father Caughey at their church, but then he probably wouldn't understand. How could a man, let alone a priest, know how she was feeling? She couldn't talk to a therapist, either. Carter would hit the roof if he saw those bills. Loretta felt like she was stuck, with no where to turn.

One chilly, rainy afternoon, Kim and Loretta were out to lunch together. Loretta had been feeling especially down, and the weather hadn't helped. She ran her fork through her salad, tossing the lettuce from one side of the plate to the other, without eating much of it.

"Are you okay?" Kim asked.

After hearing Kim's question, Loretta got tears in her eyes but tried to blink them back. "Yeah, I guess. Just a little depressed, is all." She lowered her head so Kim wouldn't see her eyes filling with unshed tears.

"Is it about Carter?"

Loretta raised her head. "How did you know?"

"You're my sister. I see how he hurts you, how he makes rude comments to you and the kids. He's very manipulating and degrading, and it's been going on for years, hasn't it, Loretta?"

"Yes, it has. And I think he's been having affairs for years, too. I caught him once quite a long time ago, because he had the receipt from the motel in his pocket and I found it. That louse of a husband of mine admitted to it when I confronted him. He didn't even deny it. He said it was a one-time thing and it would never happen again, but I still get the feeling that he's continued to cheat on me after all these years. I've never found any proof, not like the first time, but there are some things that have happened that make me believe he's still being unfaithful. He still goes out all the time and says he's meeting with clients. I could see if he went out once or twice a week, but it's three or four nights a week, and even on the weekends. It's all the time! He's hardly ever home." Once she started talking, Loretta couldn't stop the words as they poured from her mouth. It was as if the floodgates had been opened.

"But I've made a lot of mistakes, too," Loretta hung her head. "It isn't just Carter's fault. My temper gets the best of me and I have a hard time keeping my cool. It's hard for me to keep my temper in check sometimes."

Kim reached across the table and put her hand over Loretta's, and gave her a gentle squeeze. "Have you ever thought about going to counseling together?"

"I asked him about it once, not too long ago, but he just laughed in my face," Loretta said around the tightness in her throat.

"What if you were to go to counseling by yourself? The therapist could help you deal with things like your depression and your anger issues. You don't need Carter there for that."

"I know. I probably should, but what's the point? Nothing is ever going to change. Not me, not him. Oh,

Kim. It's so depressing. I never thought it would be like this." Loretta could no longer hold back the tears.

"Have you thought about leaving him?" Kim asked.

"Oh, my gosh. I couldn't do that." Loretta's eyebrows shot up in surprise. "What would the children think? What would our parents think? Where would I live? How would I support myself? I would have to get a job again, and I've been out of the workforce for so long, I'm not sure anyone would even hire me. Besides, I don't think Carter would allow that."

It wasn't long after that conversation between Loretta and Kim that she met Bernie Lehrman by accident. Loretta and Bernie met at the Speedy Clean dry cleaners when they literally ran into each other. Loretta had just dropped off her dry cleaning at the counter and had been looking in her purse for her car keys when she spun around without looking, just as Bernie was coming through the doorway. They crashed head-on into each other. On impact, Loretta dropped her purse and Bernie dropped his laundry. Bernie reached out to steady Loretta by the elbows before she fell.

They were both so shocked and flustered that they began talking at the same time.

"Excuse me, ma'am. I'm so sorry! Are you hurt?" the gentleman's eyes were wide with concern and he still had hold of her by one of her elbows.

"Oh, my gosh! I'm so sorry! Are you alright?" Loretta covered her mouth with her free hand in embarrassment and disbelief. She could feel the heat rising in her face.

They both acknowledged that they were fine, at which point Bernie bent down to pick up the items from the floor. He handed Loretta her purse—thankfully nothing had spilled out—and in one scoop, gathered up his laundry.

"I'm so sorry. It was entirely my fault." Loretta was mortified. She couldn't believe she hadn't been paying attention to where she was going and actually ran into someone.

"No, not at all. The fault was all mine. In fact, I'd like to make it up to you. If you're sure you're alright, could I invite you for a cup of coffee? My treat." The man was smiling at her.

She hesitated. Going for coffee with a perfect stranger was not something she would ever think of doing, but he looked truly apologetic and Loretta could see the kindness in the gentleman's eyes. She looked back at Sandra, the clerk standing behind the counter. She saw Sandra had been watching them and was smiling. Loretta gave her an inquiring look, raising her eyebrows, and the clerk, who obviously understood the subtle request, gave Loretta a small nod. *He must be a regular here if Sandra thinks it's okay.* Since she had nothing else to do, Loretta thought, *why not?*

"Sure. I'd like that." She smiled back at him.

"That would be lovely. There's a small café about three doors down that makes a fabulous cup of coffee. Or, if you prefer tea, they have a nice Earl Grey that you might like. Let me drop off my cleaning, and if you don't mind walking, we can leave our vehicles here while we go have a cup." He was already setting his clothes on the counter in front of Sandra, who was still watching and smiling.

"Sandra, would that be okay if we left the cars here in your lot for a bit while we grabbed a coffee?" he asked the clerk.

"Certainly, Mr. Lehrman. That would be fine." She started separating his laundry and continued to smile.

Just as they stepped outside, Loretta asked him to wait a moment. She went back into the store and asked the clerk if she knew the gentleman.

"Yes, he's been a customer for years. And he's very nice and quite a gentleman."

"Okay, I'll trust you. Thank you, Sandra." She waved at Sandra as she headed out the door.

"By the way, I'm Bernie Lehrman," he said. He extended his hand to Loretta and gave her a firm handshake. Loretta introduced herself and fell into step next to Bernie as he led the way the short distance to the café. It was a quaint coffee shop that Loretta had seen hundreds of times, but had never ventured into.

After placing their orders—both preferring the Earl Grey—Bernie picked up the tab as he'd promised. He steered them towards a table in front of the large picture window that faced the street. Loretta noticed

Bernie had held the doors open for her and even held the chair as she sat down. It had been many years since anyone had acted like a true gentleman and treated her with respect.

She was studying the man who sat in front of her, trying hard not to be obvious about it. He was a few inches taller than she was, and maybe eight or ten years older. He had warm blue eyes with creases on the outside edges ... what did her mother always call them? Oh, yes, "laugh lines." He had a full head of sandy-brown hair with a bit of grey at the temples. He was a few pounds overweight, but the extra weight didn't look bad on him at all. It seemed to give him a round, genuinely pleasant face. There was a friendly glow about him, but she couldn't tell if the glow was from the sparkle in his eyes or the perpetual smile on his lips. Probably both, she decided.

"So, Ms. Mills, are you alright? You're not hurt by our collision, are you?" asked Bernie.

"Please, call me Loretta, and no, I'm not hurt at all. How about you? Are you alright? No broken bones?" She asked. Loretta had never gotten comfortable enough with strangers to make small talk, even after all these years of listening to Carter insult her about it. She nervously stirred her coffee to at least keep her hands busy.

He winked at her and said, "No, no broken bones. And please, call me Bernie."

"Alright. Bernie it is. So, Bernie, I couldn't help but notice your watch. That's very nice." Loretta was struggling for things to say.

"Thank you. I've had it for many years now." He turned his hand so he could glance down at the watch he wore on his wrist. "I own a jewelry store here in Gaithersburg and I bought this watch as a present to myself on my tenth anniversary as owner of the store. It's a Bulgari. I like the classic look of the watch, very simple yet elegant."

Loretta noticed he wasn't bragging about the watch, although it was probably worth at least $5,000. He just said it matter-of-factly. She couldn't help but think that if it was Carter wearing that watch, he'd be waving it in front of anyone he could get to look at it, and would probably still have the price tag hanging off it.

"It truly is beautiful. How long have you owned your store?" she asked, feeling more comfortable with him.

"My grandfather started the business back in 1956, and then my folks ran it, and now it's been passed on to me. It's a wonderful shop. I'd love it if you stopped in some time to have a look around. We take pride in the fact that we have something for everyone; beautiful things and all different prices, from low to high."

Loretta watched his eyes light up as he talked about the store. She could tell how passionate he felt about it.

"In fact, I have a beautiful pair of sapphire earrings that would bring out the blue in your eyes. I would love it if someday you would stop in and let me show them to you. If sapphires don't interest you, I have an Australian opal and tanzanite necklace that would be beautiful on you as well."

"Oh, I don't know, Bernie. I don't wear a lot of jewelry," Loretta said. That was a bit of a fib, but she came with him to have a cup of coffee, not to have him try to sell her something.

"You'll have to forgive me, Loretta. Sometimes I get a bit carried away when I talk about the shop." He gave her a gentle smile and continued on. "You see, when I was born, we lived above the store, so I literally grew up in the jewelry business. It wasn't until I was married that I left my childhood home and made a home with my wife."

Loretta surprised herself when she realized she was disappointed to hear he was married. She discreetly glanced at his left hand, but there was no ring.

"And I've continued to work there all these years. I started out by polishing the glass cases when I was no bigger than the cases themselves. It wasn't until years later that I found out that my grandmother would come along after me and re-polish them. You see, I was too small to reach the tops, and too young to see that I was leaving streaks on the parts that I could reach, so she had to re-polish the glass after I polished it." He broke into a big smile as he told his tale.

"And your grandmother never told you?" Loretta asked, surprised to find that she was enjoying herself.

"No, she never did. I only found out after she passed away and my grandfather told me." They both laughed at the story of the proud young boy who was trying so hard to be helpful in his grandparent's store.

"Once I was old enough, I moved on to jewelry making. We have a small workshop in the back of the store where we work on the customer's pieces that are in for repair, but we also make a lot of our own jewelry. My father still enjoys it even though he's retired now, and so do I, when I get the rare chance. Most of the time I'm in the office with paperwork or on the floor helping the customers, but that's okay. Without the customers, we wouldn't have a business."

"That's an interesting way of looking at it," Loretta said to him. She was wondering if Carter looked at the investment firm like that, but quickly acknowledged she knew better. To him, customers were nothing more than a means to an end, and for him, the end was money.

It was two hours, another cup of coffee and an orange-cranberry scone apiece before Bernie and Loretta realized that so much time had passed. She apologized for keeping Bernie away from the store for so long, but he explained it was his day off, and he didn't have any other plans, anyway.

"But won't your wife become worried? Won't she wonder where you've been?" Loretta wanted to know more about him.

Bernie looked down at his coffee cup as he said, "No. My wife died of cancer three years ago."

"Oh, Bernie. I'm so sorry." Loretta reached over and covered his hand with her own. It felt like the most natural thing to do and she immediately felt a warmth in her heart that she hadn't felt in such a long time. He looked back at her, rested his other hand on hers, and smiled.

He patted her hand before pulling his hands back and sighed. "No worries. I will always miss her, but I've gotten used to her not being here. What about you? Are you married, Loretta?"

She looked down, subconsciously twisting the wedding ring on her left hand. "Yes, I am," she admitted. "Carter and I have been together for about twenty-three years, but we haven't been happy in many years. We simply exist together."

It was Bernie's turn to put his hand on Loretta's. "And for that, I am truly sorry. I can see already that you are a kind and beautiful lady and your husband obviously doesn't know what he has."

Loretta, surprised, looked at Bernie and saw compassion and kindness in his eyes. She returned his smile with one of her own.

⚖

Later that night, Loretta lay in bed thinking about Bernie. She had never met someone who was so easy to talk to. He seemed like a genuinely nice person, and she had enjoyed the time they spent together. She found herself hoping that she might run into him again ... well, not run into him like she did when they first met, she thought with a smile. Maybe she would swing by the jewelry store. It would be a bold move for her and completely out of her comfort zone, but she would like to see him again. Besides, she could almost picture the store after Bernie gave such a detailed description. It would be fun to see if the images she pictured in her mind were close to what the store might actually look like.

Two days later, Loretta drove to Lehrman and Sons Jewelers. It was surprising to her she had butterflies in her stomach, but as soon as she walked through the door and saw Bernie standing at a counter in the back, the butterflies were forgotten. He looked up at the sound of the bell over the door and broke into a broad smile as soon as he saw Loretta. He let the loupe that had been covering one eye fall into his hand as he wound his way from around the counter and walked towards Loretta.

"My dear! It's so good to see you again! How are you?" Bernie asked as he took hold of her hand and gave her a peck on the cheek.

"I'm doing well, thank you. And how are you, Bernie?" She could feel the heat as it traveled up her neck to her face. It had been a long time since she blushed like a schoolgirl.

"I'm very well. What brings you in today? Can I show you around the store?" He still had her hand and was leading her into the center of the store. The bright lights bounced through the glass showcases, making the gems on display sparkle like the sun hitting the ocean waves.

Loretta laughed at Bernie's enthusiasm. "Yes, that would be nice. I've been thinking about the opal necklace and the sapphire earrings you told me about. I'd like to see them, if you still have them." It was the only thing she could think of to say, and deep down, she knew it was just an excuse to come to the store to see him again, but he didn't have to know that.

"They're in the back. If you'll wait just a moment, I'll get them for you." Loretta watched as Bernie slipped through a closed door. She figured that must lead to the workshop he had told her about. As she looked around, she realized that the vision she had in her mind of what the store would look like was pretty close to the real thing. It turned out that Bernie's description of the store was on point. There were no other customers at the moment, so she was free to gawk at the jewelry on display. The cases were full of so many beautiful pieces!

In just a moment, Bernie came back holding two boxes of deep purple velvet, and wrapped with a thin pink satin ribbon. *Even the boxes are pretty,* she thought. *I can't wait to see the jewelry.*

Loretta's eyes grew large as Bernie opened the box with the earrings first. They were exquisite! Yellow gold filigree spirals formed a delicate chandelier setting. Each earring had five matching stones of the deepest blue sapphires she had ever seen dangling within the chandelier setting, with the gold wrapped snugly around each sapphire.

"Oh, Bernie! These are beautiful! The gems are absolutely gorgeous!" Loretta stood there staring at the earrings, unable to take her eyes off them. She reached out her hand as if she were going to touch them, but drew back before she could.

"These are from my own design. I'd had the idea in my head for years, but I waited until I could find the perfect stones to put in the settings. It wasn't until a few years ago that I came upon these gems. Here, let me show you the necklace." He put the first box down and picked up the second one. "This was my design as well. I was able to finish the piece about two years ago."

As he opened the box, Loretta let out a gasp as she stared at its contents. A gold necklace with a herringbone chain lay in the silk-lined box. Hanging from the center of the chain was the most beautiful gem she had ever seen. An oval-shaped Australian opal—with deep tones of blue, green, and purple— shone like it was on fire. Around the opal, which was as big as her thumb nail, were six identical stones of tanzanite. They had the exact shade of dark purple as that in the opal and were large enough to surround the opal completely.

"Bernie, I don't know what to say! This is absolutely stunning. I can't get over the way the light catches the brilliance of the opal. And the tanzanite stones are the same color as the fire in the opal! It's just fabulous. But why do you hide them in the back? Why not put them out here on display for everyone to see and enjoy?" Loretta asked.

Bernie held the box, his finger gently tracing the gold chain of the necklace. "I don't want to sell the necklace or the earrings to just anyone. Eventually, they will belong to someone who sees the true beauty of the stones, someone who will wear them with as much love and appreciation for them as I have. I can tell when someone comes through that door, if they are the right customer for these or not. If they are, then I will show them the pieces. If not, I will keep them in the back, waiting for that special person," he said, with a twinkle in his eye.

"How many people have seen your pieces?" Loretta was in awe.

"Until now, no one. You are the first." Loretta raised her head to look at Bernie as the realization of what he had said sunk in.

"You haven't shown them to anyone else?" Her eyes opened wide in disbelief.

"That's right. You, my dear, are the first." He said, as he gave her a wink.

Bernie and Loretta quickly and easily became close friends. They would meet for coffee or lunch as often as they could. Sometimes, they would take a long walk in the park or a scenic drive through the countryside. It wasn't the kind of relationship that led them to the bedroom; rather, they would sit and talk for hours, enjoying each other's company. It was as if they'd known each other for years. They shared stories from the past, both happy ones and sad ones. They talked through the feelings of loneliness that they'd both been feeling. And sometimes they didn't talk at all, and that was nice, too.

Carter had seen a change in Loretta. She didn't seem as withdrawn and quiet as she had been for as long as he could remember. She seemed almost happier, and didn't seem to ride his ass as much. He grew suspicious, wondering what that was all about. If he didn't know better, he'd think she had a little something on the side.

It had been about six months that Loretta had been seeing Bernie, when Carter finally asked her one night at dinner, to see if his suspicions held any truth. Margaret was out with a couple of friends and wouldn't be home until late, so Irene prepared dinner for just Carter and Loretta. Their meals together were usually quiet, almost silent, except for the occasional bit of small talk, but only if it was necessary.

"So, Loretta," Carter asked, trying to sound casual. "You seem to be in a good mood lately. What's up with that?"

"Nothing, Carter. Nothing at all." She speared a forkful of mushroom risotto and continued eating without looking at him.

"Hmm." He grunted at her, but left the question hanging in the air. He continued to watch her for any reactions, but she just kept eating, keeping her eyes on the dinner plate in front of her.

The next morning, Saturday, Loretta left the house early. As soon as Carter saw the taillights of her BMW heading down the driveway, he went into her suite of rooms to look around. He didn't quite know what he was looking for, maybe love letters or greeting cards, but he figured that once he saw it, he would know. He started foraging in her bedroom. There was the usual junk in the pair of nightstands that stood on either side of her bed–an old paperback, a bunch of scrunchies for her hair, a small bottle of hand lotion, and a bottle of Tylenol PM. The vanity had the same nonsense, along with various kinds of makeup and more scrunchies. *Good Lord! How many scrunchies does that woman need?* He even ran his hand under the mattress.

Carter shifted his focus across the room to the large armoire where Loretta kept endless amounts of underclothes, panty hose, scarves, and purses. He ran his hands through the mountains of bits and pieces in each of the drawers, hoping to feel something that might be hidden there, but each time he came up empty.

Carter gave a quick glance through the jewelry that was stored in the armoire, but there was nothing unexpected there either. He almost missed it, but just as he was about to shut one of the drawers, he spotted the large velvet box tucked in the back of it. He opened the box and found a beautiful Australian opal necklace. Carter knew from the looks of it that it was an expensive piece, but she sure as hell didn't get it from him. He lifted the necklace out of the box, surprised by the weight of it, and studied it. It was beautiful, for sure, but where did she get it? He dropped it back into the box, letting the hinged top snap shut, and returned it to the drawer.

Carter now had a headache, thanks to Loretta, and rubbed his head in agitation. He went for a run, since that usually helped him clear his head. So many thoughts filled his mind. *Where did she get that necklace? That had to cost a couple thousand, at least. She wouldn't have bought it for herself, not for that kind of money. She must be fooling around with some guy with deep pockets. But who? Who would give her an expensive necklace like that?*

Carter kept asking himself these questions repeatedly, the pounding of his feet on the pavement matching the pounding of his headache, but he couldn't come up with any answers. That she was always in a good mood and that she had a very expensive gift hidden away told him she had to be fooling around. No doubt about it. Maybe it was time to find out what was going on with her.

That afternoon, Carter called his former college roommate and current employee, Tony, at home.

"Listen, Tony," Carter said. "I need the name of a good private investigator. Who do you know?"

"Jeez, Carter, I don't know anyone, but I'll bet my wife does." Tony laughed at his own joke.

"Tony, I'm serious. I need the name of a good PI." He wasn't aware that he was clutching the phone so tightly that his knuckles were white.

"Shit, I don't know any PI's. I'm an investment broker, like you," Tony said. "We don't deal with that kind of secret spy stuff. Seriously, Carter. Why? What are you doing?"

"I'm not doing anything, but I think Loretta is." Carter said as he pushed the end-call button on his phone.

Chapter 8
2012

As had often been the case for most people, including Carter and Loretta, the weeks turned into months, the months into years, and before they knew it, another few years had passed.

Steven was living with his girlfriend in D.C., Danny had graduated from Johns Hopkins and was working in the family business at the Gaithersburg office, and Margaret was working on her International Relations degree at the University of Maryland. If she had her choice, she wanted to work for the State Department in Washington, but that would be a hard job to get. The competition for government jobs was fierce. Carter had only a few political clients, and most of them were associated with the local government. His political connections didn't extend as far as the state, but he promised Margaret that he would do what he could to snag a few state-affiliated connections. For now, she was living at home, studying hard and interning at a local non-profit company, hoping it would help her land her dream job in D.C.

Carter would partake in the occasional tryst, but not as much as he used to. He had lost interest since Loretta stopped accusing him of being unfaithful and the danger of getting caught wasn't there anymore. *It's like skiing down the steep side of a mountain,* Carter reasoned. *Once you've done it so many times, there's no sense of adventure and it gets boring.*

Loretta, meanwhile, had discreetly maintained her relationship with Bernie for almost three years now and couldn't be happier. One rainy afternoon while she and Kim were having lunch together, Loretta confided in Kim and told her all about her relationship with Bernie.

It surprised Loretta to see that Kim was not judgmental, but was happy for her.

"You don't think I'm a bad person for having an affair?" Loretta asked.

"Ordinarily, I wouldn't like it, but I know you have been through a lot with Carter, and if you're happy, then I'm happy." Kim reached over the bistro table and gave Loretta's hand a squeeze. Loretta gripped Kim's hand and returned the squeeze.

"His name is Bernie. He's a very nice man. He's kind and gentle, and he's very considerate." Loretta's eyes lit up as she gushed on and on about Bernie. "We can sit and talk for hours! He tells me things, but then he listens to me when I tell him about my troubles or a good book I'm reading or a pretty sweater I just bought. Bernie never criticizes me or puts me down. He makes me feel loved and appreciated. I would like for you to meet him someday."

"You know, I think I'd like that. I would very much like to meet him," said Kim with a smile.

⚖

Carter, Loretta and the kids hadn't traveled together as a family to their condo in Punta Cana in a long time, although Loretta still went whenever she could. Sometimes Kim would go with her, while at other times, Margaret or even the boys and their friends might go with her. More often than not, though, just she and Bernie would make the trip. Carter went once in a while, but never with someone from the family. As long as Loretta didn't ask, he didn't tell. He was paying big bucks for the condo, so he figured he might as well enjoy it too.

Not much had changed for Carter and Loretta. They continued to live separate lives, all the while putting on their masks and appearing to be a happy couple to the outside world. They simply existed in the same house, barely looking at one another, let alone having a meaningful conversation. When they spoke more than a few necessary words to each other, it tended to end up with snide comments getting fired back and forth, and sometimes it even led to an argument, so it was easier to avoid any form of communication, and only speak to each other when they absolutely had to.

On the rare occasion when neither one had other plans, Carter and Loretta would find themselves having dinner together at home. If Margaret wasn't working or hanging out with her friends, she would join them, but when it was just the two of them, they both brought their iPads to the table to avoid conversation. Carter would study the online financial pages while Loretta caught up with her social media accounts or read an ebook.

Carter had found out about Loretta's romance with Bernie after having her followed by a private investigator not long after he'd found the necklace. Knowing that her lover owned a jewelry store explained where an expensive necklace like that had come from. Even after all the affairs that Carter had had, it never occurred to him that Loretta could be attracted to someone other than himself.

He didn't care that she was fooling around. After all, that would be like calling the kettle black. But if he confronted her about her extramarital affair, he was smart enough to realize that she was likely to do the same to him, and that was a subject that he did not want to discuss with her.

Carter was not the jealous type, but the fact that Loretta's affair had lasted this long bothered him. In his eyes, having an extramarital affair was supposed to be a casual thing to enjoy, almost like golf or baseball. The idea was to end one game and move on to another. It wasn't supposed to last. He'd learned that lesson well after his fling with Catherine years before.

One evening, the skies opened up in torrential rains, with thunder that shook the windows and lightning that lit up the room. Margaret was working and wouldn't be home for dinner. It wasn't worth trying to leave the house to grab a bite to eat elsewhere in that kind of weather, so Carter and Loretta found themselves having dinner together. Irene had fixed them a delicious meal of beef bourguignon with garden salads and thick slices of bread from a fresh baguette. It was the perfect, comfort-food kind of meal for a rainy night.

Loretta had just returned from a week-long stay in Punta Cana, and since Margaret hadn't gone with her, Carter knew she would have gone with someone else. It could have been Kim, but Carter had a feeling that the boyfriend must have gone ... again. His mood was as dark and grey as the sky, and he decided it was as good a time as any to confront her.

Carter picked up a slice of bread and buttered it. "How was your trip, Loretta?"

Startled by the sudden voice that interrupted the silence, Loretta lifted her head to look at him. She hesitated and then said, "It was fine. The weather was pleasant, as always." She went back to her stew and her iPad.

Carter was trying to act casual and not let his anger show. "Does your boyfriend like Punta Cana?" He kept his eyes on her, wanting to see if she flinched.

She slowly raised her head to meet his gaze. "Excuse me?"

"Your boyfriend, the jeweler. I'm assuming he likes it there. After all, you've gone together quite a few times." He didn't know how many times for sure, but it didn't take a Rhodes Scholar to figure out it had probably been more than once or twice. One corner of his mouth turned upward in a sneer, his eyes little more than slits.

She looked him square in the eyes and said, "Actually, he enjoys it very much."

It surprised Carter to hear her admission. He was expecting her to deny the affair, maybe even beg his forgiveness, but he didn't think she would give in so easily.

"Carter," she said, "I'd like a divorce."

His breath caught in his throat. "What did you say?" This was definitely NOT the way he thought the conversation would go.

She looked at him calmly and repeated, "I said, I'd like a divorce."

He felt the fury instantly. He tightened his hands into fists and was breathing through his nose, like a bull ready to storm a red flag. "You'd like a divorce after all I've done for you? After all I've done for this family?" His reflexes kicked in, bringing him to a standing position. His voice got louder and louder. "You were nothing when I met you. I gave you everything you ever wanted; everything you ever needed. And you want a divorce? You ungrateful bitch!"

Loretta was just looking at him, not uttering a word. Carter pounded the table with both fists, making water splash out of the crystal glasses sitting in front of them. He stomped out of the dining room and left the house, slamming the door that led from the kitchen into the garage hard enough to knock the kitchen clock off the wall. The tires squealed on the garage floor as he backed his car out and sped off into the dark, rainy night.

Loretta quietly got up from the table and went to her bedroom, leaving Irene to clean up the meal that had barely been touched.

Carter drove around for a while, but the rain was making it too hard to see the road and the last thing he needed right now was to wrap the car around a tree. He pulled into the first bar he could find and had a drink. Luckily, the one he picked was almost empty. The last thing he wanted was a crowd. Carter asked the bartender for a Glenlivet scotch, neat, and sat at a table towards the back of the room, nursing his drink. The heavy wooden bench seats had high backs and the pendulum light hanging from the ceiling cast very little light, giving him the sense of privacy that he needed.

He hadn't expected that from Loretta. *Who in hell did she think she was? I've worked my ass off over the years just so she and the kids could have a nice home, nice cars, a vacation home in the Dominican, and this is the thanks I get? It's not like she's made it easy to be married to her. She's put me through a lot, thanks to her violent temper. Fine! If that's what she wants, she can have the divorce, but I won't make it easy for her. I'm not giving her one damned penny. I'm not supporting her and that freaking boyfriend of hers. She can get a damned job if she needs to. I don't give a shit.*

⚖️

After a sleepless night, Carter stopped in the next day to see Tommy Gleason, his father's close friend and long-time attorney. Mike Mills and Tommy were the same age and had grown up together. Carter had used his services a few times for real estate transactions, wills, and the sporadic legal questions involving the firm, but certainly not for anything along these lines. He needed to find out what a divorce would mean to him and his wallet.

"Carter, I'm not sure this is the answer you want to hear, but a divorce is going to be costly." Tommy said. "You and Loretta have been married for over 26 years, so any property acquired during that time will have to be split down the middle. And she will probably get maintenance of, say, around $6,000 a month."

"Are you kidding me? Six grand every freaking month? Holy shit! That's outrageous! What about the house, the cars, the investments? I paid for all of it!" Carter's voice steadily rose until he was almost shouting.

Tommy kept his voice low in an attempt to demonstrate to Carter that he didn't need to yell. "Well, like I said, the judge will probably split the joint assets down the middle. If one of you wants the house, that person would have to buy out the other person's interest. Otherwise, you would have to sell the house and split any remaining equity. The same would be true for the condo in Punta Cana and the investments."

Carter ran his hands through his hair as he paced in front of Tommy. "This is ridiculous. It's going to cost me a fortune. Everything I've worked for will end up either in her pocket or dissolved and sold. There has to be another way!"

"Carter, the law looks at the marital assets as joint property, and treats that property equally between the partners. It doesn't matter who earned what."

Carter sat down with a thud in the overstuffed leather chair in front of Tommy's desk. All he could do was shake his head with the proverbial steam coming out of his ears.

Unbeknownst to Carter, Loretta also went to see a lawyer that morning and gave the attorney a retainer to start the divorce proceedings. With that done, the next step was to look for an apartment. She and Kim went together to talk with a real estate agent and gave him an idea of what Loretta was looking for. Nothing too big or flashy, just some place nice, maybe three bedrooms for when the kids came to visit. Loretta wanted to stay in the Gaithersburg area and didn't want to spend a ton of money on the rent, but other than that, she didn't have any other needs or desires. For now, she would have to be careful with her money. There was no telling when or if she would get a monthly maintenance check from Carter, but she had enough squirreled away from her own investments she could live comfortably, at least for a little while. She'd been out of the workforce for many years now, so the idea of having to get a job to help with her financial status was intimidating, but if she had to, Loretta would do it.

Later that night, Loretta found Carter sitting at the desk in his home office with a small desk lamp giving off the only light in the room. He had both hands wrapped around a crystal tumbler, his thumb gently stroking the curve of the glass. He was staring out the window with a look on his face that Loretta couldn't read. She hesitated at the open doorway, took a deep breath, and knocked on the door with a gentle rap.

He took a sip from the glass in his hand, looked at her, and said, "What do you want?"

She stepped a few feet into the office. "I just want to talk to you for a minute." She decided it was best to just come right out with it. "I talked to an attorney today. I've asked him to start the divorce proceedings."

"So, this is it, huh? You're going to split up the family, just like that. Is that really what you want?" Even in the darkened room, she could see the anger in his eyes as he glared at her, before he turned back towards the window.

"Listen, Carter. You know as well as I do that this marriage fell apart a long time ago. You've been having affairs since the children were little and I just looked the other way. Neither one of us has been happy for years. That's no way for either of us to live, let alone the kids."

"And what do you think the children will say when they hear that their mother is breaking up the family?"

She would not take the bait. "I think the sooner we get this done, the better." Loretta turned on her heel and left the room, but not before she heard Carter mutter to himself, "Stupid bitch."

⚖

In the days that followed, Loretta looked at quite a few apartments before finally deciding on a two-bedroom apartment in a very nice area just outside of Gaithersburg. It was a bit pricey, but it included a modern kitchen, a spacious living area, and a loft that she was sure she could use as a spare bedroom if she needed to. The only drawback was that it wouldn't be available for another two months, but that would give her enough time to pack. The next day, after she'd had time to think and be sure of her decision, Loretta put down a deposit on the apartment. She felt nervous about taking the leap, but she knew in her gut it was the right thing to do.

Loretta was waiting for Carter as he came through the kitchen door after work later that afternoon. She'd been talking to Irene, telling her about the apartment, but as soon as they heard the automatic garage door opening, Irene gave Loretta a motherly pat on the hand and retreated to her room. As Carter walked in, he saw Loretta, who was standing with her arms crossed, one hip resting against the granite-topped island. He set his briefcase on the floor.

She needed him to understand that this was real. She was leaving him. "Carter," she said, "I just wanted you to know that I rented an apartment today. It won't be available though, for another couple of months."

He looked at her with anger in his eyes, but she was used to that. It didn't even faze her anymore.

"Fine," Carter said. "Let me know if you need help packing." He picked up his briefcase and stormed out of the kitchen. As he walked past her, his shoulder connected with hers, knocking her off balance. Luckily, she was able to catch herself before she fell. She just shook her head, more and more convinced that she'd made the right choice.

Chapter 9
2012
Loretta's Death

After an unusually calm and rational conversation, the one thing that Carter and Loretta had agreed upon was that it would be best if they kept the divorce quiet from the outside world. Loretta hadn't wanted to give the gossips in their social circle any fodder and Carter was concerned, as always, about his image. It would be best, they agreed, if they continued to attend the various church and social functions, acting as if they had the perfect family, even though the marriage was all but over. Without even realizing it, they had been doing this for many years, so it would not be hard to continue in that way.

When the kids were told of the pending divorce, the boys didn't seem too surprised by the announcement, but Margaret was shocked and became very upset.

"I don't understand. What's going to happen to us? Where will we live?" Margaret looked from her mother to her father and back again, looking for answers.

"Don't worry, sweetheart." Carter wrapped Margaret in a hug. She cried on his shoulder as he patted her back. "It'll be okay. I promise. I'll see to it, just like I always do."

Two days after Loretta put down a deposit on the apartment, she, Carter and Margaret were planning to go to a brunch that was an annual fundraiser for the local animal shelter. None of them wanted to go, but it was in keeping with their agreement that they continue to put up a front. This was a fundraiser that they had gone to for several years, and they felt it might draw unnecessary questions from others if they skipped it. None of them felt very sociable, but under the circumstances, they agreed it was still best, for appearance's sake, if they went.

Margaret had worked until late the night before, so Carter waited as long as he could, and at 7:30 that morning, he knocked on her bedroom door to see if she was awake yet. When he didn't hear her respond, he opened the door and poked his head in.

"Margaret, it's time to get up," he softly called to her. "We have to go to that brunch your mother signed us up for."

Margaret yawned and said, "I know, dad. My alarm already went off, but I hit the snooze button. Just give me a couple of minutes and I'll get up."

Carter looked at the lump in the bed, the top of her head the only part not covered by a comforter. "Alright. I'm going out for a quick run around the pond. I'll be back soon. Your mother must be in the shower now. I can hear the water running."

Margaret mumbled something unintelligible as she snuggled deeper under the covers. Carter shut the door.

Margaret had gotten out of bed and was getting ready when she heard her father calling to her. "Margaret! Come quick! Your mother fell!" As she opened the bedroom door, Margaret saw her father standing outside her room in the hallway, bent over with his hands on his knees, as if he was trying to catch his breath. "Your mother ... she's on the floor in the shower."

"Oh, my God! Is she alright?" Margaret followed as Carter ran down the hall towards her mother's bedroom suite.

Carter stopped and looked back at her. "I don't know. Maybe you'd better call for an ambulance."

Margaret ran into the first room she came to. Her mother's office, which was located right outside her mother's bedroom suite, had a phone that she could use to call 911. As she dialed, she could hear her father's footsteps pounding the carpeted floor in the hallway as he continued running toward her mother's bedroom.

"Nine-one-one. What's your emergency?" asked the voice on the other end of the phone.

"Yes, this is Margaret Mills. My mother fell and we need an ambulance." Margaret gave the call taker the address.

"Is she injured?"

"I don't know. My dad just went to her." Margaret was nervously twisting the phone cord around her finger.

"Can you see her, Margaret?" the call taker asked.

"No, but my dad said she fell in the shower and he's with her now."

"Okay, Margaret, can you go to your mother? I need to know if she's hurt at all." Margaret tried to step into the hallway to see if she could spot either of her parents, but the cord on the phone was too short.

"I'm on a landline. I'll have to grab the phone from her room. Let me put you on hold so I can get the other phone."

"Okay, Margaret. That's fine. I'll wait right here."

Margaret put the phone on hold, then ran through Loretta's bedroom and into the water closet that was located midway between the bedroom and the separate bath and shower area. As she picked up the landline by the toilet and reconnected her call with the 911 center, Margaret watched her father carry her mother from the shower. She was naked and her head was bloody. Carter laid Loretta down in the hallway, just outside the water closet where Margaret was standing with the phone pressed to her ear.

"Oh, my god! What's wrong with mom? Dad, don't move her!" As the gravity of the situation hit her,

Margaret screamed and dropped the phone to the floor. Her mother was seriously injured and looked to be unconscious.

"Dad, wait! Don't move her!" Margaret was flapping her hands at her father.

Carter ignored Margaret's pleading, picked Loretta up again and moved her into the large bedroom. Margaret watched in horror as he laid her mother on the floor next to the bed. He knelt down with his ear to her face, as if he was listening for her breaths.

"She's not breathing," he said.

Margaret ran into the bedroom and knelt on the floor next to her parents. "Daddy! Make her breathe! We have to do CPR!" Margaret tried to open her mother's airway by tilting her head back and lifting her jaw.

Carter started doing chest compressions. He looked at his daughter wide-eyed and asked, "Where in hell is the ambulance?"

"I don't know, Dad! I don't know! I'll call them again! Oh my God! They need to help her!"

With that, Margaret ran downstairs to the kitchen and called 911 from the cordless phone. A different call taker than the first one was on the phone with Margaret, asking her more questions. This time, Margaret had seen her mother and could let the call taker know it wasn't good.

"Oh my God! I think she's dead!" Margaret was screaming into the phone as she paced the floor. "My mother isn't breathing at all and there's blood everywhere! The ambulance needs to get here right away! Please, tell them to hurry!"

"Margaret, I need you to make sure the door is open so the ambulance can get in to help your mother. The police and rescue are on their way, too." The call taker was speaking with a calm and firm tone.

Margaret set the cordless phone on the kitchen counter and ran to the front door, throwing it wide open. The ambulance wasn't there yet. As fast as her legs could carry her, Margaret ran back up the stairs to her mother's bedroom. Her father was kneeling next to her mother, trying to cover her with a blanket he'd taken from the bed. He looked up at Margaret as he arranged the blanket over his wife's body, being careful not to cover her face. "She's getting cold. I need to keep her warm."

Margaret ran to the bedroom window that faced the front of the house. "I hear them. They're coming. I can hear the sirens." Margaret ran downstairs and out the front door just as the paramedics from the fire department were grabbing their medical gear from the back of the rescue squad. A police car rolled up right behind them.

Margaret was screaming. "Come on! Hurry! She's not breathing and there's blood everywhere! I think she's dead! Hurry, please! I think my mother is dead!"

The paramedics followed Margaret as she led the way through the house and up the stairs to her mother's bedroom, looking back after every few steps to make sure they were still behind her. Once in the bedroom, the medics got right to work on their patient.

Margaret and her father stepped out of the way. Margaret watched in horror as a paramedic inserted an IV into her mother's arm. Another paramedic covered her mouth and nose with a clear mask that had a tube leading to a green oxygen tank. One of them hooked up cords that led from an AED to her chest. The other talked to a doctor at the hospital through the radio.

The medics worked furiously to get her heart started again, but it was no use. Loretta Mills, wife of Carter Mills, mother of Steven, Danny and Margaret, sister to Kim, and lover to Bernie Lehrman, was dead.

A police officer gently took Margaret by the elbow and led her downstairs, her father following close behind. She sat on a couch in the living room with her hands wrapped around her waist, as her shoulders shook from the sobs. Tears flowed in a heavy stream down her cheeks. She rocked back and forth as the realization sunk in that her mother was gone. Carter sat next to her, rubbing her back in sync with her rocking.

There were so many people in the house that it looked like a circus ... a very sad, strange and surreal circus. Carter and Margaret watched as at least a half-dozen people went in and out the front door, some wearing uniforms, some in plain clothes. One man in a police uniform, who said he was an evidence technician, was there with all kinds of equipment. Another man identified himself as the medical examiner. Margaret watched the comings and goings of the strangers parading through her home without comprehension.

Two of the men in business suits identified themselves as police investigators, and asked both Margaret and Carter to tell them what had happened. Carter explained that when he'd brought a cup of coffee to his wife in her bedroom, he heard the shower running, so he knew she was getting ready for a brunch the family was supposed to attend. He left to go on a run around the neighborhood, but by the time he returned home, it was getting late, so he wanted to make sure his family would be ready to leave soon. He checked on his daughter first, and from her bedroom doorway, he could hear the water running in Loretta's shower. At that point, he thought it odd that she was still in the shower, so he went to check on her. That's when he found her, unconscious and bloody, on the shower floor. The shower room was too wet and steamy for Carter to attempt CPR, so he carried her into the bedroom. Unfortunately, he still wasn't able to save her.

Margaret, clearly in shock, could not tell them what she had seen. The men—the ones that said they were investigators—didn't press her. Her mother was dead, and she was numb.

⚖

The next few days were difficult ones for the Mills family, as they are for anyone who's suffered a loss. They went about their daily routines as best they could, their minds clouded in disbelief and sadness.

The boys looked to be handling their mother's death stoically, with no public displays of grief. Their friends came over, and they would all retreat to the basement game room, preferring to play pool or video games as an escape. Although they kept busy, Carter could tell they were very distant and uncharacteristically quiet around their friends. It pleased Carter to see that they could be so self-controlled. He had taught them well.

But Margaret was the complete opposite, preferring to stay in her room by herself with the door closed. As he passed by her room, Carter could hear Margaret's sobs. She was more like her mother, in that she was far more emotional than Carter. And all Carter could do was wander around the house, going from one room to the next, finding it hard to figure out what to do with himself. He couldn't sit still, but he couldn't concentrate on anything either.

Soon after Loretta was declared dead, the medical examiner had taken her body to their office for an autopsy. In the meantime, Carter met with the funeral home and made the necessary arrangements. Carter had also contacted the church regarding the funeral services.

Together, the family picked out the readings and the hymns that the choir would sing. There was nothing left for Carter to do.

As the news spread, it seemed like the phones would never stop ringing. Carter had turned off his cell phone and left strict instructions with Irene to just let the house phone ring. He didn't want to talk to anyone, and as a result, his voicemail and answering machine were quickly filling up with the endless offers from well-wishers who wanted to know if they needed anything. If that wasn't bad enough, it was surprising how many people felt they had to come to the house to offer condolences, since no one had picked up the phone when they called. *These people can't take the hint. Don't they know I don't want to talk to anyone?* Carter thought.

And even though Irene was on hand, there were some people that felt they had to bring over a casserole dish or a cake of some sort. The refrigerator was full, and the countertops were getting there. *Did they think the family would starve?*

At the calling hours, held a few days later, the line of people stretched through the funeral home, out the door and around the corner of the building. It seemed like it would never end. It was the longest four hours of Carter's life. If he had to say thanks for coming one more time, he thought he was going to explode. *These people have no idea what Loretta was really like. She had everyone fooled.* But he plastered the puppy dog eyes on his face, shook their hands, and accepted the hugs from the many people that came to offer their condolences to the family.

The morning of the funeral, the church was filled with so many mourners that Carter didn't think there was an empty seat to be had. The priest droned on and on about what a good, selfless and dedicated woman Loretta had been, always giving of her time to help at the church and school, always willing to head the different committees, making sure that the various functions and fundraisers went off without a hitch. *Yeah, she was a good woman, all right,* Carter thought. *A woman with a nasty streak a mile long is more like it. And what's so good about wanting to get a divorce and break up the family? I wonder what the priest would say if he knew about that. What if he knew about her boyfriend? What would the priest say about that little tidbit?* Carter swiped at the corner of his eyes with his knuckle, wiping away a non-existent tear, as the priest looked his way.

Chapter 10
The Investigation Begins

Investigator Steve "Mac" MacIntosh had been with the Montgomery County Police Department for almost seventeen years, serving the past five years as sergeant of the Criminal Investigation Division at the Division Six Headquarters in Gaithersburg. Loretta's death was certainly not the first one Mac had dealt with, but there was something about this one that wasn't sitting right with him. The husband, an upstanding member of the community and a career professional, said that his wife had slipped and fallen in the shower, that he had carried her from the shower into the bedroom, and that he tried to give her CPR. The victim had a deep gash on the side of her head, a black eye that was swollen shut, and marks on some other parts of her body that Mac just couldn't explain. And it seemed to Mac that there was an excessive amount of blood spattered throughout the bedroom suite. More blood spatter, he thought, than there should be from simply being carried from one room to the next. There was something that kept niggling at Mac, and he'd learned long ago to trust his gut. He couldn't put his finger on it, but his gut was screaming at him that something wasn't right.

Three days after her death, the coroner, George Schmidt, faxed over the results of the autopsy. Dr. Schmidt's findings confirmed Loretta had died from a skull fracture on the side of her head, above her right ear.

With the autopsy results in hand, Mac pored over the crime scene photos for the umpteenth time. To him, it seemed like the cut on Loretta's head was deeper than it should be from a fall. Granted, the victim had presumably fallen and hit the right side of her head on the low, tiled bench that ran along the length of the shower, but her skull was actually fractured. That's a lot of damage from a fall from a standing position. And what about her eye? Her left eye was a nasty shade of purple and swollen shut, for God's sake! Dr. Schmidt had explained it away by saying the force of the fall caused a ripple effect. Loretta's skull impacted with the tiled bench, and that impact had pushed her brain from the right side towards the left side of her skull, followed by her brain pushing against the back of her left eye, which, in turn, caused the swelling and bruising. To Mac, that theory just didn't explain the momentum needed to cause that much damage. *It might have been a fall,* Mac thought, *but it seems like she might have had help with the force of that fall.*

"Hey, Coop. Come here for a second." Mac waved his hand at the investigator, who was sitting at the desk next to his own.

Mac and James Cooper had been working together as partners for almost five years. When Cooper had been assigned to the team, they had quickly formed a tight bond, even though they were as different as night and day. Mac was average height, salt and pepper hair, and thirty-nine years old. Coop, as he was called, was tall, skinny and thirty-five years old. Where Mac was quiet, reserved and pensive, Cooper was much more outgoing, humorous and impulsive. He brought an infectious energy to CID that kept everyone on their toes, although at times, he could also be a pain in the ass. But even on the days when his patience was wearing thin, Mac couldn't stay upset with Coop for long. They were an odd mix, but they worked well together and worked tirelessly on their cases until they were satisfied that there were no loose ends.

"What do you make of this?" Mac asked. He had the photos splayed across his desk. "Look at the blood spatter on the walls and the other stuff. Why would there be blood on things like the lampshade? And why would it be spattered that high on the wall?"

"I don't know, Mac. What are you thinking?" Cooper asked, as he leaned over the desk to peer at the photos.

"I'm not sure, but it seems to me, if she fell in the bathroom and all he did was carry her from there into the bedroom, there shouldn't be that much blood on the bedroom walls or the nightstand."

"What did Doc Schmidt say? Did you get the autopsy results yet?" Coop asked. He had a couple of the photos in his hand and was giving them an intense study.

"He said it was an accidental death and that she died from a fractured skull." Mac said as he grabbed a magnifying glass and was scrutinizing the details in the photos.

"No shit. We knew that much." Coop rolled his eyes. "Was there anything else? Any drugs or alcohol in her system?"

"No, nothing like that at all. Just the physical damage to her body." Mac said. "I called and talked to him after I got the report. I specifically asked him about her swollen eye, but he was adamant that the fall caused the damage. He said it was caused by the impact of her head hitting the tile and her brain bouncing off the eyeball."

Coop cringed as he pictured what Mac was describing. "Then you have to let it go, man. That's all you can do."

"Yeah, that's the problem. If the medical examiner says it was an accidental death, that's pretty much the final word. But it's bugging me." Mac said. "I'd love to get back in that house and have a better look at the bedroom and shower area, but it would take a search warrant at this point, and no judge will give me a search warrant based on a gut feeling."

Coop put the photos back on the pile of papers on Mac's desk and went back to his own desk. With a sigh, Mac put the photos back in the manila folder marked with Loretta's name and set it on the edge of his desk.

Two weeks later and Loretta Mills' death still bothered Mac, but he'd had to put it aside, as there were other cases to work on. There was still nothing that said it was anything but an accidental slip and fall in the shower. That is, until the day he got an anonymous letter.

Anita, the civilian clerk, had given Mac the mail, and he looked at it with the usual lack of interest. Nothing but junk mail, a couple of invoices to be paid, and a letter in a plain white envelope addressed to Sergeant MacIntosh, with no return address. He raised his eyebrows with curiosity as he reached for the letter opener. Inside the envelope, Mac found a plain, white sheet of copy paper ... with no logos or letterhead ... typed with some alarming words.

Dear Investigator,

I was friends with Loretta Mills for years, and I can tell you, she didn't die by accident. I don't know how he did it, but her husband killed her. He's had several affairs over the years and she always looked the other way for the sake of the children. But just before she died, she told him she was in love with someone else and wanted a divorce. Even though they'd lived separate lives and even slept in separate bedrooms for a number of years, he was very angry with her when she told him this. He had also been physically and verbally abusive to her in the past. I truly believe he killed her.

Please, for the sake of Loretta's eternal peace, check into this.

There was no name, no signature, nothing that pointed out who had written the note. Mac reread the letter two more times and then stood up from his desk. With his eyes still glued to the letter, and without looking where he was going, he brought it over to Coop to look at.

"Hey, Coop. Check this out." Mac handed the letter over to his partner.

After reading it, Coop looked up at Mac, wide-eyed. "Wow!" he said. "This kind of confirms some of what you were feeling, that something's up with her death."

Mac nodded his head as he frowned. "I think it's time to call Mr. Mills in for an interview."

"Sounds like a damn good idea to me." Coop handed the note back to Mac.

"I'll see if I can get a hold of him to have him come in as soon as possible." Mac looked in the report for Carter Mills' cell phone number, picked up the phone and dialed. After four rings, he heard a brusque voice on the other end say, "Hello?"

"Mr. Mills, this is Sergeant MacIntosh, with the Gaithersburg police. I was wondering if you might have some time today to come down to the station. There are a few things I'd like to discuss with you."

"Yeah, well, my schedule is pretty full today, Sergeant. What's going on?" Mac got the impression that Carter, judging from his attitude, was no longer playing the part of the grieving husband.

"It's about your wife's death, but if you don't mind, I'd rather discuss the details with you when you come in. When can I expect you?"

"Like I said, my schedule is pretty full."

Mac knew all about this game of cat and mouse, and he would not let Mills get the upper hand. "Mr. Mills, if transportation is a problem, I would be happy to send a patrol car to pick you up, or if you prefer, I could meet you at your office."

After a long hesitation, Carter answered. "Fine. I'll be there at two o'clock. And I'll have my attorney with me."

"That would be fine. In fact, In fact, I would strongly recommend that. See you at two, Mr. Mills." Mac hung up the phone, looked at his partner with a sly grin and announced, "He'll be here at two with his attorney."

He let out a long breath and relaxed his shoulders a bit as he opened the manila folder labeled L. MILLS. He'd had it sitting on the corner of his desk since Loretta died, unable to file it away in the Completed files. He placed the anonymous letter in the file, right on top.

⚖

At 2:15, Carter Mills and Tommy Gleason approached the front door of the Gaithersburg Police Department.

Tommy stopped before going through the door. "Carter, you're going to have to answer their questions truthfully and as best as you can, but if I feel that they're stepping out of line, I'll intercept."

"That's fine. I don't plan on being here for long, anyway. I've got more important things to do, and this is bullshit." Carter yanked open the front door with more force than was necessary.

After asking for Sgt. MacIntosh, the department's civilian clerk Anita, showed Carter and Tommy to a small conference room. It was a nondescript room with a wood-laminate table in the center, about a half-dozen chairs gathered around, and a flat-screen television with a DVD player in a far corner. Both Carter and Tommy declined the cup of coffee that Anita offered them.

Anita had told Mac and Coop right away that Carter and his attorney had arrived. Mac, however, wanted to let Carter sit and stew for a while. It was another ten minutes before they entered the room.

"Good afternoon, Mr. Mills. Counselor. I'm Sgt. Macintosh and this is Inv. Cooper." Mac poured on the charm, offered them both a warm handshake and smiled cordially at the men seated at the table as he and Coop took seats opposite them. Coop placed a manila folder on the table while Mac took his time, opening up a legal-sized pad of yellow paper to a blank page before reaching into his suit-coat pocket to retrieve a pen. He would take notes, while the video camera hanging from the ceiling above the television would record the conversation.

"Thank you for coming. Just so that you're aware, this interview is being recorded," Mac said, as he pointed over his shoulder to the video camera. "We just have a few questions for you, Mr. Mills, but I'd like to start by reading you your Miranda rights."

"Miranda rights? Are you serious? Am I under arrest?" Carter, wide-eyed, looked from Mac to Tommy and back again.

Tommy reached over and put his hand on Carter's arm to silence him. "Sergeant, is my client under arrest?"

"No, he's not under arrest, counselor. We just have a couple of questions, and since it involves the death of Mr. Mills' wife, we want to make sure that his rights are protected. It's strictly a precautionary measure, at this point," Mac said.

Mac wiggled his fingers towards Cooper, who opened the manila folder and withdrew a form. Mac took the form and passed it across the table to Carter.

"Mr. Mills, this is a printed copy of your legal rights. As I read them to you, I would ask that you initial each one on this form, signifying that we have read you your rights and you understand them."

Carter looked at Tommy, who gave a quick nod of his head and reached into his coat pocket to withdraw a costly Mont Blanc pen for Carter to use.

"You have the right to remain silent and refuse to answer our questions. Do you understand what this means?" Mac locked in on Carter's eyes as he recited the Miranda rights to him.

"Of course, I understand." Carter responded snidely, maintaining eye contact with Mac.

"Okay, Mr. Mills," Mac spoke slowly, "but you also need to initial here on the lines after each right that I'm reading to you." Mac glanced at Coop out of the corner of his eye, who, judging by the slight smirk on his face, was enjoying this bit of intimidation.

Mac recited each of the rights, pausing between each one so that Carter could initial the form.

"Okay, Mr. Mills. Why don't we start by having you tell us what happened the morning your wife died," Mac sat poised with pen in hand.

"What's to tell? I saw her on the floor of the shower, carried her into the bedroom, and started CPR. End of story." Carter sat back in the chair, his hands clasped together on the table. He was obviously used to being in control and was trying to convey a sense of annoyance.

"Well," Coop jumped in, "let's back up a bit. We understand you had separate bedrooms, is that correct?"

"Yes, she and I slept in separate rooms, but that's because I snore and she's a light sleeper."

"It wasn't because there was trouble in your marriage?" Coop asked.

Carter sat up straight in his chair, but just as he opened his mouth to answer, Gleason put his hand on Carter's forearm to stop him. "My client has already answered your question, Investigator."

"Why were you in her room that morning?" Coop emphasized the word '*her*' in his question.

"Every morning, I brought my wife a cup of coffee. I'm almost always the first one to get up, so I would go downstairs to get the coffee started. When it was ready, I would bring her a cup."

"So Mr. Mills, you brought your wife a cup of coffee every day, even though you weren't necessarily getting along too well."

Carter looked irritated. "Why do you keep saying that? I loved my wife. I brought her coffee every morning, and I kissed her goodnight and told her I loved her every night. Who says we weren't getting along?"

Coop ignored the question and asked, "Mr. Mills, why were you checking on your wife that morning? Why not just leave the coffee and go about your business?"

Once again, Carter looked at his attorney, who raised his eyebrows and gave an almost imperceptible nod of his head.

Carter took a couple of breaths before answering. "That morning we were supposed to go to a fundraising breakfast. It usually takes Loretta at least an hour to get ready, sometimes more. I had a cup of coffee for her in my hand, so I left it on her nightstand. I could hear Loretta's shower running, so I knew she was getting ready. Then I went to wake my daughter, and she said that she would get up but wanted a few more minutes in bed. After that, I went for a quick run around the neighborhood. When I came back, I took a shower and then checked on Margaret to make sure she was getting ready because it was getting late. I heard music playing in her room, so I knew she was up. From the hallway outside Margaret's room, I could hear the shower was still running in Loretta's room, and I thought that was weird, so I went in. That's when I found her on the floor in the shower."

"What was weird about hearing the shower running?" Coop asked.

"The fact that she'd been in the shower for that long. It was getting late, and she needed to get a move on if we were going to make the breakfast on time."

"And how long do you think she was in the shower?"

The attorney spoke up, saying, "I believe that would be speculation on the part of my client, Investigator. I'm advising him not to answer that question."

Mac asked, "Mr. Mills, you told us you went for a quick run, is that correct?"

"Yes, that's what I just said." Carter was getting snarky.

"Where exactly did you go on this quick run of yours?" Coop's questions were dripping with sarcasm. Two could play that game.

Carter shrugged his shoulders before answering. "I don't remember. I think I ran to the pond and back. Yes, now that I think about it, that's what I did. I just ran around the pond and came back."

"Uh, huh. Did anyone see you on this run, Mr. Mills?"

"I have no way of knowing that. I didn't pay attention to who was looking out their windows or walking their dog while I was on my run. Now, if you're asking me if I stopped to speak with anyone, the answer is no, I didn't." Carter glared at Coop.

"Okay, that's fine. And how long did it take you to run around the pond and come back to your home, Mr. Mills?" Coop was laying it on thick.

"I guess about fifteen minutes or so. I don't know exactly because I didn't time it."

"Is that the route that you normally take on your run?"

"Sometimes, yes, but not always."

"If you don't run around the pond, where do you go?"

"It depends on how much time I have and what I feel like. I just run through the neighborhood, but I like to run through different streets. If I see a house that's for sale, I like to keep an eye on it. When it sells, I contact the new owners to see if they need an investment broker." Carter raised one corner of his mouth in a smile, as if he was proud of himself.

Coop asked, "You said you moved Loretta from the shower into the bedroom and did CPR on her. Why didn't you do CPR in the bathroom where you found her?"

"I tried," Carter said, "but it was too steamy, and the floor was wet. And the lighting in that room sucks. There are a couple of skylights, but it was still dark outside, and the only other overhead lights in that room are small, recessed lights."

"Are you referring to the area directly outside the shower?" Mac asked.

"Yes. The tile was slippery, so I moved her onto the rug in the bedroom."

"Mr. Mills," Coop asked, "why did you leave your wife and go down the hall to ask Margaret to call 911?"

"Because I knew I needed help. Loretta was badly hurt, and she was unconscious." Carter shrugged his shoulders, as if it was an obvious answer.

Mac locked his eyes on Carter. "I remember from the morning she died that there were three different phones within reach, any one of which you could have used to call 911 yourself. Why didn't you use one of them?"

"I don't know. I guess I wasn't thinking clearly. It was very upsetting to see my wife like that. I guess I just wanted someone to help and since Margaret was the only other one at home, I asked for her help." Carter had the decency to hang his head and drop the sarcasm when he answered the question.

Mills looked to the side at Tommy, who gave a nod and said, "I think you can understand, Investigator, that my client was under tremendous stress at that time, and probably in shock."

Coop looked at the attorney, almost as if he'd forgotten he was there, and then back to Mills. "I'm also wondering, Mr. Mills, why you were in your pajamas when the police arrived and not in your running clothes or business clothes."

"You can't be serious. You're asking about the clothes I was wearing?" Carter glanced at Tommy, but the attorney nodded, a sign that he should answer the question. Carter was bobbing his knees up and down, a sure sign he was getting agitated.

Carter shook his head. "I took a quick shower after I got back, but it was still a bit too early to get into my suit. I don't like putting on my suit until the last minute, in case I get it dirty or wrinkled, so I just put on my pajamas."

"You put on the top and the bottoms, then?"

"I don't remember."

"Do you remember, Mr. Mills, if it was the same pair of pajamas that you'd worn to bed the night before?"

"I have no idea what I wore to bed that night. Sometimes I have a couple of pairs of pajamas on my bedroom chair, so I'll just grab whatever is there. Who cares?" Carter put his elbows on the table and leaned forward, glaring at Coop.

"Did you change your clothes from the time you found your wife on the floor in the shower to the time when the ambulance arrived?" Mirroring Carter, Coop leaned on the table, steepling his fingertips together. Coop always enjoyed playing the part of the proverbial bad cop, and for a guy who rarely got angry, he played the part very well.

"No, of course not. Why would I have changed my clothes at a time like that?" Carter asked.

"If what you say is true, Mr. Mills, and you had to carry your wife out of the shower and into the bedroom, then you would have gotten soaked. Not only from the shower, which according to you was still running, but also from her blood."

"I didn't pay attention to how wet or bloody my clothes were. My wife wasn't breathing, and I was trying to save her by performing CPR. That's all I know." Carter was back to giving clipped answers.

"Speaking of the blood," Mac asked, "how do you think she got that huge cut on the side of her head, above her ear?"

"How do I know? There's a low bench, like a step, that runs along the one side of the shower. She probably hit her head on that bench when she fell. Look, if you don't mind, I need to leave and get back to my office. I have a lot of work to do." Carter stood up, and following his lead, so did Tommy.

"Okay, Mr. Mills. That's it for today, but we may have more questions for you at some point in the future. I would advise you not to leave town for any length of time." Coop extended his hand, but Carter just looked down at the hand without taking it and walked out of the room. Tommy shook hands with Coop and Mac, wished them both a good day, and followed his client out the door.

Mac and Coop walked back to their office. "Man, oh, man, Mac. This guy is lying through his teeth. Did you see how jumpy he was getting? I'd love to play poker with him some day!"

"I agree," Mac said. "But I've got more questions now than I had before. I want to talk to the medics that were on the scene that day to get their take on things. And daddy is not going to like it, but I think it's time we get the daughter in here and ask for her side of the story. I think I'll try to call her right now."

"Shouldn't you run it past their attorney to see if it's okay to talk to the daughter?" Coop asked.

"The attorney represents Carter," Mac said, while reaching with one hand for the desk phone. "He said nothing about having to go through him to talk to anyone else in the family. He'll probably say that eventually, but as of right now, as far as we know, he only represents the father. I'm going to get a hold of her and see what happens."

"Cool beans," Coop said with a chuckle. "That works for me."

Mac dialed Margaret's cell phone number, and after five or six rings, he heard the voicemail pick up. He left his name and number, letting her know he had a few questions he'd like to ask her. A few moments after he set his cell phone down on the desk, it rang, alerting him to an incoming call.

Mac recognized the number on the phone's display as being the one he had just dialed. "Good afternoon, Sgt. MacIntosh speaking."

He heard a young female voice on the other end of the phone. "Good afternoon, Sergeant. This is Margaret Mills. You just called me?"

"Yes, Margaret. Thank you for returning my call." Mac said, as he flashed the thumbs up sign to Coop. "I was hoping you might have some time today to come to the station and talk with me. I just have a couple of questions I'd like to ask you about the morning your mom passed away. It shouldn't take long."

"I don't know. My dad's not home yet and I really should ask him first." Her voice was barely above a whisper.

"No problem, Margaret. I'd appreciate it if you'd talk it over with your dad and decide on a time that's good for you. Just call me back as soon as possible and let me know when to expect you."

"Okay, Sergeant. I'll let you know. Thank you."

Mac nodded his head as he set the phone down. "She's going to talk to her father first, but I guarantee she'll be in."

"You think so?" asked Coop.

"Absolutely. Carter is nervous right now, so he'll call the attorney, and the attorney will turn around and tell Margaret to come in. I doubt very much the attorney believes that the death was anything but an accident. Even so, they don't want to raise any suspicions and refusing to talk to the police would not look good." Mac was tapping the desk with his index finger to stress the point. "Yeah, she'll be in to talk to us."

Sure enough, Mac's prediction came to fruition when his phone rang first thing the next morning. Mac picked up the phone, talked for only a minute, then broke into a wide smile as he hung up the phone.

"What did I tell you, Coop. That was Margaret Mills. She'll be here with Tommy Gleason, the attorney, at eleven o'clock." Mac said.

"Cool. But I think I'll let you play the bad cop this time. She seems like a good kid. I don't want to say the wrong thing and make her cry," Coop said, smiling.

"Thanks a lot, Coop. Then again, an interview like this calls for tact, diplomacy, and compassion. You're right. I'd better handle it." Mac laughed and slapped Coop on the shoulder as he walked past his partner.

⚖

At eleven o'clock on the dot, Anita buzzed Mac's phone extension to let him know that Margaret and the attorney had arrived. She had already escorted them into the same conference room where Margaret's father was interviewed the day before.

Mac pushed open the conference room door and went in, with Coop right behind him. "Good morning, Miss Mills. Mr. Gleason." Mac and Coop both held out their hands to offer handshakes and then took a seat. They considered Margaret a witness, not a suspect, so there was no need to read her the Miranda warnings, the way they had for her father.

Mac began the conversation by saying, "First of all, Miss Mills, let me start by saying how sorry we are at your mom's passing. We know this isn't easy for you, especially since it's only been a few weeks, so if at any time you need to take a break, or get some water or anything at all, you just let us know."

Margaret looked at the tissue she was wadding up in her hands and softly said, "thank you."

Coop, true to his word, sat back and let Mac ask the questions. "Miss Mills, just so you and Mr. Gleason are aware, we are videotaping this interview." Margaret followed his finger as he pointed to the camera hanging from the ceiling. "I'm going to ask you some questions that might be difficult. We understand that. We'll try to get through this together, as quickly and easily as we can, okay?" Mac looked at Margaret and saw a tear running down her cheek.

"Okay." Margaret wiped the tear away, but another one followed.

"Let's start with your mom's routine in the morning. If she knew she had to be somewhere by, say, nine o'clock, what time would she get up?"

"Well, that depends." Margaret said. "She had curly hair, so if she needed to go somewhere, she didn't wash her hair because it took too long to dry and style. She would just, you know, shower her body and keep her hair dry."

Mac was writing notes on his legal pad while he talked to Margaret. "Do you know if she washed her hair that morning?"

"I don't know. Her hair was wet but I don't know if she washed it or not."

"We've already talked to your father, Margaret, and he told us he went for a run that morning. Do you remember him going for a run?"

"No, not really. He's usually the first one up in the mornings, so I'm not sure because I was still in bed. I know he hasn't had a lot of time to run lately because he's been very busy, but he said he was going to go for a run that morning when he first knocked on my door. I don't know if he did, though."

"We understand your father liked to bring your mother a cup of coffee in the morning, too," Mac urged.

"Yes," Margaret said. "He usually makes a pot of coffee and then brings her some."

"Do you know if he brought her a cup that morning?"

Margaret shrugged her shoulders. "I don't know for sure, but he always does."

"Your father went for a run, and then when he got back, he made coffee and brought a cup to your mother. What happened after that?" Mac asked.

"I had hit the snooze button a couple of times, but then I got up and was getting ready when he knocked on my door again. He said my mom fell, and she was on the floor in the shower." A stream of tears fell down her cheeks, but Margaret wiped them away.

Mac reached across the table and patted her arm. "It's okay, Margaret. Take your time."

She took a deep breath and held it a moment to compose herself before continuing. "We ran down the hall, but he said I should call 911. My mom's office is right outside her bedroom, so I stopped in there to call for an ambulance."

"What happened to your father at that point?"

"He kept going to my mom's bedroom. He went back to my mom."

"So you called 911," Mac prompted.

"Yes, but they were asking me a lot of questions that I couldn't answer because I hadn't seen her yet. Also, I was on a landline in the office, and I couldn't get to her, so the person at 911 asked if I could get closer to her. That's when I put that phone on hold and went into her bedroom. I still couldn't see my dad because he was with her in the shower. I picked up the phone in the toilet room because it's close to the shower, and that's when I saw my dad carrying my mom into the bedroom."

"So, the toilet room is a separate room that's between the bedroom and the shower room, right?"

"Yes. He walked past me when I was on the phone in the toilet room, when he brought her from the shower into the bedroom." Margaret's tears continued to fall as she recalled the memory.

"Can you tell me where in the bedroom he put her down?"

"First, he put her down on the floor in front of the toilet room door, but then he picked her up again and carried her into the bedroom. He put her down next to the bed."

"If I understand this correctly, your father carried your mother from the shower area, where it's tiled, down the small hallway, and just past the toilet room where you were. And the hallway and bedroom areas are carpeted, right?"

"Yes, they're carpeted. Only the part where the tub and shower are is tiled."

"Okay, Margaret. You're doing a great job." Mac gave her a reassuring smile. "I have just a few more questions. What happened after you saw your father put your mother down in the hallway?"

"Like I said, he picked her up again, and carried her into the bedroom, and put her down next to the bed. I think that's when I screamed and I hung up on 911. Then he started doing CPR. He was doing chest compressions. I went to help my dad do CPR. I tried to lift her chin and tilt her head back, but it didn't work. She was kind of stiff. We didn't know where the ambulance was, and why it was taking them so long to get there, so I ran downstairs to the kitchen to call 911 again."

"So now your mother was near the bed instead of by the toilet room?"

"Yes. He carried her there."

"Why did you run downstairs to the kitchen to use the phone?" Mac asked.

"I'm not sure why. I guess I was freaked out because at that point I think I knew she must be dead. Plus there was so much blood on the floor where her head was." Margaret closed her eyes and took a deep breath before continuing. "I didn't want to go back and see all that, but I needed to make sure the ambulance got here. That's when I called 911 again from the cordless phone in the kitchen."

"But at some point you went back upstairs, right?"

"Yes. Dad was on the floor next to her. He put a blanket from the bed on her because he said she was getting cold." Margaret seemed to stare at a chip on the table, her voice getting softer. Mac knew the memories were still too raw, and the interview was wearing on the young woman.

"Then what happened?"

"He was asking me where the ambulance was. Then I heard the sirens, so I ran back downstairs. They were coming up the driveway, so I opened the door and yelled at them to hurry. I took them upstairs to show them where her bedroom was and they started working on her to get her breathing again." Margaret sobbed as tears flowed down her cheeks. She looked down at her hands resting in her lap, tightly clutching the tissue.

Tommy had been sitting quietly until then, but he put an arm around Margaret's shoulders and spoke softly. "Gentlemen, I think that's enough."

Mac gave a gentle nod of his head in agreement.

⚖

After the interview, Mac and Coop returned to the CID office. Brandon Powers and Patrick O'Malley were at their desks, both looking up as Mac and Coop walked in.

"Hey," O'Malley spoke up. "How did it go with the daughter?"

"Rough." Mac admitted. "I feel bad for her. Anyone who witnesses a scene like that will have some horrible memories for a long, long time."

"Yeah, that can't be a good thing to go through, but especially when it's her mother," admitted O'Malley.

Mac sat at his desk for several moments, staring at the folder in front of him without comprehending. After a few moments, with a shake of his head and a cleansing breath, he opened the folder to review the notes that he had taken during the interview. Coop was quietly going through his notes as well.

After a while, Mac broke the silence and spoke up. "What do you think, Coop?"

"There's no doubt in my mind that he killed her, but there's no way it happened the way he's claiming it did. There are too many things that just don't make sense. What are your feelings?"

"Oh, he definitely killed her. Now we just have to prove it. I think it's time to call in the big guns. I'll give the DA a call and see what he thinks."

Chapter 11
Search Warrant

Mac pushed the auto-dial button on the landline to connect to the district attorney's office and asked to speak to Montgomery County District Attorney Dennis Wozniak.

"Hey, Dennis. This is Steve MacIntosh with Gaithersburg PD. How are you?" Mac asked with a smile.

"I'm doing well, Mac. How are you doing these days? I thought you were looking to retire?"

Mac groaned and said, "Not unless I win the lottery. I still have to put my son through college."

"I hear you. Damn kids are expensive these days." Dennis chuckled at his own joke. It was common knowledge that the DA had four daughters and doted on them. He was one of those people who had a no nonsense perspective while he was on the job and could be a real S.O.B., but the minute he got home, he was a pussycat, especially where it concerned his girls. He often joked about how they had him wrapped around their fingers.

Mac got right to the point of the call. "Dennis, I have a case that I'd like you to look at. Do you remember a couple of weeks ago when Loretta Mills, wife of investor Carter Mills, died after a fall in the shower?"

"I sure do," Dennis said. "Why, what's up? Is that the case you want me to look at?"

"Yeah, if you would, I'd appreciate it. That whole thing has been stuck in my craw since she died, but the medical examiner said she died from a fall, so there wasn't much I could do. However, I got an anonymous letter in the mail a couple of days ago, asking me to look into the possibility that she was murdered. I'd like your input to see if we should go any further with this."

Mac could hear over the phone the squeak of the DA's wooden chair as he changed position. Dennis and Mac both had a fondness for antique furniture and Dennis had a beautiful roll-top desk and matching chair in his office that Mac would have given his eyeteeth to own. After a slight pause, Dennis asked, "Does the letter suggest who murdered her?"

"Yes," Mac said. "According to this letter, it was her husband. Carter supposedly killed her because she fell in love with someone else and told him she wanted a divorce."

Dennis hesitated. "Hmm. The old, 'if I can't have her, nobody can' motive. What do you think?"

"I think it's a possibility." Mac said. "She had some bruises that I can't account for and there was a hell of a lot of blood at the scene. Too much, I think. We've already interviewed Carter and their daughter, and there are things in his interview that don't make sense either. I can send the tapes of the interviews, too, if you'd like."

"Well, send me what you have and I'll take a look." Dennis said.

"Thanks, Dennis. I appreciate it." Mac hung up the phone, feeling like a weight had been lifted from his shoulders. Maybe now, with the DA's help, he could find out what it was about this case that bothered him so much.

Three days later, Mac and Coop were in a local diner having lunch when Mac's cell phone vibrated against his hip. As he looked at the phone, he saw the DA's number on the screen. Mac quickly swallowed the hot dog he'd been munching on and said hello.

"Mac, this is Dennis." The District Attorney was a down-to-earth kind of guy, never one to flaunt his title, even though he was considered the leading law enforcement officer in the county.

"I looked at the photos and reports you sent over on the Mills case," Dennis said. "I think you've got something here. There are some things that don't make a lot of sense. If you have some time in the next day or two, I'd like to sit down with you and compare notes."

Mac looked across the small table of the diner and nodded his head at Coop, who had just finished his own hot dog and was licking the mustard off his fingers.

"Sure, Dennis. How about tomorrow morning at, say, nine o'clock?" Mac gave a thumbs' up to Coop. "Great. We'll see you then."

"The DA agrees that there's something fishy about the Mills case," Mac said to Coop. He disconnected the call and set his phone on the table. "We're meeting him tomorrow morning to discuss it."

That night, Mac had trouble sleeping. His mind was like a room full of bouncy balls in motion as he lay in bed, tossing and turning. It had become a sort of habit to mull things over in his mind about his current cases on these sleepless nights, and that night, he found himself going over the facts of the Mills case. He thought about the Mills and their marriage, and it wasn't long before his thoughts turned to his own marriage.

He and Alayna had met in college, fallen in love and gotten married right after graduation. They had one son, Austin, who was now thirteen. But because of the hours and hours they spend on the job and away from family, the divorce rate is high among cops. Unfortunately, Mac became just one more number added to that statistic. Over the years, he'd missed several family functions, and had worked a number of important holidays. Finally, Alayna had had enough. When he got called into work on the night of their fifteenth wedding anniversary, right in the middle of a candlelight dinner, he could see it in her eyes. Looking back, he knew that was the straw that broke the camel's back.

Two weeks later, she had asked him to move out of their North Potomac home. "It's not that I don't love you," she had said. "As a matter of fact, I love you very much. But I don't want a part-time husband. I need you to be with me more than you're able to give."

Mac understood and found a comfortable two-bedroom apartment that was only about five minutes away from them. That was far enough for him.

Mac saw Alayna every other weekend and a couple times a week when he picked up Austin after school for a few hours. He still loved her and his heart gave a little lurch every time he saw her. He could tell from the warm smile on her face she still felt the same way towards him. Mac would give her a kiss on the cheek, just as he'd always done, and she allowed him to do that, but then she would put her hand on his chest as if she was blocking him from coming any closer. And if he was being honest with himself, he couldn't blame her. As much as he loved Alayna and Austin, he had always wanted to be a cop and couldn't even fathom doing anything else. He just wished he could have had both his family and the job, but it wasn't meant to be.

Austin seemed to adjust pretty well to his parent's living arrangements, but then again, a lot of his friends had parents that had also split up. Divorce was nothing new to the kids these days. Mac was grateful that he and Austin got along so well, thanks to their mutual love of sports.

They spent a lot of time on their weekends together watching baseball and football games on TV, and when Mac could get a hold of tickets, they would go to the Baltimore Orioles or the Washington Redskins games. Alayna was great about it, too. The games didn't always fall on his weekend, but she never gave him a hard time if he asked to switch weekends so he and Austin could go to a game. He would invite her to go too, but she always said no. "This is your time with Austin," she would say.

After tossing and turning for what seemed like hours, Mac gave up the idea of sleeping and went for an early run. The sun was just peeking over the horizon, casting the neighborhood into a pink and orange glow. He ran about a mile through the neighborhood before he turned towards his apartment and headed back.

After a quick shower and a protein shake breakfast, Mac jumped into the car and headed the few miles into work. His Ford Focus was about eight years old, but it still looked great and had very low mileage. He smiled as he thought about Coop, always busting on him to get rid of it and buy something newer, but he just didn't see the sense in getting saddled with a car loan when this car was in great condition, rarely had any mechanical issues and had been paid off years before.

As he unlocked the door to the CID office, Mac realized he still had about a half-hour before the others came in to work, so he turned on the coffee maker and made himself a cup of Dark Magic coffee. He had a feeling he was going to need the extra boost of caffeine. He returned to his desk, grabbed the manila folder labeled L. MILLS, and studied his notes on the case.

Before he knew it, Coop was coming through the doorway with a loud clap of his hands. "Good morning, boss! How's it going?" Coop asked.

Mac, who had been lost in thought and oblivious to Coop's entrance, jumped at the sudden noise. "Holy crap, Coop! You scared the shit out of me!" Mac looked down at the crumpled paper in his hands that had been smooth only a few moments before. That is, until his partner had entered the room like a tornado.

"It's going to be a gorgeous day, Mac! A good day to fight crime and catch bad guys!" Coop laughed, as he vigorously rubbed his hands together, creating enough friction to start a small bonfire.

"So, here's the thing," Mac said. He flattened his hand over the paper to smooth out the creases, but wasn't having much luck. "We've got about forty-five minutes before we have to leave to meet with DA Wozniak. Why don't we go over the case so we're on the same page."

Coop put a caramel macchiato k-cup in the coffee maker and looked at Mac. "You want one, as long as I'm here?"

"Sure, except make mine high-test. I need the caffeine," Mac said. Without looking up, he held the mug in Coop's direction.

"Another sleepless night, eh?"

Mac didn't answer him, but he didn't need to. Besides being partners, the two had become close friends, and they often confided in each other about personal matters. Coop loaded the coffee maker with a fresh k-cup. After it finished brewing, he plunked the mug on the desk in front of Mac and went back to his own desk.

They spent the next half hour looking at the photos, reports, and paperwork on the case, then gathered everything together and piled into the department-issued Crown Victoria. Mac was glad they never went undercover with that car. With its tinted windows, side-mounted spotlights, and hubcaps the size of teacup saucers, it screamed "Police!".

Dennis Wozniak was waiting for them by the time they got to the DA's office. He already had his own paperwork spread out on the large table in the conference room when Mac and Coop arrived. They exchanged hellos and handshakes and got right to work.

"I think the first thing we need to do," Dennis said, "is get a blood spatter expert to look at these photos. If we're lucky, Carter's maid hasn't cleaned the bedroom that well and they haven't painted the walls yet because there are some things I'd like to get a closer look at. It would be perfect if the blood spatters were still on the walls, on the lamp that's on the nightstand and on the nightstand itself. It looks like a lot of blood on the rug also, but it's hard to tell from the photos exactly how much blood there is. Depending on how much she lost,

I'm sure some of it must have soaked through to the padding underneath."

Now that the DA was on board, they all agreed that the best course of action would be to get a search warrant. Over the next three hours, Dennis, Mac and Coop wrote an extensive list of things they wanted to check out at the Mills' residence once they had the warrant in hand. The detectives then returned to their office at the PD and wrote up the application for the warrant. Coop called Judge Johannsen and arranged to bring the application to her before the end of the day.

Judge Evelyn Johannsen had been on the bench as a County Criminal Court judge for about sixteen years. She was as tough as nails but at the same time, had a reputation for being fair and was well-respected by both the defense and the prosecution. She didn't play favorites, and she didn't care who she pissed off. In her opinion, it was more important to be honest, fair-minded and impartial, to do the best possible job on the bench, regardless of who stood in front of her.

It was about 4:30 when Mac and Coop ran up the courthouse steps. Mac carried the folder with the warrant application and the supporting paperwork. They met Judge Johannsen in her chambers, gave her the paperwork, and took a seat while she read through it.

Mac and Coop sat waiting, occasionally glancing at each other, at the judge or their cell phones as the clock ticked off the minutes. On the bookshelf behind the judge, Mac noticed the brass scales of justice. *Funny,* he mused, *how every judge's chambers I've ever been in, the scales of justice are always on a shelf somewhere. They must all have the same interior decorators.*

After about fifteen minutes, the judge looked up, took off her glasses and sighed. "This is not what I expected, I must admit. I've met the Mills, and would never have thought Carter capable of murder. But you've brought up some good questions in your application that definitely need to be addressed. Gentlemen, you have your search warrant." She picked up a pen and signed her name on the paper.

⚖️

At six o'clock the next morning, Mac, Coop and the other two men on their team met for a briefing in the CID office before they executed the search warrant. Mac had gotten there a half hour earlier, after another restless night, and made copies of the list they had drawn up with DA Wozniack for each of the team members. Since this was most likely the only chance they would have to examine the crime scene, he wanted to make sure they missed nothing.

During the briefing, Mac assigned everyone a duty. Mac would oversee operations, while Coop, a trained evidence technician, would concentrate on the bedroom and adjoining bath area to photograph any signs of blood that remained in the rooms. He would be partnered up with Brandon Powers, an evidence technician who specialized in forensic evidence. While Coop photographed the bedroom and any remaining physical evidence, Powers would concentrate on collecting the forensic evidence, specifically the blood, for later testing in a lab. In the meantime, Patrick O'Malley would head to the basement and test the hot water tank to find out how long it takes to run out of hot, steamy water. Once he had that information, he would go upstairs to see if it was possible to hear Loretta's shower running from the hallway, as Carter had claimed. O'Malley would then help Coop and Powers collect the evidence in the bedroom suite.

Once the team discussed the specifics of the search warrant and there were no further questions, the team piled into their department-issued vehicles and set off for the Mills residence.

At 7:15, the Montgomery County Police Department, Criminal Investigation Division of Division Six Headquarters at Gaithersburg rang the doorbell of Carter Mills' home. After a moment, the curtain covering the sidelight next to the door shifted as Carter peered out to find the police on his front steps. He threw the door open and glared at Mac, who was the first in line.

"What the hell are you doing here? What do you want?" He stood firm, with one hand holding the door to block the entrance. His dark eyes darted between Mac and Coop. Mac pushed his way past Carter, barely able to squeeze between Carter and the door frame.

"Good morning, Mr. Mills," Mac said cheerfully. Once in the foyer, he turned around and waved for the other team members to come in. Carter had no choice but to step aside to make room for the men who were coming into his home, all of whom were carrying heavy bags of equipment. Mac stepped in front of Carter and held out the warrant.

Carter snatched it out of Mac's hand. "What the hell is this?" Carter looked at the folded paper in his hand with a sneer, as if Mac had handed him a pile of shit.

"Mr. Mills, that is a search warrant allowing us to search these premises for any evidence in relation to the death of your wife, Loretta Mills." Mac stood stone-faced while Carter's mouth opened in obvious surprise.

"Daddy, what's going on?" Margaret walked into the foyer, her bare feet padding across the polished marble floor. She stood next to her father, looking between him and the men from the police department. "Daddy?"

Carter was staring at the folded paper in his hand. "They said it's a search warrant. They're looking for evidence, something to do with your mother's fall." He lifted his head to look at his daughter with a strange look in his eye.

Mac recalled the way to the bedroom suite and led the way upstairs for the investigators, who were to collect evidence in that location. They got right to work, and began snapping photos and dabbing with long cotton swabs at tiny spots of blood that were, fortunately for them, still on the walls, nightstand and bedside lamp.

Mac knew they had gotten lucky. After Loretta had died, and after basic cleaning and straightening, it looked like the door to her suite had been left closed. Mac knew from experience that very often the deceased's belongings would be shipped off to the Rescue Mission right away. Other times, it would be quite a while before the family could face looking at their loved one's personal items. There was no way of knowing how grief would affect the different family members, and every family was different.

As the police investigators invaded his home, Carter stormed down the hall to his study, slammed the door closed, and called Tommy Gleason at home. He never gave it a thought that it was so early in the day.

After three rings, Tommy answered his cell phone. "Tommy. It's me, Carter. Listen, I've got a big problem here. The cops just came to the house with a search warrant. They said they're looking for evidence related to Loretta's death. What the hell do I do now?"

At the time Carter called, Tommy had been sitting at the breakfast table, reading the morning newspaper and enjoying his breakfast with his wife, Vivian. As Carter relayed his story, Tommy put the paper down, forgot about his eggs Benedict, and shifted to attention in his chair.

"Carter, what are you saying? Are you telling me they think she was killed? That it wasn't a fall?"

Vivian's head snapped up as she heard her husband's words.

"I don't know what the hell they think! All I know is they handed me a search warrant and said it had to do with Loretta's death. They're in her bedroom suite now." Carter was running his hand through his hair and pacing in circles around the study.

"Holy crap, Carter! What did you do?"

"I didn't do anything! She fell, and I gave her CPR! I tried to save her! That's it, I swear!"

"Damn it, Carter. Don't say or do anything. Just sit tight. I'm on my way." Tommy disconnected the call and slammed his hand on the table. "What the hell did he do now?"

He left the room before Vivian could ask him to explain what was going on. She was used to the interruptions. That came with the territory, when one was married to a high-powered attorney. But after hearing Carter's name and seeing her husband's reaction to the phone call, she knew it couldn't be good.

Twenty minutes later, Tommy was pulling into the Mills' circular driveway but had to stop and park his Range Rover well-before the house. The three police units parked in the driveway had prevented him from getting any closer. As he approached the front door on foot, Carter, who was still in his pajamas, ran out and met him at the base of the steps. Tommy reached out and hauled Carter by the elbow towards the front door.

"Come with me. We're going to your office." Tommy still had a firm grip on Carter's arm, but Carter wrenched it free as they crossed the threshold into the foyer.

"Listen, I ..." Carter started to say something, but Tommy was quick to cut him off.

"Shut the hell up. Wait until we get to your office, will you?" As they entered the office, Tommy shut the door behind them and turned the lock. Carter returned to pacing while Tommy stood next to the desk, his arms crossed over his chest, anger burning in his eyes as he watched Carter.

"Now, what is going on? You'd better be straight with me, Carter. Don't feed me any bullshit. Did you have anything to do with Loretta dying that day?"

"I'm telling you, no. I had nothing to do with it. She fell in the shower, so I carried her out, and I tried to give her CPR. That's it. She was dead before I got there." Carter's hair was disheveled and raised in spikes from running his hands over his scalp. Even though the morning was chilly, the sweat was building on his forehead.

"Then let me see the search warrant. I may not be a criminal lawyer, but I can read a warrant." Carter found the papers on the desktop where he had left them and handed them to the attorney. Tommy ripped it from Carter's hand as he continued to glare at Carter, then spent the next few moments studying the warrant and shaking his head in disbelief. Carter continued to pace around the room.

"If you're telling me the truth, then it's best to just let them do what they have to do. With a warrant, you can't stop them anyway, but I'd like to know why they think it was anything but an accident." Tommy was looking at Carter with as much anger as he'd ever felt towards anyone.

Six hours later, Mac and the crew left Carter's house, leaving Loretta's suite in disarray. They had removed what had been fresh sheets from the bed and left them in a heap on the floor. They left the mattress to rest at an odd angle on the bed, the cushions and coils exposed because they had taken the mattress cover as evidence. Even though Irene had cleaned the carpet after Loretta's death, now there were gaping holes where the investigators had completely cut away and removed large sections of the carpet and padding where her body had lain. The investigators had rummaged through Loretta's closet, armoire, dresser drawers, and nightstands, but had not been careful about putting things back the way they were. This kind of investigation required that the investigators and evidence technicians be thorough, not necessarily neat. Mac would normally feel bad about leaving such a mess, but sometimes it just couldn't be helped. This time, however, he didn't feel bad at all for Carter.

Once back at the station, the team got to work storing the collection of evidence in secure lockers for the night. They logged it all into the special computer program that was used to keep track of the evidence brought in or removed from the department's custody. At the Mills' house, each article had been meticulously bagged and tagged with the time the evidence had been collected, the specific location where it had been taken from, and the name of the officer who had collected it. Now, that same information was being entered into the computer as they stored each article in the lockers. It was a long and tedious task, but an extremely important one. The chain of custody and accuracy of the information could make or break a case if it were questioned during a trial. Fortunately, Mac had complete trust in the evidence technicians and knew they were doing what they had spent countless hours in training to do.

Almost thirteen hours after the day began, Mac and the team headed home. In the morning, they would compare notes and see what they had. The photos of the blood droplets found in the rooms would be sent to a blood spatter expert, while they would send the blood samples to the lab to make sure it belonged to Loretta, although Mac was sure it did. They had gathered as much physical evidence from the bedroom as they could.

Next would come the hard part—putting a case together against Carter Mills that would stand up in court. To Mac, this stage was kind of like working on a jigsaw puzzle. The pieces were all laid out, and it was up to him and his team to put it together, piece by piece, until the picture against Carter Mills was clear.

Chapter 12

After a surprisingly restful night, Mac went into the office a bit early the next day, as he very often tried to do. He needed a few minutes of quiet time before the others arrived to gather his thoughts and write up his report. He was deep in thought, typing on his desktop computer, when Coop came bursting through the door.

"Hey, boss! What's up?"

Mac's knees connected with the underside of his desk as he jumped. "Coop, I swear to God, you're going to give me a heart attack one of these days." Mac shook his head as he saw the string of jumbled letters that his twitchy fingers had typed into the report when he'd jumped at the sudden noise.

Coop laughed, placed his suit jacket on the back of his chair, and sat at his desk. "Are you working on your report for the search warrant from yesterday?"

"Yeah, trying to," he said as he deleted the unnecessary letters. "It's times like this when I find it hard to be factual and not let my assumptions take over, because there's so much that's circumstantial. On the other hand, there's even more stuff at this point that just plain doesn't make any sense. It's hard to put that in a report without making it convoluted."

"I agree with you," Coop said. "There are some things that don't add up. I see now why this case was bugging you so much. There are questions like why did he move her all that way and not start CPR in the bathroom where she fell? Why did he run to get his daughter instead of calling 911 himself when there were at least three phones in that bedroom suite, all within easy reach? I didn't believe him when he said in the interview that he needed help from his daughter. And where did all that blood come from in the bedroom, if she'd fallen in the shower? You would think that most of the blood would be in the shower, since she was in there for a while after she fell."

Once Powers and O'Malley arrived, the group closed the CID door so that they wouldn't be disturbed and got right to work comparing notes and opinions, but there was no doubt in anyone's mind that something was amiss. The evidence they collected only solidified that in their minds.

After an hour of discussion, Powers left to take the blood swabs to the forensic center for analysis. Meanwhile, O'Malley got to work making notations in the computer system as he moved each piece of evidence, left last night in the lockers, into the secure evidence room known as the vault. The vault was a rather large room accessible by only a few people in the department where the evidence was kept for secure, long-term storage. That only a few members of the department had access to the vault, allowed for safe keeping of the items, which included drugs, money and guns.

"I think we should talk to the paramedics that were on scene that morning and get their statements," Mac said to Coop. "Why don't I call over to the fire department and see if they're working today."

"Perfect. I was just going to suggest we grab a cup of coffee and a danish from that new coffee shop down the street. We can do that on the way to the firehouse."

An hour later, Mac and Coop were at the fire department walking towards the lounge with Paramedic Kevin Porter and Medic Sarah Whitman. Both had been at the Mills' residence the morning of Loretta's death.

Before they sat down in the leather armchairs, Coop helped himself to a Pepsi from the fridge. "Anyone else want anything while I'm up?"

Sarah accepted a bottle of water. Mac and Kevin both said they were good.

"So, Kevin," Mac began as they took their seats, "you pronounced Loretta dead that morning. Does anything stick out in your mind about her death?"

"Yes, definitely. A couple of things, actually."

"Like what?" Mac had his pocket-sized notebook out, poised on the wide arm of the chair, ready to take notes.

"Well," Kevin's brows pulled together as he thought back to that day. "First of all, she'd been dead for a while. Her neck and jaw were stiff, meaning that rigor mortis had started to set in."

"How long does it take before rigor sets in?" Coop asked, while munching a croissant from a package he'd found on the counter.

"It can take anywhere from two to six hours after death. She had that deep laceration on the side of her head and a nasty black eye that, at least to me, seemed to be too extreme for a slip and fall from a standing position. By the way, how do you figure she got that laceration? Was it from the fall or was she hit with something?"

"We're trying to figure that out," Mac said. "The husband claims she must have hit her head on the bench that runs along the length of the shower. We never found any piece of evidence that would leave a fracture like that if he hit her over the head with it."

"Also," Sarah said, "there was a lot of blood in that bedroom. I even said something to Kevin afterwards about how much blood was on the floor. Head wounds bleed a lot, but you would think that most of the blood would have been in the shower, if that's where she fell."

Mac and Coop were able to ask a few more questions, but then had to leave the fire department when Kevin and Sarah got dispatched to an emergency.

As they walked across the fire department parking lot, Coop jogged ahead and hopped into the driver's seat. Mac preferred to drive, given his partner's love for driving like he was at the Indy 500, but this time he just gave Coop a sideways glance, shook his head and got in the passenger side.

"So, Mac, what do you think? Do we have enough now to charge Carter Mills with homicide?" He was driving down the road, using both hands to buckle his seatbelt while maneuvering the steering wheel on his knees. Mac ignored that but discreetly tightened his own seatbelt.

"I think we do. How about you?" Mac already knew the answer, but he always liked to bounce the ideas off the other investigators and make them feel they are very much a part of the team.

"I agree, boss. We definitely have a motive, which is the fact that she had a boyfriend and wanted a divorce, but he was too proud to accept it. We have opportunity, because he killed her in the middle of the night and he made sure there were no witnesses to the actual crime. The only problem is that we don't have a weapon, other than his fists. We might not have the so-called smoking gun, but I definitely think he killed his wife and staged it to look like an accident."

Coop suddenly swerved around a cat that ran into the road in front of them. Mac grabbed the dashboard to hang on. "I'd like to survive the trip back to the station, though!" Mac looked at his partner, who had a grin on his face and was clearly enjoying the chance to unnerve his boss.

After a moment or two, Mac puffed out his cheeks, released the breath he didn't realize he'd been holding and let go of the dashboard. "I think the next step is to put it all together and talk to DA Wozniak to see if we can get it in front of the Grand Jury for an indictment."

Once safely back at the station, they spent the rest of the day writing their respective reports, stopping every once in a while to bounce ideas off each other. Powers and O'Malley had also returned and joined them.

Before they knew it, it was already after five o'clock on Friday afternoon, so they took a much-needed break for the weekend. They would rest up over the next two days and then put their heads together, starting fresh on Monday morning.

"Besides," Coop said, loosening his tie, "I've got a hot date tonight with that nurse, Brandy, from the hospital ER. I've been trying to get a date with her for about three months and I finally got her to cave and go out with me.

"That's good. I'm glad you could convince her what a great guy you are." Mac laughed but shook his head as Coop kissed the tip of his finger, touched his butt with that finger and made a sizzling sound.

Mac, on the other hand, had nothing as exciting going on over the weekend. It wasn't his weekend with Austin. There weren't any good baseball games on the television, and the only thing he had planned was a poker game late Sunday afternoon. He'd kept in touch with a bunch of guys from his high school days and even after all these years, they still tried to get together once a month on Sunday for a couple hours of poker, beer and pizza. It was Mac's turn to host, so he'd have to run to the grocery store at some point to get the beer and pretzels. They would order the pizza once everyone got there.

Mac considered himself frugal—Coop called it cheap—but he allowed himself the extravagance of having a cleaning service come in once every other week, and thankfully, they'd come earlier that week. That would save him from having to clean the apartment, which was one job he didn't care for.

According to the weather report, it was supposed to be a warm and sunny weekend. Maybe he could talk Alayna and Austin into going for a walk at Seneca Creek State Park on Saturday. He decided to give Alayna a call after he got home.

Later that evening, he called the landline at his ex-wife's home—formerly his home—and Austin picked up.

"Hey, buddy. How's it going?" It was always good to talk to Austin. He was a good kid, and Mac enjoyed talking with him.

"Pretty good. I aced that science test today."

"Awesome! I knew you had the brains in the family." Mac chuckled as he pictured Austin rolling his eyes. "Hey, I was thinking. How about taking a hike this weekend at Seneca Creek? We could all go."

"Sure, dad. That sounds great. Wait a minute, mom just came in." Mac could hear Austin's voice sounding distant as he faced away from the phone. "Mom, it's dad. He wants to know if we can all go hiking this weekend at Seneca Creek."

"I don't know, buddy. Let me talk to him." There was a bit of a pause and some scuffling noises as Austin passed the phone to Alayna. "Hi, Mac."

"Hey, Alayna. How are you?"

"I'm okay. What's up?" Alayna was never one for small talk, preferring instead to get right to the point. It was just one trait that Mac had always admired about her.

"It's supposed to be nice this weekend. What do you say we all take a walk at Seneca Creek tomorrow?"

Alayna drew in a deep breath. "I don't know, Mac. If you want to take Austin, that's fine by me, but I'm not sure I should go."

"Why not? Come along, Alayna. We've always enjoyed going to the park. We could make a day of it, like we used to do. I miss that." Mac's voice softened. "I miss you."

"I know, Mac. I miss you too, but I don't think this is a good idea."

"Okay, I'll tell you what. I'll be there at nine o'clock tomorrow morning. I won't pressure you, but that will give you time to think about going. What do you say? Will you think about it?"

"Okay, Mac. I'll think about it, but I won't promise anything." Mac broke into a wide smile, because at least it wasn't an outright "no." He felt a bit of hope. Who knows? Maybe someday he could win her back.

The next morning, Mac was up at the crack of dawn to get ready. Even after he'd gone on a run, showered and eaten his usual weekend breakfast of oatmeal with fresh blueberries, he still had almost an hour to kill. As he sat at the kitchen table, he reached for his laptop that he'd left charging on the counter the night before. He checked his email, but that only kept him busy for a few minutes. Even with the security program that Austin had helped him install, he still got plenty of junk emails. He settled on playing a few games of computer solitaire to kill time.

After losing two games and winning one, it was time to pick up Alayna and Austin. As he pulled into the driveway, Austin came bouncing out of the house and waved. "Hey, Dad!"

Mac stepped out of the car and gave his son a man hug, grateful that his now-teenage son didn't mind getting hugs from his father in public. Austin opened the backseat door of Mac's car and threw in a backpack and fishing pole.

"What's with the fishing pole and the backpack?" Mac asked as he looked at his son with a smile. He knew from experience what he was going to say. Mac retrieved the fishing pole from the back seat, opened the trunk of the car, and put the fishing pole in it.

"Well, we haven't gone fishing in a while, and we haven't gone on one of those big paddle boats in a long time. You know, the one that the whole family can sit in together. And I kinda thought that maybe we could do that today, so I brought my swimsuit and towels and stuff."

"Oh, you did, did you?" laughed Mac. He looked up to see Alayna walking towards them, with a picnic basket in hand. He waited until she was near and said, "I'm glad you came." She just smiled at him. He reached out to take the basket, with his hand wrapped around hers for a few seconds longer than was necessary, before she let go of the handle.

He put the picnic basket in the back, closed the trunk, and hopped into the driver's seat. "Alright," said Mac. "Let's go have some fun in the sun."

They spent the rest of the morning hiking in the woods and riding in a four-person paddle boat. After they ate their lunch, Austin had seen one of his school buddies fishing off the pier, so he joined his buddy, hoping to catch the big one. Mac and Alayna continued to sit together at the picnic table, enjoying the light breeze and the shade from the large pine trees that loomed overhead. Their conversation was light, enjoyable and friendly. That night, Mac went to bed with a smile on his face, happier than he'd been in a long time. He slept peacefully through the night and woke up on Sunday morning, feeling happy and refreshed.

Chapter 13

Monday morning rolled around, and Mac and Coop got right to work on the Mills case. They worked hard for the next three days, putting together a case that the District Attorney would present to the Grand Jury. With luck, they would have an indictment for murder within a few weeks. Mac felt strongly about this case, that it was up to him, the men on his team and the District Attorney, to see that justice prevails and that Carter spends the rest of his days behind bars. It was up to them to defend Loretta and avenge her death, since she wasn't here to do it herself.

DA Wozniak met with Mac and Coop on Thursday afternoon. They'd already had multiple phone conversations over the course of the week to discuss the case, but this meeting would wrap it up in a neat package for presentation to the Grand Jury. Coop set a box that was filled with a couple of large folders comprising the officers' reports, witness statements, diagrams of the house, the search warrant, and the crime scene photos on the table in the conference room.

Mac pulled an envelope from the top of the pile and handed it to Dennis. "We just got the lab results on the blood samples we took from Loretta's bedroom. Wait until you see what it says."

Dennis took the envelope and withdrew several folded papers. It took a few moments for him to skim through the report, but he raised his eyebrows as he read further down. "Well, according to this, all the blood samples matched Loretta's DNA, which is not surprising. But the interesting notation is on the sample taken from the headboard. It says there is blood and tissue in that sample. I'd like to see what kind of tissue it is. I'd like to send that sample to an expert I've dealt with before. He can determine exactly what that tissue is and where that tissue came from within Loretta's body. It could very well be skin cells, but from where, is the question. It could be from her head, her lip, or it could even be something like brain cells. I'm sure this guy will be able to tell us."

Dennis put the lab report back on the table and said, "So, gentlemen. Tell me what you have."

"We're convinced he killed her and then staged the whole thing to look like an accidental fall in the shower," said Mac. "To sum it up, this is what we believe happened. In the early morning hours, they were in the bedroom and got into an argument. Carter lost his temper and hit her with an unknown object, which is what caused the large laceration and skull fracture on the side of her head. That would also account for the amount of blood spatter on the walls, lamp, nightstand, and other objects in the bedroom. She fell to the bedroom floor but, nice guy that he is, he walked away and left her there. She bled out right where she landed on the rug, which accounts for why there was so much blood in that one particular spot. Then, after at least two hours, he went back into the bedroom, discovered that she was dead, and decided to stage her death to look like an accident. He wrapped her in the bed sheet, which was probably already bloody, and carried her into the shower. We believe he used the bed sheet so that he didn't leave a blood trail between the bedroom and the shower. He then replaced the sheets on the bed with a fresh set.

"He apparently always brought Loretta a cup of coffee in the morning, so he did it again that morning, to make it seem like a 'normal' morning." Mac wiggled his index fingers to simulate air quotes. "Then he claims that he then went out for a run through the neighborhood. We believe he did indeed leave the house at that time, but it was not to go on a run. It was to get rid of the murder weapon, the missing pillow, and the bloody sheets that were originally on the bed. When he got back home, he carried her into the shower, turned it on, then ran to get Margaret so that he could use her as a witness to the fact that Loretta had been in the shower and that he had carried her from there, into the bedroom.

"His story, however, is that Loretta had already been in the shower when he brought the usual cup of coffee to her bedroom. It was after that he says he went for a quick run in the neighborhood, came back, showered, and put his pajamas back on, even though they would be going out to breakfast in a short while. He said he could hear from the hallway that the shower was still running, so at that point, he allegedly went to check on her and discovered her laying on the floor in the shower. He said that the shower area was too wet and steamy for CPR, which was why he had to move her into the bedroom.

"We've proven that there's no way there could be that much steam in the bathroom in the time it took him to bring her some coffee, go for a run, take his own shower and then go back to Loretta's bedroom suite to check on her. That's verified from the tests that we did on the morning of the search warrant, because we proved that the hot water tank starts to run cold after twenty-two minutes. If he did everything he claims he did that morning while she was supposedly in the shower for that entire time, there's no way the shower would still be steamy." Mac gave a sharp rap on the table for emphasis.

"And if she fell in the shower like Carter claims," Coop pointed out, "there wouldn't be that much blood on the bedroom floor. She would have bled out in the shower well-before he carried her into the bedroom."

Dennis nodded his head as he said, "Gentlemen, I'm sure we can present a charge of second degree murder to the Grand Jury because, in my opinion, he acted recklessly in a fit of rage, and he had no regard for her life. I'd like to add a charge of tampering with evidence as well, because he moved Loretta's body and he got rid of the weapon, his pajamas, a pillow, and the sheets on the bed to cover-up the homicide. I'll try to get this expedited and in front of the Grand Jury within the next two weeks."

True to his word, DA Wozniak was able to present the case against Carter Mills to the Grand Jury two weeks later. Dennis walked into the County Courthouse on that Wednesday morning, a few minutes before nine o'clock, stopped by his office long enough to pick up the case paperwork he'd gotten from Sgt. MacIntosh and Inv. Cooper, and continued on to the Grand Jury room. Mac and Coop were already there, waiting in the hallway outside the jury room.

"Good morning, gentlemen. How are you, on this fine day?" Dennis reached out to give both investigators a firm handshake.

"Doing well, sir. How are you?" Coop asked.

"I'm doing well. Very well, indeed. Thank you for asking. Well, are we all set to get the ball rolling this morning?" Dennis straightened his already-straight tie with his free hand, keeping a tight grip on the case file in the other hand.

"I believe so," said Mac. "I'm confident we'll get the indictment. No question in my mind."

"In that case, let's get started." Dennis said. Coop opened the door, letting the DA and Mac go in ahead of him.

The grand jury room consisted of a raised stage with a couple of dozen seats occupying the area where the jury was to be seated. A large table and a podium were placed in front of and facing the jury for the prosecution's use, with witness chairs next to the table. Off to the side was a television used for things such as viewing surveillance videos. Dennis set the file on the table and took a seat, while Mac and Coop took their seats behind the DA. The eighteen or twenty jurors who had been milling about returned to their seats when they saw the DA had come in.

After a few moments, DA Wozniak stood up and walked to the podium to address the jurors.

"Good morning. I hope you are all well, this fine day," Dennis said with a genuine smile on his lips. "My name is Dennis Wozniak, and I'm the District Attorney for Montgomery County. I understand you have all been serving in this particular Grand Jury session for a couple of weeks now, so I won't rehash all the rules. I'm sure you know by now that any business conducted here is to be kept in the strictest confidence. Anything discussed, and any action taken, is not to be shared with anyone, not family, not friends. And if you don't mind, please refrain from using your cell phone while the Jury is in session. It seems like they've become extensions of our arms these days, but we can't have the distraction. We're dealing with people's lives here, and that's much more important than texting your partner and asking him or her to take a pound of hamburger out of the freezer."

Mac watched the juror's faces as Dennis talked to them. He was a kind and gentle man with a warm smile, but there was something about him that commanded respect and it showed as the jurors kept their eyes glued to him. A few chuckled at his last comments.

"Remember, ladies and gentlemen, your job is not to decide guilt or innocence. Your job is to decide if there is reasonable cause to believe a crime has been committed. I will also ask you to determine if there is reasonable belief that it was the suspect who committed the alleged crime, and if so, what charges are appropriate. You'll notice I said 'alleged' crime. That's because, in this great country of ours, everyone is innocent until proven guilty."

"And with that being said, if there are no questions, I think we should begin." Dennis looked around the room at each juror, and over his shoulder to Mac and Coop, who were sitting behind him. "No questions? Excellent. Let's get started."

For the rest of the morning, Dennis showed the evidence gathered by the police department to the jury. They reviewed the statements, the photos, and the diagrams depicting the blood spots in the bedroom. It didn't take long for them to hand down an indictment, charging Carter Mills with the charges they had sought, second degree murder and tampering with evidence.

By seven o'clock the next morning, Sgt. Macintosh, Investigator Cooper and two uniformed officers were banging on the thick wood and leaded glass front door of Carter Mills' opulent home. It took several moments for a sleepy-eyed Irene to come to the door, still tightening the belt on her bathrobe. As she opened the door, the color drained from her face and her eyes grew wide when she realized there were police officers standing in front of her.

"Good morning, Irene," Mac stepped forward. "We need to speak with Mr. Mills."

"Now what the hell do you want?" Carter rounded the corner and stopped next to Irene. "It's alright, Irene. I've got this." She took a few steps back, which gave Carter the chance to slide into the doorway, blocking the entrance. "I asked you a question, Sergeant. What— do—you—want?" He enunciated each word with fire in his eyes, as if he were speaking to an insolent child.

Mac reached into his suit coat pocket and withdrew a folded piece of paper. "Mr. Carter Mills, I have a warrant for your arrest. You are being charged with second degree murder and tampering with evidence in the death of your wife, Loretta Mills. Please turn around, Mr. Mills."

"Are you serious? Have you lost your freaking mind?" Carter instinctively stepped back as the two uniformed officers stepped through the doorway. "I didn't kill Loretta. She fell, you asshole. I tried to save her. I tried giving her CPR. Get away from me!" Carter frantically looked side to side as the officers stood on either side of him, each one grabbing his wrists and bringing his hands behind his back. The click of the handcuffs securing Carter's wrists seemed to echo in the large foyer. Irene stood watching the scene unfold, her eyes wide, one hand resting against her chest.

"Irene! Call my attorney! Call Tommy Gleason!" Carter was shouting orders at Irene, who seemed to be frozen in place. "Now, damn it! Now, Irene, go call Tommy Gleason!" With a stricken look on her face, she turned and headed down the hall at a quick pace.

Even though he was handcuffed, one of the officers still held firmly onto Carter's forearm and pulled him back as he tried to head down the hallway, attempting to follow Irene.

Mac heard a soft whimper and looked towards the top of the stairs to see Margaret with tears streaming down her cheeks, one hand covering her mouth, the other arm wrapped around her middle, as if she was giving herself a hug. She'd been watching the scene unfold as they placed her father in handcuffs, under arrest for causing her mother's death. He couldn't imagine the pain the young girl was going through, and how much pain she would have in her future. The father in him wanted to console her, but the cop in him knew he couldn't cross that line. He was here to do his job and make an arrest, no matter how difficult the consequences would be for Margaret.

They took Carter to the police department, still in his pajamas and slippers, where he was fingerprinted and photographed. He had refused to talk to Mac and Coop, opting instead to "lawyer up." This interview would have been just a formality anyway, since they'd already interviewed him once before, but it's always helpful for them to get a suspect to talk as much as possible.

After being in the holding cell for a few hours, alternating between sitting and pacing, they handcuffed Carter again and brought him before Judge Johannsen for arraignment. Mac and Coop found seats in the back of the courtroom. The attorney, Tommy Gleason, stood by Carter's side and entered a plea of not guilty on his behalf. Carter stared straight ahead at the judge. His mouth was closed, his lips a thin line. Only the wide-opened look in his eyes gave away the shock he must have been feeling.

Coop leaned over to whisper in Mac's ear. "Looks like he took his attorney's advice and is going to keep his mouth shut. The man's so arrogant, I wouldn't have been surprised if he tried to get mouthy with Judge Johannsen."

"You're right about that. I wouldn't put anything past him." Mac shook his head. "But it's not over yet. In fact, I'll bet you a beer after work tonight that he opens his big mouth before the arraignment is finished."

"You're on!" Coop said, a bit too loudly. He and Mac exchanged a fist bump to seal the deal as Judge

Johannsen looked their way with one eyebrow raised in admonishment.

The judge asked for a bail recommendation from DA Wozniak. "Your honor, I would ask that no bail be set for Mr. Mills. In my opinion, he is a flight risk. He has unlimited funds at his disposal, the family condo in Punta Cana, and a passport. I ask that he be remanded without bail."

"Your honor," interrupted attorney Gleason, "my client promises he isn't going anywhere. He has a thriving business where others depend on him for their livelihood. His daughter still lives at home, and his two sons are living nearby. He has no intention of leaving them. My client promises to stay right here, with his loving family, and would be willing to post a reasonable bail as a way to show the Court his intentions."

The judge didn't hesitate. "I agree. He is a flight risk. However, I think one million dollars bail and surrendering the passport will suffice." Judge Johannsen picked up the gavel and smacked it down on the wooden pad with a resounding bang that echoed off the walls of the courtroom.

"Are you serious? One million dollars? Where in hell am I going to get that kind of cash?" Carter was beside himself with anger, his face burning red. A vein in his forehead became more and more prominent the louder he yelled. Tommy tried to get his attention by pulling on his elbow, but Carter was not having any part of that, as he continued to yell at the judge. "This is freaking ridiculous! I didn't kill Loretta! Judge, you have to believe me! I tried to save her! I gave her CPR!"

Judge Johannsen pointed the gavel at Carter, saying, "Mr. Mills, control yourself or I'll remove the bail entirely, and you'll be remanded *without* bail. It's your choice."

"Holy shit, Judge. This isn't right! I tried to save her! I tried to give her CPR, for God's sake! This isn't right!" Tommy tried to calm Carter down, squeezing his shoulder, and telling him to be quiet, to no avail. Within seconds, Carter had two court security officers on either side of him, pulling him towards the door that would lead to the court's holding cell. Carter looked over his shoulder at the judge in one last attempt. "Please, judge. Please don't send me to jail. I didn't kill my wife!"

Judge Johannsen looked down at the folder on her desk that contained the paperwork for the next case to be called. The message to Carter was clear...she was not interested in hearing him plead for his freedom.

Mac and Coop got up from their seats to leave. "I'll take a nice cold bottle of Flying Dog, old buddy." Mac nudged his partner in the shoulder as Coop looked back at him with a wry smile.

⚖

After work, all the investigators met at a local bar called Jimmy's Saloon. It was a popular hangout for cops who wanted to unwind a bit after the pressures of the day. Badges came off, and they did not acknowledge rank, making it easier to leave the job back at the office. Coop and Mac took a couple of stools at the bar while Brandon and Patrick headed to the pool table a few feet away.

"Okay, Sandy. Set 'em up. A bottle of Flying Dog for Mac, here, and a Sam Adams for me. We're celebrating tonight."

"Really? What are you celebrating?" Sandy had been the evening bartender for years, long enough to know what they would drink without them having to place their order. She reached into the cooler, grabbed the beers, and plunked them on the bar in front of the detectives. She didn't even bother with the glasses, knowing they wouldn't use them, anyway.

"We're celebrating because we're the best damn detectives this city has ever seen, that's what." Coop took a lengthy pull on his beer.

"Oh, yeah?" Sandy responded with a twinkle in her eye. "And what did you do today, Captain Courageous?"

"Not just today, my love. We are the best *every* day!" Coop slapped the top of the dark wooden bar for emphasis. "How about asking Jimmy if he'd throw a dozen Buffalo wings in the fryer for me? I'm starving."

Mac leaned on the bar with a smile and watched his partner, who could eat all day, every day, and never gain a pound. "Ah, what the hell. Sandy, as long as Jimmy's taking orders, have him throw one of his special cheeseburgers on the grill for me, would you?"

Brandon and Patrick had finished their round of pool and joined Mac and Coop at the bar. It wasn't long before some of the other regulars started showing up and the conversation turned to the Mills' arrest.

"I don't think he ever thought he'd be arrested," said Mac. "He's so freaking arrogant, he probably figured that he'd literally get away with murder. That he's so much smarter than anyone else. It's very satisfying to see someone like that get knocked down a few pegs."

"I'll tell you one thing," Coop said with a wide smile, "while Mills was getting arraigned, the vein in his forehead was bulging so much, I'll bet you could bounce a quarter off of it!"

"No doubt!" chimed in Brandon with a smirk.

"Holy shit." Patrick was staring at the television screen resting on a shelf in the corner of the bar. "Hey, Sandy. Can you turn that up?" The others turned to see what Patrick was looking at.

A news commentator was standing in front of the Montgomery County Jail, while a banner was running across the bottom of the screen announcing Breaking News.

Sandy used the remote to turn up the volume. "... was arraigned this morning on murder charges in the death of his wife, Loretta Mills. Carter Mills is a well-known investment adviser from Gaithersburg who is being accused of beating his wife to death after an argument, although his attorney contends that she tragically slipped and fell in the shower. This is a developing story, but we'll have more information as it becomes available."

"Wow!" Mac said, "that story didn't take long to get out."

Later that night, Mac was sitting on the couch, his stocking feet resting on the coffee table, while he nursed a bottle of beer, more warm now than cold. He'd been looking at the television, but his mind was a million miles away as he thought about the Mills case. Mac was barely listening as yet another mindless sitcom ended and the eleven o'clock news came on until he realized that Carter Mills' arrest was the leading story. He sat up straight as he recognized the photo displayed on the screen behind the young blonde commentator as that of Carter Mills. The commentator had added a few more details from what was said on the news earlier in the day, but the initial statement that Mills had posted bail and was now out of jail, is what surprised Mac. *He could gather up enough money in one afternoon to post a million dollars bail? I knew he was rich, but I didn't know he had that much cash available. I wonder if he had it all lined up ahead of time, just in case he got arrested. Unbelievable!*

⚖

Over the course of the next several weeks, Mac and Coop continued to work on the case, tying down any loose ends. Dennis Wozniak insisted on prosecuting the case himself, and asked Assistant District Attorney Kimberly Coville to be his assistant, called the second chair.

Carter, meanwhile, had hired two of the top criminal attorneys in the area, Julie Fletcher and Bruce Keegan. Family friend Tommy Gleason would be part of the legal team, although his area of expertise was real estate and civil law, not criminal law. But as a favor to Carter's father, Michael, he would do what he could for Carter's defense.

Right away, Julie and Bruce requested a suppression hearing to determine whether the evidence had been collected legally by the police department or not. This was an often-used tactic by defense counsel, hoping to have the evidence deemed inadmissible before the trial. If it was successful and the evidence was thrown out, one of two things could happen. The first was that the prosecution would have a much more difficult time at the trial of proving guilt without their key evidence. Second, the defense could make a move to dismiss the case, because, simply put, without the incriminating evidence, there was no case.

The defense attorneys, prosecution attorneys and Judge Johannsen were all present for the suppression hearing.

The defense counsel began the proceedings. "Your honor, we believe the evidence collected by the police after Mrs. Mills' death should be suppressed. The mission of the first responders when they entered the house that morning was strictly a life-saving mission, not a criminal one. The police had a right to enter the home to save Loretta Mills' life, but they did not have consent from my client or a warrant to search the premises and gather evidence. Therefore, any and all evidence, including blood samples, photos or any other items collected that day when Loretta Mills was pronounced dead should be suppressed."

Dennis then argued that the police had a right to search for and collect evidence under exigent circumstances, which, in this case, was the large amount of blood in the bathroom and bedroom. "That," he explained, "and the fact that the items were also in plain view, gave police the leeway to collect evidence without consent or a warrant. Let it be known, however, that the defendant gave verbal consent when the evidence technician entered the house carrying his equipment and told the defendant that he would collect evidence from the scene."

Judge Johannsen listened to the attorneys while looking at the photographs taken that morning. She then announced her decision. She agreed with the prosecution that there was a need to investigate the death under exigent circumstances, that the blood on the bedroom walls was inconsistent with a fall in the shower. And, the judge ruled, that the evidence was in plain sight, which made that a legal search. "The police could not wear blinders to what they saw that morning. Anyone of a reasonable, questioning mind would have believed that the amount of blood found in the shower and in the bedroom, especially on the walls and floor, would have provided an indication as to the manner of Mrs. Mills' death. However, I will add that although the blood is proof of the violent nature of Mrs. Mills' death, it does not show the manner of death, be it homicide or accident."

"Regarding the consent to search," continued Judge Johannsen, "Mr. Mills was told that an evidence technician would be present and a reasonable person in today's world, thanks to television and the internet, would believe that the technician, who appeared with his equipment, would take photographs, blood samples and measurements. We've all seen CSI counselors. I find that all evidence collected regarding the death of Loretta Mills is admissible in the trial of Carter Mills." With a loud crack of her gavel as she hit it against the wooden block, Judge Johannsen closed the suppression hearing.

Chapter 14
Trial Days 1 and 2
Jury Selection

The trial was scheduled to begin on a crisp Monday morning in mid-October. It had been six months since Loretta Mills died in her bedroom suite of the family home.

Prior to the trial, Mac, Coop, Dennis, and Kimberly had met several times to outline their plan of attack for the trial. The prosecution always goes first to call witnesses to the stand and Dennis agreed to call Mac, as the lead investigator, as the first witness. The rules of the court say that any potential witness may not view the court proceedings until after they gave their testimony. This is so they couldn't be accused of skewing their knowledge of the case based on something they may hear from a lawyer, the judge, or another witness.

So once he gave his testimony, Mac could sit in on the rest of the trial, or at least, as often as his schedule allowed. This would be one of the biggest cases of his career, and he didn't want to miss a minute of the trial, if he could help it.

The prosecution and the defense had each drawn up their own lists of witnesses that would be called to testify, and shared their lists with each other. This is so both sides could prepare questions for those witnesses.

The prosecution would call several professionals to testify about the evidence that had been collected. A pathologist, the coroner, and a blood spatter expert would all be asked to share their interpretation of the evidence. The medics that were present the morning Loretta died were on the list to testify and Dennis would also call the Mills' housekeeper, Irene Stapleton, to the stand.

The defense counsel had only a few people on their list. Most of them seemed to be friends with the Mills family, so they were most likely going to be called as character witnesses. But Mac noticed, with a heavy heart, that Margaret Mills was on the list to testify for the defense. He knew her testimony would be a difficult one to listen to.

After months of preparation, the day of the trial arrived. The first order of business was to pick the jury, which would be comprised of twelve jurors, and anywhere from two to four alternates. This step takes a bit of time, because both the prosecution and defense ask each prospective juror specific questions. They will then try to determine which candidate would be fair and impartial, based on their answers. They would release any person from jury duty if they had any preconceived opinions about the case or the defendant, or if they were biased. Ultimately, those picked to be on the jury would need to make their decision of guilt or innocence based solely on the evidence presented during the trial. They could not base their decision on something they heard in the news or on social media.

Late Tuesday morning, after almost a day and a half of jury selection, Dennis called Mac at the police department, letting him know the jury had been selected.

"Really?" Mac couldn't help but be surprised. "After all the media exposure the case has had so far, I thought it might take longer than that to pick the jurors."

"It's no surprise that almost everyone that was questioned had heard of the case, but there were quite a few who had not formed an opinion on it. So, of those that fell into that category, we picked sixteen people we felt would be impartial. We went through well over a hundred candidates, but I think we've got a good jury. We'll be starting the testimony this afternoon and as you know, you're the first witness I'd like to call."

"Excellent. We'll be there." Mac hung up the phone and turned to Coop, who was sitting at his desk, typing on the computer.

"Hey, Coop! They've picked the jury, so the trial is going to start this afternoon. Let's go grab a bite to eat now so we can head over to the courtroom in plenty of time before it starts."

In one swift movement, Coop stood up and swung around to grab his suit jacket that was hanging on the back of his chair. "Sounds good to me. Let's go."

The trial wouldn't start until two o'clock, so Mac and Coop had a couple of hours to kill before they headed to the courthouse. Because of the nerves brought on by the anticipation of the trial, Mac wasn't very hungry. Coop, however, was the complete opposite and could eat at any time, under any circumstances. After tossing a few suggestions back and forth, they decided on a nearby local diner. Mac settled for a bowl of cheddar broccoli soup while Coop ordered an open-faced roast beef sandwich with green beans, mashed potatoes, and gravy.

When the food arrived, Mac looked at Coop with disbelief. "How can you eat all that food in the middle of the day? If I ate all that, I would be so stuffed I'd have to take a nap afterwards."

"I can eat all day, every day and not gain a pound. In case you haven't noticed, I have a pretty high metabolism. And you, my friend, are just getting old." Coop laughed and shoveled a forkful of mashed potatoes in his mouth.

Mac could only shake his head with a slight smile as he tore open his packet of saltines.

After finishing their lunch and paying the tab, it was time to head to the courthouse. As they neared the car, Mac walked ahead and jumped into the driver's seat, not wanting to stress his already frayed nerves with Coop's erratic driving. After all, he wanted to make sure they got there in one piece. When it came time for him to testify, Mac didn't want to testify via Zoom from a hospital bed.

As they arrived at the courthouse, they were both surprised at the number of people that were waiting outside. A slew of people appearing to be news reporters, camera technicians, and curiosity seekers crowded around the lawn and front steps of the courthouse. Off to the side were a few young people, one with purple hair and a couple of others with baseball caps on backwards. Many of the young men were wearing their jeans hanging so low, the waistbands were hugging the bottom of their ass cheeks.

"If I ever dressed like that with my underwear hanging out for all to see," said Mac, "my father would have dragged my ass back into the house. Then he would make sure I didn't leave until I changed into something more respectful."

"I hear you. My mother would have done the same thing," Coop said with a chuckle.

Mac drove past the crowd towards the reserved parking spots in the back of the building. These were for judges and their staff, members of the District Attorney's office, police officers, and other officials. Only a few places were left. Mac pulled into an open spot at the back of the lot and put the Gaithersburg Police plaque on the dashboard.

"Good Lord," said Mac. "Did you see all those people? I've never seen a crowd like that waiting for a trial to start. Not here, anyway."

"Look at it this way, Mac. As the lead investigator, you're going to be famous! Just wait and see." Coop gave Mac a fist bump on the shoulder. "You'll be getting job offers from all over the country! You might even get to star on your own TV program, like 'Law and Order'."

Mac gave Coop a sideways glance, and said with a chuckle, "You're an idiot."

After showing their credentials, a court security officer opened the back door to let them in. "Are you here for the Mills trial?" asked the burly officer.

"Yep," Coop said, nodding his head.

"You and everybody else in the county," the security officer said. As they stood there, he ran a metal-detecting wand over their bodies. Both were carrying their department-issued hand guns on their hips, but after carefully checking their identification, the security officer waved them through.

"The trial's going to be in Judge Johannsen's court, room 134. Down this hall, turn right, you'll see the DA is already here."

Mac and Coop thanked him and headed down the hallway. They were already familiar with where that courtroom was located because they had been to the courthouse so many times before, during the normal course of business. This time, however, it stood out because it was the only courtroom to have so many people waiting outside the door. DA Wozniak and ADA

Kimberly Coville were whispering together. Farther down the hall, all three defense attorneys were conversing in a small circle, while Carter Mills and his daughter Margaret were sitting near them on a long bench. Mac watched out of the corner of his eye as Carter fidgeted, obviously not able to get comfortable on the hard wooden bench. One minute he'd be leaning over with his elbows on his knees, the next minute he'd straighten up and wipe his palms on his trousers. A few minutes later, two other young men arrived. Mac assumed they must be Carter's sons since they looked like him.

A few minutes past two o'clock, a court clerk propped the door open, and then walked back into the courtroom. She took a seat to the right of the judge's chair, which was at the head of the room. A bailiff was standing to the left of the bench. The people that had gathered in the hall, both defense and prosecution, filed into the room and took their respective places.

Members of the defense proceeded to the table in front of, but to the left of the bench, while the prosecution headed to their table situated to the right side. The jury would sit on the far right side of the courtroom, on a raised dais, called the jury box.

As a witness scheduled to testify, Mac couldn't observe any part of the trial until after his testimony, so he stayed outside in the hall. He would have to wait a short while until they called him as the first witness of the trial.

Coop continued on to the courtroom. Neither side would call him to testify for this trial, so he would be in attendance as often as he could.

There were approximately fifty seats in the gallery. Coop noticed, as he found a seat at the farthest edge of the gallery, that a small section had been designated for the media's use, and those seats were already taken. He watched as the rest of the seats were being filled by Carter's immediate family members that had been waiting out in the hall. News reporters that didn't find seats in the media section, and other people that were, most likely, just curious onlookers took the rest. There were still several people that were standing in the back and milling about, too late to grab a coveted seat in the gallery.

Judge Johannsen arrived a few minutes later and greeted each of the attorneys by name as she approached the bench. Her ability to remember names and faces was another quality that accounted for the respect she had earned within the judicial world. The judge looked towards the gallery and did a double-take. Her brows creased together in a frown.

"Bailiff," the judge called, signaling to the uniformed man at the side. The judge covered up her microphone with her hand out of habit, even though she hadn't powered it on yet. "There seems to be an abundance of people here today. Why don't you see if you can open up another room and have a TV monitor set up so that they can watch the proceedings from there. I can't have this many people standing around during a murder trial. Family members can stay here, but the media and everyone else who doesn't have a seat will have to go to the auxiliary courtroom."

Judge Johannsen turned on her microphone. "Ladies, and gentlemen, we'll take a thirty minute break so that we can set up an auxiliary room for those wishing to watch the trial. Family members may stay in this room if you wish. However, I would ask that the media and anyone else who can't find a seat in this room, to please find a seat in the other room. Members of the media who are not using laptops may stay, but I would ask those with laptops will have to go to the other room. However, you will all be able to watch the proceedings live from the other room via a television screen that we're in the process of setting up now."

One of the local news personalities stood up and asked, "Judge, would it be possible for the media to stay here in this courtroom?"

"No. There are too many of you, and I find the clicking of the keyboard to be very distracting. I would rather have you go to the other room. Thank you." Judge Johannsen stood up and left the bench.

And with that, Coop could hear several groans as the bailiff led a large group of people out of the courtroom and down the hall. Still, most of the fifty seats in the gallery were occupied by family members, curiosity seekers and members of the media who were using cameras or taking handwritten notes the old fashioned way. Coop even noticed one man who was there with a sketchpad, already drawing an excellent likeness of the judge.

After a forty minute delay, the trial was ready to begin. The bailiff asked that everyone rise as the judge entered. She took her seat at the bench and turned on the microphone. The courtroom fell quiet as Judge Johannsen informed everyone that there would be no talking during testimonies and that no one would be allowed in or out while court was in session. She found it to be very distracting when doors were continually opened and closed during a trial, and she would rather everyone's concentration remain on the trial, rather than on the gallery.

Judge Johannsen also stressed that no one was to contact the jurors for any reason. Although they would not be sequestered during the trial, they could not communicate with anyone regarding the trial itself.

She then explained that she had asked the media to observe the proceedings from another room because she found the constant clicking of the keys to be a nuisance. She further explained that, after receiving a request to film the trial from some members of the media, she had consulted the civil rights law, and has decided not to allow cameras, including cell phones, in the courtroom. A few more people left, taking their cameras with them.

The judge then asked the bailiff to bring the jurors into the courtroom. Coop watched as the sixteen men and women that comprised the jury filed into the courtroom and took their seats on the dais. He noticed that a couple of the jurors seemed to be wide-eyed, with the "deer in the headlights" look, although most seemed to be calmer, at least on the outside. A few held water bottles, some hung on to coffee cups.

Once everyone took their seats in the jury box, there was an eerie quiet in the courtroom. The judge seemed to be focused on something she was writing at the bench. After a few moments, she put her pen down and addressed the court.

"Ladies and gentlemen, the defendant, his counsel, and the District Attorney are all present, so we may begin." The judge lifted her hand towards the prosecution's table, giving him consent to begin with his opening statement.

DA Wozniak stood up, walked to the podium, and introduced himself to the courtroom. He then turned to address the jury. "I'd like to begin by telling you that this will be a hard trial to hear for many reasons. The defendant, Carter Mills, is a prominent member of the Gaithersburg community and a very successful investment broker, but don't let that influence you. We have charged him with murder in the second degree, which means we believe he intentionally caused his wife Loretta's death. He is accused of a heinous crime, of killing his wife of almost twenty-eight years, and staging the murder to look like she slipped and fell in the shower.

"During this trial, we will discuss a few hours in history and a few hundred square feet on the second floor of their home. You will see some disturbing photographs of the crime scene and of the victim, Loretta Mills. We will call on several people who will give testimony that, I expect, will be difficult for you to hear.

"We will tell you the details of a marriage that was falling apart. To the people outside of their family, the Mills' appeared to be the perfect couple, and yet, in reality, they lived very separate lives. When Carter had any number of business functions to attend, he went alone, refusing to bring Loretta. They never went out to dinner anymore, or to a show or even to the movies, just the two of them. They owned a condo in Punta Cana, but hadn't gone together as a family in several years. Make no mistake, they each traveled to Punta Cana, but they went at separate times and with separate groups of friends or family. And they had been sleeping in separate bedrooms for quite a while. Carter has told the investigators during an interview that he slept in a separate bedroom out of consideration for his wife, to spare her the effects of his loud snoring. The truth is that they couldn't stand to be with each other anymore. Loretta had even gone so far as to put a deposit down on an apartment two days before her death. Her intention was to get away from her husband, the accused killer, Carter Mills.

Carter turned to whisper into the ear of his attorney, seated at his side. The attorney whispered something back and gave a chopping motion with his hand, as if he was telling Carter to stop.

"You will learn that the cause of Loretta's death is not in dispute. However, the *manner* of her death is what we will determine during this trial and there are two choices as to what happened that ill-fated day. Either Loretta fell accidentally, or as we believe, she was beaten to death by her husband and left to die on the bedroom floor.

Dennis held up a photo of the wound on Loretta's head. Several audible gasps could be heard from the jurors and the gallery. "According to Carter Mills' statements, Loretta fell in the shower and hit the right side of her head on an eighteen-inch-high tiled bench that ran along the base of the shower wall."

He next held up a photo of her face with a substantial bruise to her left eye. "You see here an injury Loretta sustained to her face. This injury was from when her head was hit so violently on the right side that her brain bounced to the left side of her skull, leaving her left eye so swollen and bruised that it was swollen shut. This type of injury had to have taken over an hour to develop on Loretta's face.

"Look at the large bruise to her nose, and the other bruises on her face and both cheeks. These injuries have nothing to do with a fall." Dennis pointed to the areas in the photo as he described the various injuries.

Dennis held up yet another photo. "And this photo shows the bruising on her arm. But interestingly enough, there are no bruises on her legs, back or buttocks. After an alleged fall that left this much damage, you would think that there would be bruising elsewhere on the body. How could a fall in the shower split Loretta's skull open and give her so many injuries, but none on her back or buttocks? No, these injuries did not come from falling in the shower."

Dennis held the photos in the air and shook them for emphasis. "Loretta Mills received these wounds from a beating and from trying to defend herself." Dennis returned the photos to the table with a slap.

"The medics that responded that morning will describe to you what they encountered when they arrived on scene and treated Loretta. They tried to save Loretta's life, but unfortunately, she was beyond help. They could not open her airway because rigor mortis was already setting in. The AED showed there was no electrical activity coming from Loretta's heart. It was clear almost immediately that she was dead and had been for some time."

Dennis moved over to an easel that held a large drawing of a floor plan and picked up a wooden pointer. "This is a floor plan showing the second floor of the Mill's home. Carter Mills has already told the police during an interview that he discovered his wife on the floor of the shower after she had suffered an apparent head injury. He picked her up and moved her fifty to sixty feet into the bedroom." He used the pointer to show the path on the diagram that Carter had taken that morning.

"Once he discovered his wife's body," Dennis simulated quote marks with his fingers as he said the word 'discovered,' "Carter left Loretta lying there in the shower. He ignored the six landline and cordless phones within easy reach and went to his daughter Margaret's room, intending to ask her to call 911, rather than to make the call himself. He then went back to his wife's shower and her body, and waited until he heard Margaret come into the bedroom. Luckily for him, Margaret had picked up the phone in the nearby water closet, which is a separate room between the shower and the bedroom."

Dennis had walked back to the floor plan on display and pointed out the path that Carter had taken that morning. "Then he carried Loretta from the shower and down this small hallway towards the bedroom. He briefly set her down just outside of the water closet, where, at that moment, his daughter was talking with the 911 center. He made sure his daughter could see him because he needed a witness to this elaborate scheme. Then he picked Loretta up again, carried her past the large armoire and put her on the floor with her head and shoulder wedged against the bed."

The room was eerily quiet as the DA then walked back to the prosecution's table and held up a photo of the skylights in the shower room. "Carter Mills claims he had to move her because the lighting was better in the bedroom, that the shower room was too wet and hazy because of the steam. He claims he wasn't able to perform CPR on her in those conditions, so he had to move her to the bedroom. He made sure that Margaret was there to watch as he carried her mother's body out of the shower room, down the hall and into the bedroom.

"Margaret called 911 a few times during this incident and you will hear the recording of those calls. I know they will be difficult to listen to because you will hear Margaret screaming into the phone as her father carried her mother's body past her and into the bedroom. You will hear her screaming 'Oh, my God, there's blood everywhere.'

Dennis walked away from the easel, but kept the pointer in his hand, using it to gently tap the palm of his other hand.

"The Gaithersburg police interviewed Carter Mills a couple of weeks after Loretta's death. Ladies and gentlemen, you'll hear that interview on tape, and you will hear the responses that Mr. Mills gave regarding his wife's death. You will hear him claim that the night before her death, they said they loved each other before they went to bed, as they supposedly did every night, even though they maintained separate lives and slept in separate bedrooms. Even though she had signed the lease on her own apartment, to live in her own place without him, they supposedly expressed their love to each other before they went to bed every night.

"In this recording, you will hear Carter Mills say that he prepared a cup of coffee for Loretta, brought it upstairs to her bedroom and left it on her nightstand. Then he went for a quick run around the neighborhood pond the morning of her death. When he got back, he showered and put his pajamas back on. You will hear him say on the tape that he did this because they had planned to go to a fundraising brunch that morning and he didn't want to get his suit and tie wrinkled. He then went to make sure that Margaret was getting up, and he claimed he could still hear Loretta's shower running from the hallway outside Margaret's room. Surprised that she would still be in the shower, and thinking that they were going to be late, he went to Loretta's room and called out to her. He knocked, but there was no answer, so he went in. That's when he found her on the floor of the shower.

"We believe that the beating took place before daylight while it was still dark, which is why the defendant didn't see all the blood that was in the bedroom. The blood spatter was coming from left to right from the area near the bed." Dennis showed with a sweep of his arm how the blood went from left to right. "There was blood spatter on the headboard and on the water bottles and children's photographs that sat on the nightstand by the bed. There was blood spatter on the lamp in Loretta's bedroom. However, there was no blood at all on the coffee cup that Carter Mills said he brought to his wife that morning, just before he discovered her body in the shower. There is absolutely no doubt whatsoever that a violent beating took place in that bedroom before the fall was staged.

"Ladies and gentlemen, during this trial, you will hear testimony from a few different experts. Experts in areas like blood spatter analysis and forensic pathology, and I ask that you listen carefully to their testimony.

Things like blood spatter patterns are identifiable to experts. They tell a story to these experts. And if you listen to these experts, the story the evidence tells them is one of violence. There was violence in the bedroom the morning that Loretta Mills was killed.

"You will hear from evidence technicians and police officers from the Gaithersburg Police Department. They will tell you about the blood spatter and the blood swabs they took from the walls of the bedroom, the items on the nightstand, and from the shower.

"I would also like to point out the second law Mr. Mills is charged with, that of tampering with physical evidence. This charge stems from when he moved the body to alter the evidence. There was a tremendous amount of blood on the bedroom carpeting from when he'd beaten her and left her to die, but he had to find a way to account for all of that blood. That's why, when he moved Loretta's body from the shower, he had to place her body in the exact spot where she had died only hours before.

"He also changed the sheets on Loretta's bed because they had to be covered in blood as well. The live-in housekeeper had told us during an interview that there were different sheets on the bed from when she last changed them. She also said the bed wasn't made the way she made it. The evidence photos will show there were only three pillows on the bed when the first responders arrived. And yet, the housekeeper told us there should have been four pillows on the bed.

"Ladies and gentlemen of the jury, there are so many things you will hear during this trial that point to a horrific beating. Carter Mills' story that his wife died from a fall in the shower is pure fabrication and absolutely ridiculous. I ask that you consider the photos showing the massive wound on the right side of Loretta's head. Look at the time of her death. By the time the first responders arrived, she had already been dead for several hours. Consider the blood spatter in her bedroom. There is no reasonable explanation for her blood to be on the ceiling, lamp, nightstand and headboard unless it was from a violent beating. And yet there was no blood found on the coffee cup the defendant had placed on the nightstand, right before he claimed to have discovered her body. Listen to Loretta's beloved daughter screaming while she was on the phone with the 911 center. She was hysterical, screaming that there was blood everywhere.

"When you hear the evidence, ladies and gentlemen, you will see that this is a man, regardless of his social standing, who beat his wife to death. Please, don't let him get away with it. Thank you."

With that, the judge called for a twenty-minute recess.

⚖

The court reconvened after the quick break. Once the bailiff called the court to order, attorney Julie Fletcher approached the podium. Mac didn't know her personally, so once he had found out that she would represent Carter Mills, he had Googled her name to find out more about her. The search revealed that she was from the DC area and had only been practicing criminal law for about seven years. Based on the number of news articles, though, Mac could tell that she'd represented a substantial number of criminals in those few years. Apparently, her preference was to represent major felony clients, especially accused killers. Although he hadn't read where she'd taken many cases to trial, he read where she'd gotten reduced charges for her clients and they were given corresponding reduced sentences. From a defense perspective, taking a plea to a lesser charge and reduced sentence would be preferable to going to trial where the original charge and corresponding heavier sentence were possible if there was a conviction. Then again, that also showed that she had a lack of criminal trial experience.

Julie appeared to be a rather petite woman, about 5'2" and maybe 120 pounds, but as soon as she spoke into the microphone, her voice resonated throughout the courtroom. "Good afternoon, ladies and gentlemen." Coop raised his eyebrows in surprise. The deep, authoritative voice did not match her size.

"My name is Julie Fletcher, and my job is to make sure that justice is done. I will show you that this is a case of a totally innocent man who is being charged with a crime that never happened. In fact, there isn't a crime in this case at all. It was merely a tragic accident. Mr. Mills loved his wife. He could never bring harm to Loretta." As she was speaking, Julie held up a family photo taken a few years before and slowly turned around the courtroom so that the judge and jury could see the Mills family smiling, forever frozen in time.

"It is my belief that the police twisted the facts, and I take issue with the competence of the police investigation. Now, don't get me wrong ... I have a great deal of respect for police officers and the work they do. But I will give you the details surrounding this case, and what the police did and didn't do during the investigation."

Coop looked to the side and gave a questioning glance to the reporter seated next to him, one eyebrow raised.

"We've also asked various experts to look at the evidence, and you'll hear from those experts. One expert we've talked to feels that the blood trail went from the bathroom to the bedroom, not the other way around, like the prosecution suggests. Another witness is a crime reconstruction expert, who has said that this was an incomplete investigation. This witness admits that 'it could be' a homicide." Julie used her fingers to signify air quotes, "but that is only an opinion, and the experts are not always consistent in their opinions. Ladies and gentlemen of the jury, you must remember that you cannot convict someone on 'it could be'." Again, Julie made the air quotes with her fingers. "A guilty plea has to be beyond a reasonable doubt. There can be no 'could be' in a guilty plea.

"The Montgomery County medical examiner, Dr. George Schmidt, ruled the death an accident. He was on the scene the morning of Loretta's death and said at that time that it was an accident. He later performed an autopsy and said again that it was an accident. On her death certificate, he said it was an accident. Then, for some reason, three months later, he changed his ruling to homicide. I believe the police kept pressing and pressing, until eventually, Dr. Schmidt saw things their way. Personally, I don't trust anyone who changes their opinion based on other people's opinions. Ladies and gentlemen of the jury, please keep that in mind, but understand that during this trial, I intend to thoroughly question Dr. Schmidt.

"The accusations leveled at Mr. Mills by the police have compounded the tragedy of Loretta's death. Not long after Loretta's unfortunate death, the police interviewed Mr. Mills. During that interview, he admitted to them he couldn't explain the amount of blood found in the bedroom that morning. They have been unrelenting in trying to find fault with his statements ever since. You'll soon see that I can give a logical explanation for the blood and what's more, I will call on a witness who can explain the blood."

Julie casually walked over to the defense table and took a sip of water. She then turned to the diagram of the floor plan that was still displayed on the easel near the jury.

"Margaret Mills made the first call to 911 at 7:25 A.M. Loretta Mills was pronounced dead by the medics at 7:42 A.M. The district attorney has already said that you will hear the 911 calls that Margaret Mills made, and you will hear the terror, the agony and the heartbreak of those calls. I have listened to those calls several times, and I get upset every time. But those calls don't tell you where Margaret is. She didn't pick up the phone in the water closet, as the DA claims. That phone was dead. It had been disconnected, and that's why Carter had to ask Margaret to make the call to 911. He couldn't use the phone that he was closest to when he was bringing his wife out of the shower area.

"Carter Mills has already told the police that he carried Loretta out of the shower and placed her on the floor outside of the water closet. But then he picked her up again and moved the body to the bedroom, where there was more light and it wasn't as slippery as the tiled floor in the shower area. Margaret then helped him try to give Loretta CPR in the bedroom.

"The DA's theory is that Carter Mills set this whole thing up and used his daughter to verify his phony story. That's absolutely outrageous! It is not a made-up story. It's the absolute truth!

"The police have charged my client with evidence tampering because they allege, among other things, that he changed the bed sheets. And yet, they didn't take the sheets or pillows that were on the bed as evidence. The DA wants to focus on the blood at the scene, but it's my belief that the blood was spattered throughout the area when the EMTs took their gloves off. The police didn't take the blood-soaked carpet or the blanket that Carter had placed over Loretta. Maybe the blood came from the blanket when the EMTs whipped it off her body.

"Ladies and gentlemen, there is not a snowball's chance in Hades that the DA will come even remotely close to proving their case. There is no weapon, and certainly no motive. This was a loving family that suffered a catastrophic loss because of an unfortunate accident. Thank you for your attention."

Julie walked back to her seat at the defense table. With that, Judge Johannsen announced that testimony would begin, and invited the prosecution to call their first witness.

DA Wozniak stood up and gave a nod towards the judge. "Thank you, your honor. I'd like to call Sgt. Steve MacIntosh to the stand." The bailiff opened the door to the hallway and called for Mac to come into the courtroom. Mac approached the bench and nodded a greeting to the district attorney and the judge. After being sworn in by the bailiff, to tell the truth, the whole truth, and nothing but the truth, Mac took a seat at the witness stand.

Dennis began questioning Mac. "Good afternoon, Sergeant. For the record, would you please tell the Court your name?"

"Yes, sir. My name is Sgt. Steve MacIntosh."

"And can you tell us a bit about yourself, Sergeant?"

"I've been with the Montgomery County Police Department for seventeen years, and I've been stationed in Gaithersburg for the past five years or so, as sergeant of the Criminal Investigation Division."

"As I understand it," said Dennis, "you were the lead investigator on this case. Is that correct?"

"Yes, sir. That's correct."

"Can you explain to the Court why you began the investigation into Loretta Mills' death, why you thought it needed to be investigated in the first place?"

"I was working the morning Mrs. Mills died, and was present at the Mills' home, after the call came out. There were some things about the scene that didn't feel right to me. Things I couldn't logically explain."

"Can you be specific, Sergeant?"

"Well, it seemed to me that, if she had fallen in the shower, there was too much blood in the bedroom. There was blood on the wall and the nightstand and I didn't understand how or why it was there. Plus, there were injuries to her body that didn't seem right for someone who had taken a fall from a standing position."

"Why did it take a couple of weeks after her death for you to begin your investigation?"

"The medical examiner's autopsy report said that her death was an accident, that she'd died from a head injury, and that the injury resulted from a fall. There wasn't much I could do if they were the findings from the medical examiner. But not long after her death, I received an anonymous letter saying that she had been murdered and that her husband was the killer."

Carter had been sitting quietly next to his attorneys, but when he heard Mac's testimony, he shouted out, "that's ridiculous!" His attorney, Bruce Keegan, quickly leaned over and whispered in Carter's ear. Although Carter's response couldn't be heard, he was obviously upset and gestured towards Mac with his hand. After a whispered conversation with his attorney, he stopped talking, but he continued to glare at Mac.

"Please continue, Sergeant," urged Judge Johannsen.

"Sergeant, is this the letter you are referring to?" Dennis held a letter that was enclosed in a clear plastic bag towards Mac, who took it from the DA and glanced at it.

"Yes, that's the letter."

"Sergeant, would you read the letter out loud to the court?"

Mac gently cleared his throat and began reading. "I was friends with Loretta Mills for years, and I can tell you, she didn't die by accident. I don't know how he did it, but her husband killed her. He's had several affairs for years and she always looked the other way for the sake of the children. But just before she died, she'd finally told him she was in love with someone else and wanted a divorce. Even though they'd lived separate lives and even slept in separate bedrooms for several years, he was furious with her when she told him this. He had also been physically and verbally abusive to her in the past. I believe he killed her. Please, for the sake of Loretta's eternal peace, check into this." Mac handed the letter back to Dennis.

"Your honor, I'd like to introduce this letter as exhibit one. Please go on, Sergeant."

"After I received the letter, I contacted you, um, DA Wozniak for a second opinion," Mac lifted his hand towards Dennis, "and I showed you the letter and the crime scene photos ..."

Suddenly, Attorney Fletcher jumped out of her chair, yelling, "Your honor, I object to the term crime scene. At the time those photos were taken on the morning of Loretta Mills' death, they did not deem it a crime scene."

"It has since been determined to be a potential crime scene, counselor," said the Judge. "Objection overruled. Please continue, Sergeant."

"Like I was saying, I showed the crime scene photos and the letter to the DA, and he agreed it was worth checking into. We both felt that there were some questions that needed answers. After a thorough investigation, we put the case in front of the Grand Jury, and at that point, we received an indictment."

"As part of your investigation, did you interview the defendant?" asked Dennis.

"Yes, we did. I called Mr. Mills and asked him to come in for an interview. He came in later that same day."

"Your honor," said Dennis, "I'd like to play the videotaped recording of the interview with Mr. Mills, for the Court." The bailiff took the disk that Dennis had been holding and placed it in a DVD player. All eyes turned to the televisions in the Courtroom as the recording played.

Once the recording ended, Dennis stood up to address the Court. "There is one item I'd like to point out, your honor. The defendant said in the interview that he had to move his wife because it was too dark in the shower area of the bathroom for him to perform CPR. I'd like to submit into evidence this report from the National Weather Service. It shows sunrise was at 6:06 A.M. on the day of Mrs. Mills' death and it also shows that the weather that day was warm and sunny. The 911 call to report her death was more than an hour later, at 7:25 A.M. That contradicts Mr. Mills' claim that it was dark in the bathroom. I would also like to submit into evidence this photo, taken the morning of her death, that shows the skylights in the shower room. You'll notice they are perfectly clear and face the east. There would have been plenty of sunshine shining through those skylights that morning."

Dennis turned to Judge Johannsen and said, "no further questions, your honor."

Julie Fletcher stood up from the prosecution's table and walked towards Mac. "Sergeant MacIntosh, in your career as a police officer, have you ever seen anyone die from a fall before?"

"Have I ever *seen* anyone die from a fall? No, I have never been a witness to anyone that fell and died. But if you're asking me if I've ever investigated a death from a fall, then the answer is yes, I have."

"Okay, then. How many deaths from a fall have you investigated, Sergeant?"

"Off the top of my head, I would have to say only two or three, not including this one."

"And of those two or three, Sergeant, how many did you pursue as possible homicides?"

"I would say none, other than this one."

"In your career as a police detective, how many homicides have you investigated, Sergeant?"

"Again, I don't know the number exactly, but I would have to guess at least two dozen. And that would be over the last fifteen years of my career, and not all from within the Gaithersburg area, of course, but within the County."

"Of those two dozen homicides, Sergeant, how many have you solved?"

"All of them," Mac said matter-of-factly.

"You say 'all of them,' Sergeant, but how many were actually convicted?"

"All of them," Mac said again. He did, however, glance at Coop in the gallery with a flash of humor in his eyes.

Fletcher looked at the judge and proclaimed, "I have no further questions, your honor."

"You may stand down, Sergeant," said Judge Johannsen. She rapped the gavel on the wooden block and declared that the Court would reconvene at nine o'clock the next morning.

Chapter 15
Trial Day 3

The next morning, Mac and Coop sat at their desks discussing the case, the same way they'd been doing for months. They'd been over and over the details countless times, but it solidified in their minds the fact that they'd left no stone unturned.

They had worked for months to get the Carter Mills case ready for trial, and Mac knew it was as ready as it would ever be. This had been one of the biggest cases in his career, and he had planned to be at the trial every day until it was over. Coop would try to go as often as he could, but he was also trying to cover the workload, thus allowing Mac to sit in at the trial. Mac was the one that pursued the case and brought it to fruition, so Coop had said that it was only fair that Mac be the one to go.

Mac stood up and reached for his suit jacket, that was hanging on the back of his chair. "It's almost time to head out. Are you coming, Coop?"

"Sorry, Mac, I can't today," said Coop. "I told the lieutenant I'd have the report typed up today on that burglary at Mama P's Pizza from Saturday night."

"How's that coming along? Any good leads?"

"Yeah! I almost forgot to tell you. Yesterday, I looked over the surveillance video, and you're not going to believe this, but just before he broke in, the suspect tossed a soda bottle to the side of the building. I asked O'Malley to go back to see if he could find it, and he did. As soon as I get a chance, I'm going to send that to the lab. It's a long shot, but I'll see if they can analyze it and maybe find some DNA. If there are any, I'll have them run it through the database, and see if we can get a match. How cool is that?"

"That's perfect! Great catch!" Mac grabbed his car keys and headed towards the door. "I'll see you later."

Mac was lost in thought as he drove to the courthouse. The air was crisp and a bit chilly for this time of year, but he had always loved the fall. There was something about the reds, yellows and oranges of the changing leaves he liked. Or maybe it was because the heat and humidity of the Maryland summers made him sweaty and uncomfortable, where the cooler temperatures of the fall were much more enjoyable. Or it could be the memory of the homemade apple pies that Alayna used to make after they went on their traditional family outing of apple picking every fall. The smell of those pies baking filled the house with one of his favorite smells. Mac didn't even realize he had a smile on his face as he thought about those pies. *Maybe he could talk her into making one, for old times' sake*, he thought.

After he parked the car in the back parking lot, Mac ran up the steps of the courthouse, and felt a nervous energy coursing through his body, bringing his thoughts back to the present day. He was a bit early, so he stood outside in the hall, waiting for the door to the courtroom to open. Not long after, Brandon Powers came over and stood next to Mac.

"Hey, Sarge." Brandon greeted Mac with a smile. "I guess I'm the first witness of the day. I got a call from the DA last night to be here first thing in the morning."

"Lucky you! I gave my testimony yesterday, so I'm allowed to sit in the gallery and watch, starting today. I have a feeling the defense is going to try to poke holes in every single thing they can, but I firmly believe this case is solid. You and O'Malley did a great job on the evidence, so they won't get far with that." Mac gave Brandon a confident nod of his head.

"I hope you're right. There's no doubt in my mind that this guy killed his wife. I just hope we've got enough to put him away."

Mac entered the courtroom and was able to find a front-row seat in the gallery in front of the judge. *Kind of like sitting at the fifty-yard line,* he thought to himself. Mac watched as members of the media and other spectators casually wandered in. Within a half-hour, the District Attorney and his assistant Kimberly Coville, along with Carter and his attorneys—Julie Fletcher and Bruce Keegan—entered the courtroom. It was another ten minutes before the Judge and the jury took their seats.

"I apologize for the delay this morning," Judge Johannsen began. "A juror has been dismissed, but we have chosen an alternate juror to take their place. The juror did nothing wrong. It's just that it's a troublesome case, and a very emotional one. So now, without further delay, we'll start the trial for today. DA Wozniak, you may call your first witness."

"Your honor, I would like to call Officer Brandon Powers as my first witness." Dennis turned around, nodding to the bailiff to open the door. The officer walked in, buttoning his suit coat, and approached the bench.

Brandon stood in front of the courtroom with his hand on a bible while the bailiff swore him in.

He responded, "I do," and took his seat at the witness stand.

"Good morning, Officer," began Dennis. "Please state your name and credentials for the record."

"My name is Ofc. Brandon Powers, and I'm with the Gaithersburg Police Department, assigned to the Criminal Investigations Division in the capacity of an Evidence Technician."

"Thank you, Officer. First, I'd like to draw your attention to the photos and floor plans on display." He pointed to a group of tall easels displaying several photos and a black and white drawing of a floor plan. "Do you recognize them?"

"Yes, sir. I recognize them as the photos of the Mills' residence, both the outside of the home and also of the second floor, specifically Loretta Mills' bedroom and bathroom. And the floor plan seems to be of the same residence."

"And why do you recognize them, Ofc. Powers?"

"Because I was on scene at that home as one of the first responders the morning of Loretta Mills' death."

"And what exactly was your involvement that morning?"

"Well, sir, I was there originally as an officer and then as an evidence technician."

"What do you mean 'originally as an officer and then as an evidence technician'? You had a dual role that morning?"

"Yes, sir. Any time we have an unattended death, the evidence technicians are called to the scene per department policy. But since I was already on scene as the responding officer, I switched hats, so to speak, and performed ET duties."

"I see," said Dennis. "Ofc. Powers, what are your qualifications as an evidence technician. What kind of training have you had?"

"Well, I've had experience as an evidence technician for about seven years now, and have had extensive training at the County, State and Federal levels. I'm trained in the various collection and handling of evidence as well as the storage of evidence, whether it's blood, fingerprints, or solid objects like clothing and weapons. I also maintain my ET certification by taking classes several times a year, totaling about a hundred hours of training annually. And our department is nationally accredited, so our standards are quite high."

"That's good to know. Thank you. Let's go back to that morning, if we can. Do you remember when you arrived on the scene?"

"Yes, I do. It was about four minutes after the call came out. I was in my department issued vehicle and as soon as I heard the call being dispatched by the 911 center, I headed right over to the Mills' residence. I wasn't too far away."

"What was happening when you arrived?"

"Well, the rescue squad had just gotten there. The medics were getting their equipment out of the squad truck, and a young lady was at the doorway to the house, crying for us to hurry. She kept saying that she thought her mother might be dead. I followed the medics into the house and up the stairs to where the victim, Loretta Mills, was lying on the floor in her bedroom."

"Then what happened?" Dennis asked.

"The medics started working on Mrs. Mills. I heard one of them asking Mr. Mills what happened, and he said that his wife had fallen in the shower. Once he said that, it drew my attention from Mrs. Mills to the shower room, which was behind me. From where I was standing, I could hear the shower was still running, so I walked towards the shower room."

"And what was the condition of the shower room when you went in there?"

"The shower head was on the floor of the shower. It was the type of shower head that has a long hose so it can be removed from the wall unit and held in your hand. I noticed there was some blood on the floor of the shower and the room itself was steamy. The water was still running, so I shut it off. I went back into the bedroom and Lieutenant Porter, the paramedic, looked at me and shook his head. At that point, I went back to my car to get my ET equipment."

"What do you mean, 'Lieutenant Porter shook his head'? What did that mean to you?"

"I took it to mean that there was nothing they could do, that she was dead."

"Then what did you do?"

"I went back to my vehicle and got my ET equipment, and then started processing for evidence, beginning with the shower room. I took photographs to start, but the steam in the shower room was fogging up my camera lens, so I moved to the hallway and the toilet room to take photos and then the bedroom. After several minutes, I went back to the shower room and saw that the steam had cleared enough that I could resume taking photographs in there."

"And are these the photographs that you took that morning, Ofc. Powers?" Dennis handed a pile of photos to Brandon.

Brandon was quiet for a moment as he leafed through the photographs. "Yes, sir. They are."

"Can you explain what we're looking at in these photos?"

"I took these photos to show the different rooms and the condition they were in at the time of the incident, and then I went back to take close-up photos of the blood on the floors and walls within each room. In those photos, you'll see the forensic rulers I used to mark the scale of the smaller spots of blood."

"Your honor, I'd like to submit these photographs as exhibits two through forty-three." Dennis handed the stack of photos to the juror in the front row and asked, "if you would be so kind as to look at the photos, and then pass them on."

Mac watched each juror as they studied the gruesome photos. Some looked through them quicker than others, and most had frowns on their faces, but at least nobody shied away from the sight of all that blood. Although the photos were difficult to look at, the jurors seemed to understand that they had a responsibility to look at them.

"Okay, Ofc. Powers, did you take these photos?" Dennis handed Brandon some more photographs.

Brandon leafed through the photos in his hand. With a heavy sigh, he acknowledged they were also photos he had taken that morning.

"Can you explain what these photos are?"

"Yes, sir. Those are photos of Loretta Mills and the injuries she sustained the morning she was killed."

"Objection, your honor!" Julie Fletcher jumped up from her chair so fast it skidded backwards across the floor with an obnoxious scraping noise. "The allegation that Mrs. Mills was killed has yet to be determined. In fact, that is the whole point of this trial!"

Judge Johannsen, nodding her head, acknowledged Attorney Fletcher by saying, "Objection sustained. The jury will disregard the use of the word 'killed'."

Brandon glanced at Mac with a small smile, almost as if he was proud of himself for throwing that in. He handed the photos back to Dennis, who passed them to the jury.

Again, Mac watched the jurors as they looked at the graphic photos. This time, the look on each of their faces was unmistakably one of horror.

Dennis walked back to the prosecution table and took a sip from a water bottle that had been sitting on the table, giving the jurors time to look at the photos.

Turning back to look at Brandon, Dennis asked, "Okay, Ofc. Powers. We now know that you took photographs that morning. Did you collect any other evidence?"

"Yes, sir. I collected blood swabs, a couple of water bottles, some framed photographs that were on a nightstand, and I also took a sample of the beverage that was in the coffee cup. And I took the cup as well."

At that, ADA Coville reached into a large file box that was on the floor and pulled out some plastic bags, each containing the items that Powers had mentioned, except for the beverage. She set them on the table in front of her.

"Why would you take the framed pictures for evidence?" Dennis pointed to the items seen on the table.

"Because there was blood spatter on them."

"Is that why you took the water bottles and coffee cup?"

"Partly because of the blood spatter, yes. It's also standard procedure to have any beverages tested to make sure someone did not taint it with drugs or some other foreign material."

"Objection, your honor!" Attorney Fletcher stood up, raising her hand in the air. At least this time, she didn't scrape her chair across the floor. "There's absolutely no evidence whatsoever that there were illegal drugs or any foreign substance of any kind in the water or coffee on Loretta's nightstand, or anywhere else for that matter."

Brandon turned to talk to the judge. "May I explain, your honor?"

Judge Johannsen looked at Dennis for his approval. He nodded his head.

"That is correct, that there were no drugs in the coffee or the water, and I don't mean to imply that there were. What I'm saying is that we collect any food or beverages at the scene of a death as a matter of protocol. There may or may not be anything wrong with those items, but we won't know until it's analyzed. We collect it just to be thorough in our investigation. That's our policy."

"Thank you, Ofc. Powers. Let's move on, counselor." Judge Johannsen nodded towards the District Attorney.

"Please explain to the jury how you collect blood evidence, Officer."

"Well, I use a swab, which is basically a large Q-Tip, and swipe the blood with it, trying to get as much blood and therefore DNA on the swab as possible. I then sealed each individual swab in its own sterile container to avoid any kind of contamination. Then it's carefully labeled and taken back to the police station. From there, depending on the type of case and if we considered it necessary, we may send the blood samples to the forensics lab for analysis."

"And how do you collect the other evidence?"

"It's collected with the same type of care. Each item is placed in an evidence bag, carefully and separately, to avoid any kind of contamination."

"So, in summary, Ofc. Powers, you took photographs that morning of each of the rooms in the en suite bedroom, you took close-up photos of the blood spattered onto various items throughout the involved rooms and you took photos of Mrs. Mills and her injuries. Then you collected several items that may or may not have been of any interest in this investigation."

"That's correct, sir."

"How do you keep them all straight? Do you have a way to keep track of where you got each piece of evidence?"

"Yes, I do. I write the information on the bags to identify what it is, but I also write in a notebook exactly where the item was collected and at exactly what time. Then, when I get back to the station, I transfer all of that same information into the department's evidence computer program. Once that's done, I store the evidence in secure temporary lockers."

"And who has access to these secure lockers, Ofc. Powers?"

"Well, everyone in the department has access to the lockers, but only when they're left open. That's so that we can use them to store any evidence that's brought in. But once the locker has evidence in it, the submitting officer locks the locker and then the only people that have access to the locked lockers are the evidence technicians assigned to work in the evidence room. There are three technicians who have the keys to these lockers ... myself and two others. Not even the chief of police can access them once they're locked."

Dennis stood in front of the judge and said, "Your honor, I have no more questions."

Judge Johannsen called for a twenty-minute recess. Almost everyone in the courtroom stood up to at least stretch their legs, while a few of the spectators headed out of the courtroom towards the hallway. Mac heard a few deep cleansing breaths as people moved about. He felt certain that this would be one of those trials that would wear on everyone's emotions.

When court resumed, the defense took their turn to question Ofc. Powers. Attorney Julie Fletcher approached the bench and called him to return to the witness stand. After being reminded by the bailiff that he was still under oath, Brandon took his seat.

"Ofc. Powers, why did you stop collecting evidence that morning? Did you decide you'd collected enough?"

"No, ma'am." Brandon shrugged his shoulders and said, "The medical examiner informed me it was an accidental death and there would be no need to continue. At that point, I packed up my equipment and left."

Julie selected one of the evidence bags from the table and held it up. "According to the printout from the computerized evidence report, you collected this water bottle at 9:08 that morning, and yet the information written on the evidence bag shows it was collected at 9:05. How do you account for the discrepancy in time, Officer?"

Brandon chuckled a bit and responded, "Well, ma'am, my handwriting isn't the best, and sometimes the tail on my five is too long and it ends up looking like an eight. Towards the end of that long, thirteen-hour day, I may have looked at the number too quickly and misread it when I logged it in the computer."

Julie gave Brandon a sneer, asking, "And how many other mistakes did you make by rushing through this investigation?"

Dennis stiffened as if he was going to speak up, but before he could, Brandon smiled, seemingly unphased by her attempt at intimidation, and said, "Well, ma'am, like I said, my handwriting isn't the best, but that has nothing to do with my experience and skill as an evidence technician. I know some well-respected surgeons, and we all know that doctors are famous for having bad handwriting, but as long as they're good with a knife, I couldn't care less what their shopping list looks like."

A few people in the courtroom tried without success to stifle their chuckles. Julie, her cheeks getting red, turned to the judge. "Your honor, I fail to see the levity in this situation. I would ask that you remind the witness that this is no laughing matter."

"Counselor, I doubt very much that the witness is making a joke about the situation. He's merely making a point in answer to the question that you brought up. Please continue."

Julie pinched her lips together into a thin line as she walked towards the witness stand. She lowered her voice, obviously peeved, but asked the next question. "Officer, did anyone give you direction on what items you were to take?"

"No, ma'am. It's up to the evidence technicians, based on their training, to take what is pertinent to each individual investigation. I also have my own system when I collect evidence. I take photographs of the overall scene from a distance first, then I move in to take close-up photos of specific evidence and where each item is located, like the coffee cup sitting on the nightstand. At that point, and again, depending on the case, I will take any measurements before I collect and bag the evidence."

"Exactly how far away from the bed was the large blood stain where Mrs. Mills was found when you arrived?"

"That I don't know, ma'am. At least, not exactly, although I can give you an educated guess if you'd like. Before I could make any sketches or take measurements, I was told that the death was accidental."

"Well, Ofc. Powers, do you know how far apart the stains were on the wall?"

"No, ma'am. Again, that's something that would have required a lot more processing, but it's not something that's done when it's deemed an accidental death, especially when the medical examiner is on scene and telling me that there was no need to continue collecting evidence."

"So, your investigation is not what I would call thorough." Julie turned to the judge and said she had no more questions before Brandon could give a rebuttal to her snide comment. She then moved towards the defense table, but not before she turned to Powers and flashed him a dirty look. With a smile and a nod in Julie's direction, he stepped down from the witness chair.

"In that case, I suggest we break for lunch. Court will resume at 1:30." Judge Johannsen gave a bang of the gavel.

⚖

At 1:30, the court reconvened, with Dr. George Schmidt being called to the witness stand. This time, Assistant District Attorney Kimberly Coville began questioning the doctor after the usual swearing in.

"Good afternoon, Dr. Schmidt. Can you tell us, as the Montgomery County Medical Examiner, what your credentials are?"

"Certainly. I've been the chief medical examiner for almost ten years now. As well as being a medical doctor, I am also a forensic specialist, which means I examine and evaluate physical evidence to determine the cause of death."

"Doctor, can you tell us what types of things you do to determine the cause of someone's death?"

"I work with blood and other biological fluids, as well as several things such as hair, gunshot residue, drugs, and fibers. There are many different chemical, microscopic, or physical tests I can perform on the evidentiary items I just mentioned and, based on the results of those tests, I can then determine the cause of death. I would also like to add that I am not only a forensic specialist, I am also a certified pathologist, meaning, in layperson's terms, I examine bodily fluids and tissues to determine things like diseases."

"Thank you, doctor. Did you perform the autopsy on Loretta Mills?"

"Yes, counselor, I did."

"Were you able to determine an approximate time of death, Dr. Schmidt?"

"Yes. She died between 4:30 A.M. and 5:30 A.M. on the day that they pronounced her dead."

"They called 911 at 7:30 that morning, but you're estimating that she died at least two hours before 911 was called?" Dennis asked.

"Yes, that's right."

"Doctor, how did you come by that time frame?"

"According to the autopsy report that began at 9:30 that morning, her rectal temperature was ninety-two degrees. Rigor mortis had begun to set in."

"Did she have any illegal drugs in her system, or was she intoxicated in any way?"

"No, she had nothing like that in her system at all. No alcohol, illegal drugs, or even prescribed medication. Nothing at all."

"And will you tell the court, please, what else you found because of that autopsy?"

"Well, most notable was a large laceration in the hair and skin on the right side of Ms. Mills' head that was approximately five inches long. Her left eye was bruised and swollen shut. She had bruises along the left side of her forehead and nose, on the lower right side of her neck, and some scratches on her left cheek." As he described each injury, Dr. Schmidt was brushing his hand across his own head and face to point out where the injuries were. "She also had some slight bruising on her right cheek, and a slight cut on her lower left lip."

"Did she have any other injuries, doctor?"

"Yes, she had some bruising on her right arm and a bit on her left index finger, which was also broken."

"Doctor, did Mrs. Mills have any bruising anywhere else, say, on her back or butt?"

"No, she did not. She had no injuries on her torso at all."

"Wouldn't that be unusual for someone to fall in the shower from a standing position?"

Attorney Fletcher bolted straight out of her chair, shouting, "Objection, your honor! That's purely speculation on the witness's behalf!"

"Overruled. As an experienced doctor and medical examiner, I believe he's qualified to determine if it's more common that someone would land on their back or butt after a fall. Please answer the question, Dr. Schmidt."

"From my experience," said Dr. Schmidt, "that would be very unusual, especially when there are no drugs or alcohol involved. Most people, when they slip and fall, will land on their back or butt if they fall backwards, or their knees or hands if they fall forwards. Seldom would they fall either forward, backward, or even sideways and land directly on their head. A person's natural instinct is to protect themselves by putting their hands out when they fall. In this situation, the shower itself was rather small. I find it highly unlikely that Mrs. Mills would have fallen without hitting the walls that were only inches away from her."

"Dr. Schmidt," said ADA Coville, "You said that the laceration to Mrs. Mills' head was to the right side, but it was her left eye that was swollen shut. Can you explain how that would happen?"

"The skull fracture traveled from above the right ear and down to the left eye socket, which then caused the black eye when the fracture entered the orbit. There was also some bruising on the left front and left side of the brain." Dr. Schmidt was again showing on his own head where the injuries were. "You'll see this type of pattern most often when the head hits a fixed, or stationary, object. However, the same pattern can be seen, although not as often, if a solid object that isn't stationary strikes a person. An example of this type of injury would be something like shaken baby syndrome."

"Were there any other injuries, Doctor?"

"Yes. She had a fracture of the C4 vertebrae, which, again in layperson's terms, is a broken bone in about the middle of the neck."

"Doctor, can you tell us how long before her death these injuries occurred?"

"Not exactly, because even after someone dies, some bleeding from the tissues can still occur. However, I can say with certainty that, based on the amount of bleeding in the area of the skull fracture, that injury occurred well before she died. The cervical fracture also occurred at about the same time as the skull fracture."

"In conclusion, Doctor, what did the autopsy reveal to be the cause of death for Mrs. Loretta Mills?"

"The autopsy showed the cause of death to be from head injuries that were not the result of a fall."

"Thank you, Doctor. No more questions." As Kimberly returned to the prosecution table, she gave a nod to the defense counsel.

Attorney Fletcher stood up and walked towards the witness stand, her back as straight as an arrow and her eyes as piercing as the tip of that arrow.

"You said that rigor mortis was beginning to set in. Is that correct?"

"Yes, counselor, that's correct."

"Your honor, I'd like to submit the medical report filed by the attending medics from the morning of Mrs. Mill's death. This report filed by the medics state they could move the victim's arm to insert an IV. How do you explain that, Doctor?"

"Rigor was setting in at the time of the autopsy, and that was some four to five hours after death occurred. It takes at least two hours before rigor mortis begins, and about twelve hours before it's at its peak. When the medics were working on Mrs. Mills, it would have been at the two- to three hour mark."

"Dr. Schmidt, do you know why there was a broken bone in Mrs. Mills' neck? Was she strangled to death?"

"No, I don't know what caused her broken neck. I would have had to be there when it happened. And no, she had not been strangled."

"Can you tell the court how you know that?"

"There was no bruising on her throat that would be consistent with strangulation, and the hyoid bone, which is a cervical bone near the jaw, was not fractured. When an adult has been strangled, the hyoid bone will be fractured. That was not the case with Mrs. Mills."

Julie stood in front of the doctor with her arms crossed in front of her. "So she could have broken her neck when she fell."

"As I said, counselor, in order to know that, I would have had to be there when it happened."

Julie took a yellow sheet of paper from the top of the pile on the defense table.

"Dr. Schmidt, is this the certified death certificate for Loretta Mills?"

Dr. Schmidt took the paper and, after taking a brief glance at it, he handed it back to Julie. "Yes, it is."

"How come it is an amended death certificate, doctor? It appears that the option of accident is crossed out and homicide is now checked." Julie was using air quotes at each of these words. "If you aren't sure of the cause of death, why didn't you just check undetermined or even pending?"

"Because it is my belief that Ms. Mills' death is not considered undetermined. It is a homicide, which is why I checked that box on the amended death certificate. The amended certificate shows that Ms.

Mills was injured by an object, not from a fall. And in both the original report and the amended report, the manner of death is listed as blunt force head injuries. If I may explain, because there is a difference between the cause of death and the manner of death, and it can be confusing. For example, a gunshot wound to the head may cause a person's death, but it may be the person got shot by someone else or that he shot himself. The cause of death, being a gunshot wound, is the same in this case, but the manner of death is different. In this example, the manner of death could be a homicide or it could be a suicide or even an accidental shooting. In the case of Ms. Mills, it is my determination that the cause of death was blunt force trauma to the head, and the manner of death is homicide."

"And Dr. Schmidt, were there any new facts that led you to change your mind on the manner of death, or did you just have a new opinion for some reason?" Julie raised one eyebrow in an attempt to be condescending.

"Counselor, as a trained medical professional," Schmidt said, matching her tone, "I have to rely on both fact and my well-trained and vastly experienced opinion in order to make a determination. Since I wasn't there at the time she lay dying, I had to piece the puzzle together to the best of my ability. And after all the test results came in, which took time, I might add, and after consulting with blood spatter experts and after carefully studying the autopsy report, I felt obligated to amend the original death certificate from accidental to homicide." Dr. Schmidt was not going to back down.

"But you agree, doctor, that her black eye came from a head injury, not from something like a punch in the eye during an altercation, is that correct?"

"Indirectly, but yes, counselor, that is correct."

"No further questions, your honor." Attorney Fletcher returned to her seat.

⚖

DA Wozniak stood up and called Dr. Anthony Santangelo to the bench. After being sworn in, Dr. Santangelo gave his credentials, explaining that he was a nationally recognized pathologist and has worked on some well-known cases throughout his lengthy career. At seventy-eight years old, he'd been in the business for many years, more than he cared to admit, he explained with a slight smile. He continued by saying that he'd been involved in the investigations into the deaths of President Kennedy, Dr. Martin Luther King and John Belushi, among others.

"Doctor," began Dennis, "have you seen the autopsy reports and evidence technician reports concerning the death of Loretta Mills?"

"Yes, I have."

"And what were your findings?"

"It is my belief that she suffered a homicidal assault with at least one hefty blow to the side of her skull, with more injuries to her nose and the left side of her forehead. This fatal blow to her skull ripped through the skin down to the bone, which resulted in the skull fracture. I looked closely at the photos of the wound and determined that the irregular edges of the wound signified a sharp object did not cause it. The wound was the result of tearing from the blow."

Mac took a quick glance at the jury and saw several of them cringing at the detailed description that Dr. Santangelo was giving.

"The injury," Dr. Santangelo said, "would have had cleaner edges if it resulted from a fall in the shower as the defense suggested, and yet there wasn't anything in the shower that would have caused Mrs. Mills' injuries."

"Doctor, as an expert, you also looked at the blood samples recovered from the bedroom. What were your findings?"

"It has already been determined from the lab results that all the blood belonged to Loretta. However, there was one unique sample that had been recovered from the headboard. I looked closely at that sample because it had additional tissue and I was able to determine that tissue was brain matter."

"And you're sure that it was brain matter, Doctor?"

"Yes, indeed. If you were to compare tissue collected from a person's stomach or skin or heart or liver or brain, they would all be made up of different cells, even though it's the same person. In that one sample, there were two distinct types of cells ... one was from her blood, the other from her brain."

Dennis returned to the prosecution table. "Your witness, counselor."

Julie Fletcher stood up. "Why didn't you talk to Mr. Mills before writing your report, Doctor?"

"I didn't need to, counselor. I read the interview reports from both Mr. Mills and Margaret Mills, I read the autopsy report, and I talked with DA Wozniak and the police investigators. Besides, my job is not to figure out 'whodunit'. My job is to figure out what happened. All the other things might be interesting, but that's for the lawyers to piece together, not the doctors."

"Doctor, how certain are you of these findings of yours? How many times have you been proven wrong before?"

"I'm very confident in my findings. I must admit, however, that I was wrong once that I know of in my career, although I suppose I could have been wrong other times without being made aware of it."

Attorney Fletcher stomped back to the defense table *with a look on her face*, Mac noticed, *that would stop a clock.*

With that, Judge Johannsen adjourned court until the next morning.

Chapter 16
Trial Day 4

At the start of the fourth day of the trial, ADA Kimberly Coville stood up with a computer disc in her hand. "Your honor, with your permission, I'd like to play this for the court. It's a recording of the calls Margaret Mills made to the 911 center on the morning of her mother's death."

The bailiff took the disc and put it in the CD player, adjusting the volume so that everyone could hear.

Not another could be heard sound in the courtroom while the chilling calls from Margaret were played. They heard Margaret begging the ambulance to hurry, screaming into the phone that there was blood everywhere, that she thought her mother was dead.

When the recording was finished, Kimberly waited a moment before calling her next witness. She did this not as much for the dramatic effect but more to give herself and the people in the courtroom a chance to regain their composure. It had been a difficult recording to listen to.

She then called paramedic Kevin Porter to the stand as the first witness of the day.

"Lt. Porter, would you please tell the court a bit about yourself?" Kimberly's voice was soft, the 911 call seeming to still be playing on her mind.

Kevin cleared his throat. "Yes, I'm Lieutenant Kevin Porter of the Gaithersburg Fire Department. I hold the rank of lieutenant, but I'm also a paramedic and I supervise the medical personnel. I've been a medic for fourteen years."

"And can you tell the court about your involvement with Loretta Mills on the morning of her death?"

"When the call first came out, it was dispatched as an unconscious person after a fall. We responded from the fire department and were on the scene in just under four minutes. A young female, who I understand was Margaret Mills, was outside the home, crying and yelling for us to hurry. She said she thought her mother might be dead."

"Did you speak to her at all, Lt. Porter?"

"No, I didn't. I just grabbed the gear from the rescue squad and followed Margaret into the house. She led myself and my partner, Medic Sarah Whitman, upstairs."

"And what did you find when you got upstairs?"

"As soon as we got to the bedroom, we saw a female lying on the floor right up against the bed and a male kneeling next to her."

Kimberly held up a photo of the bedroom with the bed in the center. "This is the bedroom, is it not?"

Porter acknowledged it was. She then passed the photo to the jury.

"Do you remember what Mrs. Mills looked like? What condition she was in?"

"Yes, I remember very well. She was lying on her back, naked, and partially covered by a blanket. Her head was right up against the bed frame, with her body positioned along the side of the bed. She had a large laceration on the right side of her head, a large hematoma ... a bruise ... around her left eye, and she wasn't breathing."

"What did you do at that point?"

"Well, the first thing I did was to ask Mr. Mills what happened. He said that he had found Mrs. Mills on the floor of the shower and then he carried her into the bedroom. Sarah ... uh, excuse me ... Medic Whitman and I began resuscitation techniques. Medic Whitman hooked up the leads to the AED and then tried to open the airway by intubating Ms. Mills while I was doing chest compressions. And, because Mrs. Mills' head was up against the bed, we had to move her a bit so that we could keep working on her."

"What does that mean, to intubate?"

"That's when we put a tube partway down the patient's throat to keep the airway open. Then after we put an oxygen mask on the patient, the oxygen can be forced directly into their lungs."

"Do you recall what Carter Mills wore that morning?"

"Yes," the medic said. "He was wearing light blue pajama pants and a white short-sleeved tee shirt, like an undershirt."

"And what condition were his clothes in? Do you remember?"

"Yes, I do remember. His tee shirt appeared to be damp, and there was some blood on it."

"Getting back to Mrs. Mills' condition, can you tell us, Lt. Porter, what you found from a medical standpoint?"

"We could not intubate her because her jaw couldn't be opened. The AED showed that there was no electrical activity, or in other words, no heartbeat. At that point I talked to the hospital by phone and got permission to terminate resuscitation attempts."

"Why couldn't you open her jaw?"

"Rigor mortis had started to set in."

"Objection, your honor!" interrupted attorney Fletcher. "Is the witness also a medical examiner?"

Kimberly looked at the judge. "Your honor, one wouldn't have to be a medical examiner to determine if someone is deceased. The witness has already testified that as a paramedic, he's had extensive training and fourteen years of experience. That would be enough that he would be able to tell and would need to know when someone was beyond help."

"I would agree," Judge Johannsen said. "Objection overruled."

"So, Lt. Porter, have you had training on how *not* to contaminate a scene?" asked Kimberly.

"Yes, I have. Extensive training. For anyone in the medical field, it isn't always about contaminating a scene. It also has to do with making sure we aren't exposed to anything that would harm us."

"With that in mind, did you get any blood on yourself while you were working on Loretta Mills?"

"No, I did not."

"No further questions, your honor." ADA Fletcher walked back to her seat.

This time, attorney Bruce Keegan stood up from the defense table. "Falling in a bathroom is a fairly common event, is it not, Lt. Porter?"

"Yes, actually it is."

"And not usually serious, is it?"

"No, not usually, although elderly people have a tendency to break bones, no matter where they fall." Porter said.

"Just answer the question, please. Did you speak to Mr. Mills that morning?" Keegan had a pen in his hand and was tapping it into the palm of his other hand.

"Yes, briefly." Kevin would now be careful and not give too much information in his answer.

"And what did you speak to Mr. Mills about Lt. Porter?"

"I asked him what happened to his wife, and he told me she had fallen in the shower. He said that he had to move her from the shower into the bedroom so he could perform CPR on her."

"And did you speak to Margaret, their daughter?" Tap, tap, tap with the pen.

"No, because she was pretty much hysterical. She was crying and screaming that we needed to help her mom. Although, once we started working on her mom, she stood off to the side, crying, but not screaming or saying anything."

"What about Mr. Mills, Lt. Porter? What was his condition?" Tap, tap, tap.

"Well, he didn't really say anything other than what I've already said. He just moved aside to stand with Margaret when we got there so we could start working on Mrs. Mills."

"That doesn't answer the question, lieutenant. What condition was he in? Was he weeping at all?"

"No, not to my recollection."

"Can you tell the court what he looked like that morning and what condition his clothes were in?" Still tapping the pen in his hand.

"Like I said, he had some blood smeared across the front of his tee shirt, and it seemed kind of wet from water or something. Not dripping wet, just kind of damp."

"Objection, your honor," interrupted ADA Coville. "Asked and answered."

"Move it along, counselor," the Judge said.

"Did Mr. Mills have any injuries, Lieutenant?"

"Not that I noticed, but quite honestly, I was focused on Mrs. Mills and her injuries. I didn't examine Mr. Mills."

"Did you come into contact with any of the blood that was in the bedroom or bathroom that morning, Lt. Porter?"

"No, not at all."

"How about any of the other emergency personnel? Did your partner or any police officers get blood on them?"

"Not that I'm aware of. Medic Whitman and I were the only two first responders to touch the victim and neither one of us got any blood on us." The tapping stopped, but now Keegan was using the pen as a pointer.

"Let's go over the things that you did that morning. Once you stepped into the bedroom and saw Mrs. Mills, what did you do?"

"Well, the victim ... Mrs. Mills ... was lying on the floor on her back with her head near the nightstand and her body was alongside the bed. From just below the breasts down, she was covered by a blanket. She had head and facial trauma, she wasn't breathing, and she had no pulse. I pulled the blanket off of her and then started CPR. I continued doing CPR for a minute or two and then stopped to put a cervical collar on her. Then my partner and I put her on a backboard so we could safely move her away from the bed."

"Were you wearing gloves, Lt. Porter?"

"Absolutely. We always put them on before we give any kind of medical care to a patient. We are trained to be extremely cautious with blood-borne pathogens, so we always wear gloves."

"What about taking the gloves off? How do you take them off?"

"We're also trained in how to take them off. There's a specific way to pull the first glove down towards the fingertips. Then you have to hold on to that glove with the glove on the other hand, and pull the second glove off the same way. That leaves both gloves inside out, with any contaminants still on the inside of the gloves."

Keegan handed a pair of gloves to Lt. Porter. "Would you please demonstrate how you put them on and take them off?" Porter did as he was asked, carefully putting the gloves on and taking them off again.

"You just mentioned that you 'pulled' the blanket off, Ms. Mills. Can you show us how you did that?"

"Well, I don't think 'pulled' was the right word. I pushed it off of her and let it sit on the floor next to her." Kevin showed with his hand how he swept the blanket to the side.

"Was there any blood on the blanket?" asked Keegan.

Lt. Porter thought for a moment, then responded, "I don't believe so. At least not very much, if any. She didn't have any bloody wounds on her torso that would have transferred to the blanket."

"No further questions, your honor." Keegan walked back to the defense table as Kevin got down from the witness stand.

After a brief break, the prosecution called Medic Sarah Whitman to the stand. ADA Kimberly Coville began the testimony by asking Sarah to identify herself to the court.

Sarah explained she has worked for the Gaithersburg Fire Department for about five years, although she'd been a medic for almost twelve years.

"Can you tell us what your involvement was in treating Loretta Mills on the morning that you were called to the Mills' home?" Kimberly asked.

"Yes, I can. I was driving the rescue squad that morning, and when we pulled up to the house, a young woman was outside screaming for us to hurry. Kevin and I grabbed the equipment off the squad and followed her into the house. We ran upstairs and found Mrs. Mills on the floor, with Mr. Mills kneeling next to her. We had to ask him to move so we could start working on her."

"Did you notice what Mr. Mills wore that morning?"

"Yes. He had on a white tee shirt that was kind of wet and had blood on it, and pajama pants. I think they were blue."

Kimberly asked the witness, "did you see a shirt anywhere that would have matched the pajama pants?"

"No, not that I recall," said Sarah, looking puzzled. "But I didn't really look for something like that. I was focused on the patient. I only noticed Mr. Mills and what he was wearing because of the blood on the tee shirt."

"Can you describe Mrs. Mills' physical appearance when you first got there?" asked Kimberly.

"Definitely. I noticed she had a good sized laceration just above her right ear and her hair was really bloody around that laceration. The rest of her hair was wet, as well. Her left eye was so swollen it was shut, and she also had some scratches on her face. Other than the injuries to her head, I didn't see any injuries to the rest of her body. And she was naked, so I could see her whole body. But she had bruises on her fingers, and some of the fingers looked bent."

"What condition was the room in? Did you happen to look around?"

"Yes, I did a little because, as first responders, we're trained to look at the environment around the patient. Sometimes it helps us figure out what's wrong with them. I saw that there was a lot of blood on the floor around Mrs. Mills' head. And I could see down the hallway into the bath area, so I went in there to look for any kind of medications that she may have taken."

"Did you find any medications?"

"No, I didn't. But I did see a phone on the floor of the toilet area. I remember that because I thought it was kind of strange to have a phone right next to the toilet." Sarah gave a wry smile and shrugged her shoulders.

Kimberly walked back to the prosecution table. "No further questions, your honor."

Judge Johannsen nodded to Attorney Fletcher. "Your witness, counselor," but Fletcher was already standing up, ready to question the witness.

"Ms. Whitman, who was the first one to enter the home?"

Sarah hesitated for a moment. "I believe it was Lt. Porter, but I'm not positive."

"And when you got to the bedroom, what did you see?"

"I saw a woman, Mrs. Mills, laying on the floor on the other side of the bed, and a man, Mr. Mills, kneeling next to her."

"Objection, your honor." Dennis spoke in a calm, almost fatherly voice. "Asked and answered." "Sustained. Move it along, counselor." Judge Johannsen gave a twirling motion with her pen.

"Okay, Ms. Whitman." Attorney Fletcher pushed a sheet of paper towards Sarah. "Is this your sworn statement?"

The medic took only a moment to confirm that it was. "Yes, that's my statement."

"And do you recall that in this statement, you said that you grabbed Ms. Mills' right arm and applied a tourniquet?"

"Yes, I did say that. I put on a tourniquet because I was going to start an IV, but I never got that far."

"So her arm must have been flexible enough for you to put on the tourniquet."

"Yes, it was. But the AED showed that there was no electrical activity, and Kevin was on the phone with the hospital. They told us to suspend life-saving measures, so we stopped working on her before I could start the IV."

"Ms. Whitman, your partner, testified that he 'pushed' the blanket off Ms. Mills. Is that how you would describe it?"

"I guess so. It's not like he flung it in the air, or anything."

"Was there any blood on the blanket?"

"No, not that I saw."

"And how about the phone that you've already testified you saw on the floor of the toilet room? Was there any blood on the phone?"

"I don't know. I didn't stop to look that closely at it."

"But you went all the way into the shower room, is that correct?"

"Yes, I did, to look for any medications that might have been on the counter or in the medicine cabinet."

"And what did you see when you got into the shower room, Ms. Whitman?"

"Well, I didn't see any medications, but the floor was wet and the door to the shower was open. I could see the shower head was on the floor."

"Did you see any blood in the hallway, between that shower room and the bedroom?"

"Yes," agreed Sarah. "There was quite a bit of blood in different spots on the walls and the floor by the toilet room, so I stepped around it."

"No further questions, your honor." Julie turned and walked back to the defense table.

With a firm rap of the gavel, Judge Johannsen ended the day's testimony. "Ladies and gentlemen, I think that's enough for today. We'll reconvene at 9:30 tomorrow morning."

Chapter 17
Trial Day 5

On Friday morning, Mac was at the courthouse, bright and early. As the week went by, he'd noticed fewer and fewer spectators coming to watch the trial. Where it had been standing room only on Tuesday, there were a few empty seats today, so he was able to grab a chair front and center, with a good view of the trial.

Once everyone was settled and the judge, jury, defense and prosecution took their respective places, DA Wozniak stood to begin the day's proceedings.

The next witness called to take the stand was Irene Stapleton, the Mills' housekeeper. After being sworn in, Dennis asked her to describe to the court how she came to be with the Mills family. Irene explained that shortly after she became a widow, she moved into the Mills home as a live-in housekeeper and cook. She had been with the Carter family for seven years by the time Loretta died. She considered herself a part of the family since she'd had no children of her own and even though Loretta was technically her employer, she explained that she and Loretta enjoyed each other's company and grew to be very close.

Dennis began questioning Irene by asking her about the bed in Loretta's room. Irene acknowledged she made the bed every day, but changed the sheets and comforter once a week, normally on Mondays. There were four sleeping pillows on the bed, she explained, two that would match the sheets, and two that would match each other, usually in a contrasting color. Dennis showed her an evidence photo of the bedroom that was taken the Thursday morning after Loretta had died. Irene studied the photo and said that the sheets that were on the bed that morning were not the ones that she had put on a few days prior to Loretta's death. She also testified that there were three pillows in that photo, and yet there were always four pillows on the bed. One pillow was missing.

"Do you know," Dennis asked, "what happened to the sheets that you had put on the bed on the previous Monday?"

"No," she admitted, shaking her head. "I didn't know what happened to those sheets. I never saw them again. But I do know that I threw away the sheets that were on the bed when Loretta died. Some of her blood was on them and I would never use them again knowing that. No matter how many times I washed them, they would never be clean." Irene glanced at Carter out of the corner of her eyes.

"Mrs. Stapleton, do you recall if Mr. Mills generally wore matching pajama tops and bottoms?"

"I didn't usually see the family that late at night because I went to bed earlier than they did. Once in a while, though, I might see one of them if I was getting a late-night snack or a glass of milk because my room was off the kitchen. But that didn't happen very often. Still, to answer your question, I don't recall ever seeing him wear just the pajama bottoms without the matching top. He always wore the matched set. I did his laundry, also, and there was always a matching pair of pajama bottoms and tops that I would fold and put in his dresser drawer."

"And do you know what happened to the pajama top that would have matched the pajama bottoms that Mr. Mills was wearing the morning of Mrs. Mills' death?"

"No, I don't. I believe there used to be a top to the pajamas, but I have no idea what would have happened to it. I never saw that again, either."

"Do you know what happened to the tee shirt he wore that morning?"

"Yes, I threw it away. I wasn't sure I would get the blood out of it, and frankly, it wasn't worth trying. I threw it into the same garbage bag as the sheets and put it all in the garbage pail outside."

"Now, you describe your relationship with Mrs. Mills as being a close one, is that right?" asked Dennis.

"Yes, that's true." Irene looked down and clamped her lips together.

"Did she ever confide in you?"

Irene was leery, but said, "Yes, I suppose she confided in me about some things."

"Did she ever discuss her relationship with her husband with you?"

"Yes, she did, but I don't want to break her confidence."

"It's okay, Mrs. Stapleton. I understand, but you also swore to tell the truth."

"Well," said Irene, "they argued a lot, and if they weren't arguing, they just plain ignored each other. She told me she missed the old days when they got along. She liked it better when they went out together or with other couples and had fun."

"I have no further questions, your honor." Dennis took a seat, turning the floor over to the defense counsel.

Bruce Keegan began to question Irene, asking her if she cleaned up the blood in the bedroom and bathroom. Irene looked down at her hands in her lap, pausing before she spoke.

She choked out the words, "Yes, I cleaned up the blood as best I could. I used soap and water in the shower and a steam cleaner on the rugs in the hallway and the bedroom. It was one of the hardest things I ever had to do."

"Just answer the questions, please, Mrs. Stapleton." Bruce said gently.

Bruce showed Irene another evidence photo, this one of pajamas that laid in a heap on the floor of the bathroom, near the shower stall.

"Do you recognize these pajamas?"

"Yes, I believe they are Loretta's pajamas. I did the laundry for the family almost every day. Whatever they put in their hampers, I washed, but I didn't really pay attention to what I was washing each day. They all had so many clothes."

"Do you know if these pajamas were the ones she may have worn to bed the night before she died?"

"I would have no way of knowing that because I didn't see her before she went to bed that night."

"Mrs. Stapleton, are you still working for the Mills family?"

"No, I am not. I left about two months after Mrs. Mills died. She and I were good friends. It hurt me a great deal to see that room where it happened. I just couldn't stay any longer."

"One last question, Mrs. Stapleton. Do you have any memory problems?"

"No, I do not," Irene said, lifting her head and jutting out her chin.

"No further questions, your honor."

⚖️

After lunch, Dennis called Patrick O'Malley to the stand. He was sworn in. Then, like the other witnesses before him, he told the courtroom about his credentials and his training. Dennis began the questioning by asking O'Malley if he could explain why the police felt it was necessary to execute a search warrant for the Mills' home.

"Once it was determined to be a suspicious death," O'Malley said, "there were things we needed to do during the search warrant that they didn't have a chance to do it on the morning that Mrs. Mills died."

Dennis then asked him what his role was on the day they executed the search warrant.

"Did you go into the basement to check the hot water tank, Ofc. O'Malley?"

"Yes, I did."

"What were you looking for?"

"We needed to find out how long the hot water would last before turning cold. The defendant had stated that the bathroom was steamy when he found his wife in the shower, but he also said that the shower had been running for a long time."

"Objection, your honor!" Attorney Fletcher was back to jumping out of her chair when she raised an objection. "The witness has no way of knowing what is considered a 'long time' since he wasn't there at the time."

"Overruled, counselor. The witness just stated that he is quoting your client, and I do recall Mr. Mills saying that same thing. Please continue, Ofc. O'Malley."

Julie sat down with an audible "hmph." Judge Johannsen, hearing the attorney, glared at her.

"When I initially tested the temperature of the hot water in the tank, it measured 130 degrees. However, most people don't turn the hot water all the way up. The most comfortable temperature is about 105 degrees, so I turned the water on and measured it to be at 107 degrees. Then I let it run until I could feel it turning noticeably colder and that was after twenty-eight minutes. I measured the temperature of the water at that point to be eighty-nine degrees."

Mac noticed that a couple of the jurors looked at each other with raised eyebrows. This was a key point that would poke a hole in Carter's testimony about the bathroom being steamy after all that time, and they obviously picked up on it.

"After you took the water temperatures, did you do anything else, Ofc. O'Malley?"

Patrick explained to the court how he joined the rest of his team upstairs and measured the dimensions of each of the rooms that make up the bedroom suite. He then took precise measurements of things like the size of the shower and the height of the step that Carter surmised she fell against. He also assisted Ofc. Brandon Powers, by photographing the blood spatters up close, and noting the exact location of each of them that was still present in the rooms.

O'Malley then talked extensively about taking a large number of photos of those blood spatters and taking swabs of them for later analysis. He spoke of the blood on the fabric headboard, the window blinds, a garbage pail that was near the nightstand, and a box of tissues that had been sitting on the nightstand. He described cutting away a large piece of the carpet and padding from the area near the bed because of the large blood stain that soaked through to the wooden sub-floor underneath.

"The rug looked like it had been cleaned, but there's always trace evidence left behind. Also, because she had lost so much blood, it had soaked through to the pad underneath, so I took that as well."

Dennis returned to the prosecution table and waved his hand towards Julie. "Your witness, counselor."

Julie began asking O'Malley her question before Dennis even finished talking. "Ofc. O'Malley, did you finally get to take measurements of the bedroom and bathroom?" Julie was getting snarky.

"Yes. I was able to take measurements on the day of the search warrant using a CAD computer program."

"And do you measure from wall to wall or do you include the placement of the furniture in these measurements?"

"Of course I include the furniture. The computer program that I use measures everything in the room and can present a 3D drawing using those exact measurements."

"How can you be sure the furniture was in the same position when you took the measurements and photos on the day of the search warrant as they were on the day of Mrs. Mills' death?"

"I'm confident it was all in the same position."

"You're confident, Officer?"

"Yes, I am. The photos from the day of the death are identical to the photos from the day of the search warrant. There were no visible indents in the rug, either, that would show that they had moved the furniture."

"No further questions, your honor." Julie walked back to her seat, with a scowl on her face.

"Your honor," DA Wozniak stood to address the court. "The prosecution rests its case."

Chapter 18
Trial Day 6

Mac woke up on Monday morning and headed into the office. He took one look at his desk and groaned when he realized the mound of neglected paperwork had gotten to where it was almost ready to tip over. Trial or no, he couldn't put it off any longer. He had to dive into the work that was waiting for him. It would mean missing at least the morning of testimony at the trial, but it couldn't be helped.

By the time his stomach growled, letting him know it was approaching early afternoon,

Mac had gotten through most of the things that needed his immediate attention, so he and Coop decided to make a mad dash to the courthouse, hoping to catch the bulk of the afternoon testimonies at the trial.

Coop had managed to jump into the driver's seat with a laugh before Mac could get there. Mac just shook his head and sat in the passenger seat. After a quick discussion about lunch, they decided to grab a submarine sandwich from a fast-food place and eat in the car on the way.

As they slid into a parking spot behind the courthouse, Mac looked at Coop with surprise in his eyes. "What the hell are you doing?"

"What?" Coop brushed a few stray pieces of shredded lettuce onto the floor of the car.

"Look at how you parked. You're taking up three spots. You've got the front end of the car in the spot on the one side of us and the back end on the other side."

"That's what we call a catawampus parking job, boss."

"A cata ... what??"

"Catawampus. That just means a bit crooked. Cockeyed. You know, a little kitty-cornered. This way, no one will park next to us, and we can easily get out."

"Good Lord," whispered Mac, more to himself than to Coop. He reached for the door handle and climbed out of the car.

They had gotten to the courthouse just moments before the afternoon session of the trial was starting. They found their seats as the judge took the bench.

"It must be our lucky day, Mac!" Coop gave Mac a back-handed slap on his shoulder. "We couldn't have timed that any better if we tried!"

If the trial had started before they had gotten there, the doors would have been closed and they wouldn't have been able to enter the courtroom, which meant they would have had to watch the trial from the auxiliary room.

Mac leaned over to the reporter, who had been covering the case by sketching since the first day. "I wasn't here this morning. Did I miss anything?"

"Not really," the sketch artist said. "Defense counsel called a couple of friends and family members that testified about what a good person Carter Mills is. You know ... how much he loved his wife, wouldn't hurt a flea, could leap tall buildings in a single bound and rescued little old ladies from burning buildings."

Mac and Coop both chuckled. "Yeah, right," Coop filled in. "A real humanitarian."

The next witness called by the defense was a blood spatter expert named John Foote. Mac elbowed Coop. "He's the one I was hoping to hear today."

Julie asked the witness to give his name and credentials for the record.

"I own an independent forensic consulting firm and I've been a bloodstain pattern analysis expert for over twenty years. A large part of what I do is to provide blood stain analysis for legal cases such as this one and I've testified in court for the defense and prosecution close to 100 times. I've written several articles related to blood stain and blood pattern analysis and I teach a course about this at my local college."

"Can you explain, Mr. Foote, what bloodstain pattern analysis is?" Using her laptop, Julie projected a diagram onto the screens around the courtroom of different shapes of blood droplets.

"Certainly. It's the study of the physical characteristics of blood stains. There are different types of blood stains and distinct patterns of blood stains.

Cast-off blood stains refer to blood that is released from an object in motion. If you had blood on your hand and waved, the blood would be cast off your hand and onto another object, for example, a wall. Alternatively, impact patterns occur when a force, or impact, is applied on a source of blood. This can occur, for example, if there was a pool of blood on the floor and a person was to step in it. The blood droplets would move through the air in an entirely different pattern than that of the cast-off blood. In addition, the angle of the blood hitting that other object must also be considered. Blood that hits a wall at ninety degrees will be more round, whereas a droplet that hits the wall at, say, twenty degrees, is much more elongated."

"Mr. Foote, allow me to demonstrate." With that, Julie approached an easel that was set up at the side of the courtroom with a large pad of white paper resting on it. She reached down below the easel, and picked up a two-inch-wide paint brush and a small, clear pitcher that appeared to have a dark liquid in it. After dipping the paint brush in the liquid, Julie swung her arm in a wide arc so that the dark liquid splashed across the paper.

Many of the jurors and spectators recoiled as the liquid, which they could now see was a dark red, ran down the paper, leaving long streaks of what looked like blood. Judge Johannsen banged her gavel. "Order! Order in the court! Counselor! What is the meaning of this? What in heaven's name do you think you're doing?"

Julie Keegan, looking over her shoulder at the jurors and seeing their stunned expressions, tried to explain. Quickly, she said, "Your honor, this is not blood. It's only water with a bit of red food coloring. I'd like to show the court what the witness was saying about the difference in how blood can take different shapes when it's spattered on a wall."

"Counselor, I believe that's what your diagram is for. If you pull anything like that again, I will hold you in contempt of court. Please leave the theatrics to the professionals."

Julie hung her head and quietly said, "My apologies, your honor. It won't happen again."

John Foote spoke up. "Your honor, with all due respect, I'd like to comment on the attorney's attempt at displaying blood spatter. Had I known about this ahead of time, I would have dissuaded her from doing this, not because of the shock factor, but only because the type of liquid must also be considered when doing an analysis. You see, there is a big difference in the consistency of water versus blood. Although I appreciate the attempt, water will react differently than blood when it's spattered on a wall or other object."

"Thank you, Mr. Foote," Judge Johannsen nodded at the witness. "The jury will disregard this display by the prosecution. Bailiff, please remove the easel and the other items."

Coop leaned in towards Mac and whispered, "Wow! For a second there, I thought that was actual blood. She's lucky the judge doesn't throw her out for that."

"I agree," Mac said in return. "That was a dumb move."

As the bailiff did as he was asked to do, the judge motioned to Julie. "Now, if we may continue, please proceed, Counselor."

Julie's face was bright red. "Thank you, your honor. Again, my apologies." She took a deep breath before speaking again. "Mr. Foote, have you seen the photographs taken at the Mills residence?" The attorney handed the witness a pile of photos.

Foote rifled through them and confirmed, "Yes, I have seen these."

"And what is your professional opinion?"

"As I understand it, there weren't many photographs taken at the time of her death and in my opinion, the photos taken during the search warrant were limited in what they showed. And, no offense to the officers, but there was a potential for contamination the morning of the death because there were so many people entering the bedroom with street shoes on, with no protective covering.

"I will also add that Mrs. Mills had a large laceration on her head, and head lacerations will bleed a lot. We must also consider that if a person has an abundant head of hair as Mrs. Mills had, that can also affect the patterns of the blood stain."

"Mr. Foote, I'd like to draw your attention to the photos again. Can you give us your professional opinion of each one?"

As he looked at the crime scene photos, Julie portrayed the same photos on the television screens for the judge and jury. John explained the blood stain patterns on each one. He explained that the pooling of blood in the bedroom shows that Loretta's head, or at least an object heavily saturated with her blood, was on the floor. He pointed out several spatter stains that showed diluted blood, most likely from the water in the shower. But when he was asked about the bloody spots on the wall in the bedroom, he said he couldn't tell what object might have made the transfer of the blood stains. They could have come from Mrs. Mills' head or possibly the medic's gloves when they removed them. There was no way, after the fact, to determine what object would have transferred the blood.

"Mr. Foote," said Julie, "can you tell what direction the blood stains on the various walls were coming from?"

"Certainly. It shows that Mrs. Mills was moved in the direction going from the bathroom to the bedroom."

Julie was looking very pleased with the testimony of her witness. "Can you tell if Mrs. Mills was moved from the bedroom to the bathroom?"

"No. I have seen no blood evidence to show that she was moved from the bedroom into the bathroom."

"Mr. Foote, to clarify, you're saying that Mrs. Mills fell in the shower and was then carried into the bedroom?"

"What I'm saying, counselor, is that the evidence is not conclusive in showing how she was wounded, but it does indicate Mrs. Mills was bleeding when she was moved from the bathroom into the bedroom, and not the other way around."

Julie turned to give DA Wozniak the stink eye, and said, "No further questions, your honor."

ADA Kimberly Coville stood up from the prosecution table, with an identical bunch of photos in her hand. "Mr. Foote, I'm curious why you would say that the photos taken during the search warrant were, and I quote, 'limited in what they showed'. As you can see, every one of them is shown with a forensic scale to show the size of the blood spatter, and the accompanying diagrams specify where in the rooms each one was photographed." Kimberly fanned them out and displayed them in front of Foote, as if he was to choose a card for a magic trick. "What exactly is limited in these photos?"

"What I meant was that the photos don't tell us the story of how they got there. The photos show only the position of the spatters on the walls." John was starting to look annoyed by this line of questioning.

"And when you say there was possible contamination from the people who were in the room that morning, what were you referring to? Was there any evidence of contamination? Did you see any photos of, say, bloody shoe prints?"

"No, that's not what I said." John said vehemently. "I didn't say there was contamination. I said there was a *potential* for contamination. And no, I did not see any proof of contamination or bloody shoe prints."

"So, I must say that your unbiased opinion sounds pretty biased to me."

John raised his hand as if making a point, but before he could respond, Kimberly cut him off. "I have no further questions for this witness, your honor."

And, with that, Judge Johannsen adjourned the trial until the next morning.

Chapter 19
Trial Day 7

On Tuesday morning, what would be the seventh and last day of testimony during the trial, the defense called their final witness ... Margaret Mills. It was the one testimony that Mac had been dreading. Margaret sat on the witness stand wearing a simple black dress, her long hair cascading down her back, with a few strands tucked behind her ears. Sometimes when she looked down, her hair veiled the expression on her face. The pain of her loss was quite clear.

Mac listened with a heavy heart while Margaret sobbed uncontrollably. Tears were running like a river down her cheeks as she told the court about the morning of her mother's death. She talked about seeing her father carry her mother's lifeless body from the shower area into the bedroom and about making the phone calls to 911. That, despite the parade of people coming in and out of her house, none of them could save her mother.

Julie Keegan, her head held high, seemed as if she'd forgotten the previous days' debacle over the simulated blood as she greeted the judge when court had begun that morning. But even she spoke in hushed tones when she questioned Margaret about that fateful day. It was not an easy testimony to listen to. Margaret had to take quite a few breaks to regain her composure throughout the retelling of the story.

Mac glanced at the jury for their reactions and saw many of the women with tears wetting their cheeks. Even a couple of men seemed to have trouble holding their emotions in check, appearing to be more fidgety than they had been until now. Mac was struggling also, but the only reason he could hold it together was because the initial shock for him was over. He'd seen Margaret the day her mother died and had also heard her version of the story when they interviewed her. He knew firsthand what she had gone through, and his heart ached for the young lady.

One could almost feel the tension in the courtroom. The air was heavy after listening to Margaret as she struggled to answer the questions. When her testimony was finished, the court broke for lunch, a much needed break. Very few conversations took place as the jury filed out, and Mac knew the emotional drain had to be taking its toll on them. He didn't envy their positions.

When the court came back from lunch, the Judge announced they would begin closing arguments. With that, she invited DA Dennis Wozniak to take the floor.

"Ladies and gentlemen of the jury, this has been an emotionally draining, confusing, and complex case. You've listened to five days of testimony from several people. You've listened to the first responders that were present that day. You've listened to various people that offered their professional and educated opinions as to what happened in that bedroom on the day that Loretta Mills died. You've also heard the testimony of the medical examiner who did the autopsy on Loretta Mills.

"We have a man who has been an affluent and well-known member of the community for many years. His wife was also a well-known member of the community because of the volunteer work she did for their children's schools and for the church they belonged to. But what most people saw of this family in public is not the same as the people they were in the privacy of their multi-million dollar home, behind closed doors. Carter Mills had had multiple affairs during his marriage. Likewise, Loretta also had at least one long-term affair we know of.

"There was some violence in the home, physical on one or two occasions, but mostly it was verbal abuse until eventually that violence led to one final and fatal argument. During that last argument, it is our contention that Carter Mills murdered his wife and staged it to seem like it was an accidental fall in the shower of her bedroom suite.

"Loretta told him she wanted a divorce and had even put down a deposit on an apartment, but he couldn't stand the thought of that. He got angry. Very angry. It angered him so much that he beat her and he killed her. He staged it to look like it was a fall that took his wife's life, but he made a few mistakes along the way and these mistakes tell the actual story of what happened. Don't be fooled by any of the smoke and mirrors that the defendant and the defense counsel tried to present.

"He claims that when he brought Loretta a cup of coffee that morning, he heard her shower was already running, so he left to go for a jog through the neighborhood and around the local pond. We could find no witnesses who saw him on that run, even though we spoke to several residents along the course of this supposed jog. He testified that when he came back, he got in the shower in his own bedroom suite. Even though they would be going out soon after, he uncharacteristically put on a pair of pajama pants and a t-shirt instead of the suit that he would be wearing just a short time later. Then he said that he went to see if his family was getting ready for the brunch they were supposed to attend. He claims he could hear Loretta's shower was *still* running, so he went to check on her. And after all that time, he claims the shower room was *still* steamy. So steamy, in fact, that when he realized she wasn't breathing, he had to move his wife from the shower to the bedroom in order to do CPR. Ladies and gentlemen, it's impossible to have so much steam in the bathroom after all that time. One factor he didn't consider was that after roughly twenty-eight minutes, the shower ran cold. The police investigators have proven that too much time had passed and there wouldn't be any steam by the time he says he went on a run, came back, showered, dressed and then found her.

"Remember the photos, ladies and gentlemen, that show those horrific injuries on Loretta Mills' head. We believe what truly happened that morning is that a few hours before he allegedly found her in the shower, he'd hit her with an unknown object and fractured her skull. You'll recall that Dr. Schmidt, the coroner, testified that there were blows to her head and injuries to her neck and hands that were not caused by falling in the shower.

"He beat her in the early morning hours and left her lying unconscious and bleeding on the floor of the bedroom. As she lay there dying, she continued to bleed, and all of that blood left a large puddle on the carpet. After a couple of agonizing hours, Loretta died on that floor, in a pool of her own blood.

"When he went back to her room, a couple of hours after their altercation and found her dead, Carter Mills realized he had to account, somehow, for that large blood stain on the floor. He came up with a plan. That's when he decided to stage it, so it looked like she fell in the shower. He needed to get her into the shower, but the problem was the blood. So he wrapped her up in the sheets that were on the bed at that time. These were the same sheets that their housekeeper distinctly remembers putting on the bed just a couple of days before this incident. He knew that by wrapping her up in the sheets, he wouldn't leave a trail of blood as he carried her from the bedroom to the shower. You'll remember that Mr. Foote, the blood spatter expert, testified that there was no blood on the walls that would show that Loretta was carried from the bedroom into the shower. That's because there wouldn't be any blood spatter if he had wrapped her up in the missing sheets. He then left his dead wife in the shower while he put the next phase of his plan into action.

"As I just mentioned, he claims he went for this supposed jog in the neighborhood before he came back to the house and allegedly found her in the shower. We don't believe it was a jog he went on. We believe it was at this point that he got rid of the weapon he used to split her skull open, along with the blood-stained sheets and the fourth pillow. I admit, we haven't been able to find these items, so exactly where he went, we haven't been able to determine. We believe he may have thrown these objects in a neighbor's garbage can, or in the woods, or maybe in the pond. Even if we were to dredge the entire pond and find an object, we would have no way of knowing if that item was the one he used to murder his wife. Any blood or tissue left on that object would have been washed off long ago. But we believe it would not have been a jog he went on that morning. It was a trip to dispose of the missing evidence.

"When he got back, he turned on the water in the shower, waited for the steam to build up and then tried to make it look like he had just found her. He ran to his daughter's room, telling her that her mother had fallen in the shower and was hurt. Even though he had to pass five or six phones before he could reach his daughter, he told her to call 911. Then, with his daughter in Loretta's bedroom suite as a witness, he carried his wife's dead body from the shower. He carried her back into the bedroom and then he positioned her in the exact same bloody spot where he'd left her to die a few hours earlier. He must have been thanking his lucky stars that his daughter had gone to the water closet to use the phone in there and ran past the large blood stain on the side of the bed. That gave him a chance to position his wife's body in that same bloody spot.

"We heard testimony from the first responders that Loretta was already in the beginning stages of rigor mortis by the time they got there. They testified her jaw had stiffened enough to make it difficult for them to intubate her. It's a scientific fact that it takes at least three hours after a person dies before rigor starts to set in.

"According to several people that were on the scene that morning, her hair was very wet from the shower we know was running. There is no disputing that fact. And yet, Margaret testified that when they had to go out early in the morning, her mother didn't like to wash her hair because it took too long to dry and style. Now, that's not something I can relate to," Dennis said with a smile as he patted his own thinning hair. "But apparently when the hair is thick and curly, as Loretta's was, it's a time-consuming task she tried to avoid when she was in a rush. Then why was she in the shower without a shower cap, causing her hair to become soaked shortly before they were due to leave? That's very uncharacteristic of Loretta, and it makes little sense.

"Margaret also testified that one call she made to the 911 center was from the phone in the water closet. The prosecution would like you to believe that Carter hadn't used that phone to call 911 himself because it was out of order. Ladies and gentlemen, who would you rather believe? A distraught, heartbroken daughter of the victim who was only answering the questions that were asked of her, or the individual who was trying to fabricate a story to cover his crime?

"We've heard testimony about the blood spatters in the bedroom. They also tell a story. The shape and angle of the blood spatters on the wall and nightstand show they came from the area near the bed. That's where the beating took place. There was blood spatter on the nightstand, the picture frame, the wall, and the headboard. And yet there was no blood on the coffee cup. That tells us she was beaten and her blood went flying *before* he brought her the cup of coffee.

"We heard testimony from a world-renowned pathologist that there was brain matter found in one of the blood droplets on the headboard. It takes a lot of force for brain matter to travel that kind of distance. The same kind of force that would split her skull.

"Ladies and gentlemen of the jury, all these things tell a story that differs from the story that Carter Mills wants you to believe. I ask you to look at the evidence, the injuries that she sustained, the story that was fabricated to cover up her murder, and find Carter Mills guilty of second degree murder.

"Consider the fact that he tried to cover up the murder by throwing away what would have been a bloody pillow and the bloody sheets that were on the bed. We listened as the housekeeper testified that on the morning of the murder, there were different sheets on the bed from the ones that she herself had put on the bed only a couple of days before.

"The fact that there was an absence of blood on the sheets that were on the bed that morning also tells a story. When there was so much blood spatter throughout that area of the bedroom, and yet there was no blood on the sheets, that can only mean one thing. He took off the bloody sheets that were on the bed after he killed his wife, and then put fresh sheets back on the bed.

"He also threw away the top to his pajamas, because it would have been covered in blood from the beating and from carrying her into the shower. That's why the witnesses that were at the Mills' residence have testified that he wore a tee shirt that morning.

"He moved his wife's body not once, but twice, from the bedroom to the bathroom and then, using his daughter as a witness, back into the bedroom. For that, for moving his wife's body and for disposing of the other items, you need to find him guilty of the additional charge of tampering with evidence.

"Regardless of the picture that the defense is trying to portray, theirs was not a happy marriage. When Loretta had finally had enough and started making plans to leave him, Carter's ego and his temper couldn't let that happen. So he killed her in cold blood. Ladies and gentlemen, you must find Carter Mills guilty of murdering his wife and evidence tampering. I ask that you find justice for Loretta."

With that, Dennis thanked the jury and returned to the prosecution table.

Judge Johannsen gestured with her hand towards the defense counsel. "You may proceed, Counselor."

Julie Fletcher stood up and faced the jury. "Ladies and gentlemen, please don't believe anything the DA has told you. Her husband did not kill Loretta Mills. Her unfortunate demise resulted from a dreadful slip and fall in the shower. She slipped, fell, and hit her head on the marble step in the shower. It was simply a tragic accident.

"The DA would like you to believe that the marriage between Carter and Loretta Mills was a loveless marriage, but this is not true. They would like you to believe that Loretta had planned to divorce her husband, but there were no divorce proceedings entered into court.

"Carter admitted in his police interview they said they loved each other every night before they went to bed. Yes, they slept in separate bedrooms, but that's because he loved his wife so much that he wanted to make sure she slept well at night. You see, like a lot of us, Carter Mills had a problem with snoring. He would rather sleep in a separate bedroom than have her go on without getting a good night's rest. He's not the selfish killer the DA would lead you to believe. Rather, Carter Mills loved his wife dearly and would do anything in his power to make her happy.

"There is absolutely no evidence Carter killed his wife. As a matter of fact, he tried to save her. After he found her lying on the floor of the shower, he tried to call 911 himself from the nearest phone, the one in the water closet, but it was not working. So, instead of wasting any more time, he ran to get his daughter and asked her to call 911. Then he went back to his wife and gave her CPR. But Carter needed better light and traction in order to do CPR, so he carried her from the wet shower room into the bedroom. He was trying to save his wife. You see, the shower room was wet and yes, it was steamy from the shower. In fact, one of the police officers testified that the room was indeed steamy, and he had shut the water off in the shower because of that steam. The steam, he testified, made it difficult for him to photograph the shower area, so he had to wait for the steam to clear before he could resume taking photos.

"The prosecution would like you to believe that the blood spatters on the walls and around the room were from a beating. That's not true. We believe that the blood spatters came from the first responders carelessly removing their gloves and also from when they roughly tossed aside a blood-soaked blanket that Carter had put over his wife to keep her warm. He put the blanket over his wife because he loved her.

"Ladies and gentlemen, let's not forget the alleged murder weapon. To put it simply, the prosecution has no weapon and they certainly have no motive. And to compound the issue, I have a problem with a coroner who changes his mind, months after making a ruling on the cause of death. Initially, he deemed it an accidental death from a fall, but after talking to his cronies, Dr. Schmidt changed the death certificate. I, for one, am not fond of a professional who can't make up his mind.

"And what's this nonsense about rigor mortis setting in? One medic on the scene that morning testified that she could move Loretta's arm when she applied a tourniquet because she was going to insert an IV. That would mean that her muscles hadn't tightened up, which is what rigor mortis is.

"Please, ladies and gentlemen of the jury, I beg you to look at this trial as the sham that it is. Carter Mills is not a killer. He's the victim of unfortunate circumstances cooked up by the police and the district attorney's office. We had witnesses that testified to the fact that the Mills' were nice people, active in the church and community. Carter Mills loved his wife dearly and misses her each and every passing day. You must see this and acquit him. Thank you.

With a smug look on her face, Julie returned to her seat.

Judge Johannsen called for a fifteen-minute break. The jurors had been given a lot of information in the closing arguments, and she had learned over the years that having just a few minutes to decompress was a helpful tool before they began deliberations.

After the break, Judge Johannsen began instructing the jury. She let them know that the standard of proof has to be beyond a reasonable doubt, that all twelve jurors need to agree with the verdict. If it was not a unanimous verdict, it would result in what's called a hung jury. If that happened, there may be a retrial if the district attorney's office chose to try the case again.

She let them know they would need to look at the evidence and the credibility of the witnesses in order to find Carter Mills guilty or not guilty. They were not to consider the opening and closing arguments as evidence, but rather, consider them to be the summary of the case from each point of view.

Last, she reminded the jury of the charges and explained in detail what each of them was. With a sharp snap of the gavel, she asked the jury to leave the courtroom to begin deliberations.

Over the next few days, the jurors had several questions. They had requested clarification on the charge of second degree murder, they asked to hear the police interview with Carter Mills again, and they wanted to hear snippets of different testimonies from various witnesses.

On Monday morning, after four days of deliberation, the jury announced they had reached a verdict. As soon as Dennis Wozniak was told, he called Mac to give him the news.

"Hey, Mac. The jury just came back with a verdict. I thought I'd let you know in case you wanted to go to court to hear it firsthand."

"Hell, yeah!" Mac couldn't believe it had taken this long. "I'll be there in twenty minutes. Don't let them start without me."

"You bet. I'll tell them to wait for you." Mac could hear the humor in Dennis' voice.

Within fifteen minutes, Mac and Coop were walking at a near-running pace down the hall to the courtroom. They got there at the same time as Dennis, who shook hands with both of them.

"How are you two doing? You must have had one hell of a weekend." Dennis already knew about the latest case that the detectives would have been working on all weekend long.

"Totally beat," said Coop with a sigh.

"I believe it! But you did one hell of a job. My congratulations to you both." It had been all over the news about a double homicide at a local restaurant in the early morning hours on Saturday. Mac, Coop and their team had located and arrested the suspect within twenty-four hours. The suspect, a former employee of the restaurant, had gone there intending to rob them. Tragically, he'd left two men dead before running away with $200 of the night's proceeds. It was a senseless crime, fueled by the suspect's need for drugs.

"It looks like there's a ton of people here already. Let's go find a seat." Coop and Mac had luck on their side as they grabbed two of the last seats remaining. They waited only a few more minutes before the judge took the bench and instructed the bailiff to have the jury enter the courtroom. Carter Mills was already seated at the defense table with his attorneys, Julie Fletcher and Bruce Keegan, on either side of him while Tommy Gleason sat in the front row of the gallery behind them. Carter's children and a few close family friends were sitting with Tommy.

After they took their seats, the jury foreperson passed a paper with the verdict written on it to the bailiff, who passed it to the judge. She read the note before turning to the foreperson.

"Mr. Foreperson," the judge asked, "has the jury reached a verdict on the charge of second-degree murder?"

"Yes, your honor we have. We find the defendant, Carter Mills, guilty of second degree murder."

Margaret Mills jumped up from her seat and screamed, "No! Daddy, no!" A rush of excitement swept through the courtroom. A mix of voices fill the courtroom. Some, appearing to be Carter's supporters, were crying out in disbelief, while others, obviously supporting a guilty verdict, were shouting "Yes!" with some even pumping the air with their fists.

Judge Johannsen banged her gavel in an attempt to quiet the courtroom. "I will have order in my courtroom." The judge talked over the crowd, as the bedlam quieted somewhat, "Mr. Foreperson, has the jury reached a verdict on the charge of tampering with evidence?"

"Yes, your honor. We find the defendant guilty of tampering with evidence."

Judge Johannsen continued to rap her gavel at the bench, calling for order. "Mr. Mills. You are to be remanded without bail until sentencing."

The bailiff and court security stepped forward and attempted to place Carter in handcuffs. He was twisting and turning, trying in vain to turn back to face his family. The words he was trying to speak were lost in the chaos as the security officers finished placing him in handcuffs, turning him away from the gallery and his family.

Margaret was reaching over the railing of the gallery in an attempt to hug her father before the officers led him away. Steven and Danny stood on either side of her, trying to hold her by the shoulders. Both brothers had looks of astonishment on their faces.

Others that were with the family twisted to look at each other, some crying, some stone-faced and shaking their heads in disbelief.

Julie Fletcher was trying to talk to Carter, *probably telling him she'll file an appeal right away,* thought Mac. As usual, she had a look on her face that would stop a clock.

A few people, appearing to be reporters, quickly headed out the doors to broadcast the news. Mac looked through the gallery and he could tell who was there supporting the prosecution by the looks of relief and some smiles. Others, appearing to be the ones supporting Mills, looked wide-eyed, some with their mouths open, and some crying. They seemed to be surprised, looking from one to the other.

Coop grabbed Mac's shoulder and enthusiastically squeezed in a clutch that was almost painful.

"You did it, boss. Great job!"

"Not me. *We* did a great job." Even as tired as he was, Mac couldn't help but feel energized after hearing the verdict. "Come on. Let's go tell the rest of the team. I think we should go for a drink at Jimmy's after work. It's on me."

"Now that's an offer I can't refuse!" Coop led the way through the crowd to the door. Mac looked back to see Carter being led by court security through a side door to the holding cell for prisoners. His voice carried over the rest of the noise in the courtroom as he screamed repeatedly, "I tried to save her! I tried to save her, damn it! This isn't right!"

Mac then looked at Margaret. Her hands were covering her face, her shoulders shaking as she sobbed into her hands. Steven hugged her as he ran a hand up and down her back, trying to comfort her.

⚖

Five weeks later, Dennis called Mac with the latest news. "Hey, Mac. I thought you'd want to know. Judge Johannsen just sentenced Carter Mills to twenty-five years to life."

"Cool. I wasn't sure he'd get the max, but I'm glad he did. He deserves every bit of that sentence. Maybe now Loretta will rest in peace."Mac picked up the thick Mills file that had been sitting on the corner of his desk, and with a satisfied smile on his face, placed it in the drawer of the tall metal filing cabinet marked "Closed Cases."

Chapter 20

Carter would go to the North Branch maximum security prison in less than a week's time to serve his prison sentence. Steven, Danny and Margaret had wanted to see him before he left, but Carter was adamant that they not visit him. "I'd feel better," he said, "if you didn't have to see me in prison garb." He did, however, ask to have Tommy Gleason come.

That idea did not thrill Tommy, but for the sake of Michael and Suzanne, he would go to see their only son. The elder Mills were humiliated and ashamed, refusing to visit Carter in prison. They were turning their backs on him.

Tommy sat at the cubicle and watched through the plexiglass divider as a prison guard escorted Carter into the room. Another guard stood watch at the doorway.

Once Carter took his seat at the table across from Tommy, they picked up their handsets. This would allow them to communicate through the divider. Tommy waited for Carter to speak first since he had nothing he wanted to say to Carter.

"How are my parents?" Carter asked.

"Dealing with this situation as best they can," Tommy said with a scowl on his face. Carter had enough decency to look down at the table in front of him.

When Carter raised his head to look at Tommy, he had tears in his eyes. "Listen ... I need to tell you something. Now that the trial is over, I need to tell you I killed Loretta."

"Carter, if you're trying to appease your conscience, you're talking to the wrong guy. You need to talk to a priest or a therapist, not me."

"No, please, just listen for a moment. I need to tell you why I killed Loretta. I couldn't tell you before. I didn't want to tell you before. But now I think it's important that you understand why I did what I did."

"Yes, I know why you did it, Carter. It's because you're an asshole and you treated her like shit. After all those years of you cheating on her, she'd finally had enough. She wanted a divorce and you couldn't stand the thoughts of her leaving you, so you killed her. And yes, she had a boyfriend. She was happy with him, but you couldn't stand the thoughts of her being happy. Well, Carter, I hate to tell you, and somebody should have told you this a long time ago, but it isn't all about you. The sun does not rise and set because of you."

"Would you please just listen to me? You won't ever have to hear from me again, but I'm asking you to listen, just this one last time. Please?"

Tommy was glaring at Carter, but he didn't get up to leave. It wasn't very often that Carter said please, so Tommy stayed put. Carter continued.

"What you didn't know is that Loretta was abusive. She was mentally disturbed. It's been that way for years, but she kept it well hidden. I wasn't even aware of it until after we'd been married for a while."

"What are you trying to say, Carter?" Tommy had a look of pure disgust on his face. "You're calling her mentally disturbed and abusive and she's not even here to defend herself. What is wrong with you?"

"It's true. Please, just hear me out. You can check it all out once you hear what I have to say."

"Fine, I'll listen, but if I hear any more bullshit, I'm leaving, Carter. I mean it." Tommy, now angrier than ever, was pointing at Carter through the plexiglass with the index finger of his free hand.

"She would get very angry and she would hit me. Loretta never hit the kids, thank God, but she would hit me. She would hit me in the chest, my back, my ass. She'd leave marks, sometimes using her fists, sometimes using a book, a trophy. Whatever she could get her hands on. But she knew better than to hit me in the face or arms where someone would see it.

"Like I said, it didn't start until after we'd been married for a few years. The first time she tried to hit me was after she caught me cheating on her the very first time. And she never hit me when the kids would see it or hear it. Usually, the kids were either very young, and could sleep through anything, or, after they were older, it didn't happen unless they were at sleepovers with their friends."

Carter could see from the look on Tommy's face he didn't believe him.

"Tommy, I've taken pictures of the bruises as proof. Not all of them. I missed the first few years, but I have quite a few from the last ten years that we were married. The pictures are in the wall safe in my home office. I'll give you the combination and you can see the photos for yourself. They're all dated."

"This is ridiculous. Carter, I'm done listening to you!" Tommy slammed the handset into the cradle and stood up.

"I'm telling you the truth. I swear to God. Look!" Carter dropped the phone with a loud thud and stood up so quickly, the guard immediately walked towards him, anticipating a problem. Carter pulled a photo from his back pocket and slammed it against the plexiglass divider so that Tommy could see the picture. It was a photo of a man's chest with a bruise on the left shoulder. The bruise looked to be the size of a softball—or a fist—and was a nasty, dark purple splotch.

Only part of Carter's face was visible, but it was clearly Carter in the photo.

Tommy stared at the photo. After a moment, he slowly sat down and picked up the phone again, without saying a word.

The guard, sensing that there was no longer an issue, retreated to his place near the door. Tommy looked from the photo to Carter's eyes and back to the photo, with a look of confusion showing on his face. Carter sat down and picked up the phone.

Tommy sat there, processing this information. His voice was softer as he asked, "If what you're saying is true, why wait until now? Why didn't you tell me this before?"

"I'm a grown man, Tommy. I didn't want to admit that my wife was beating me up and there was nothing I could do about it. Even after all this time, you can still see the discolorations on my body from where some of the bigger bruises were. I've been beaten so much, it takes a long time for them to go away. I have bruises, on top of bruises, on top of bruises."

"Even if I believe you, which I'm still not sure I do, why did you have to kill her? Loretta was filing for divorce. Why not just get a divorce and be done with it?"

"I'll admit, at first I didn't like the idea of a divorce, and I was furious. But after I thought about it, I realized I shouldn't let my pride get in the way any more than it already had. I should have gotten help ... I should have gotten her some help, but because of my pride, I just couldn't bring myself to admit what was happening. I couldn't admit it to myself, let alone to anyone else.

"That night, the night I killed her, we had gotten into a huge argument. I'm not even sure what it was about, but it started in my office, and we argued for a long time. We just kept yelling at each other."

"Why didn't Margaret or Irene intercept with all that yelling going on?" Tommy asked.

"Margaret wasn't home until later because she was out with friends, and Irene didn't hear it because she was in her room and we were on the other side of the house. We ended up going upstairs and Loretta headed towards her bedroom. I followed her into the bedroom, still yelling at her. I should have just walked away, and I regret to this day that I didn't. Anyway, we were still arguing, and she started to hit me. She was acting like a madwoman. It was the worst it had ever been. I kept trying to block her punches and push her away, but she wouldn't stop. She just kept coming at me.

"At some point, though, she was swinging a five-pound hand weight at me she'd picked up from somewhere in the bedroom. She was aiming at my head. I lost it. Before she could hit me with it, I grabbed the weight from her. We grappled for a bit because she kept trying to get it back. But then, somehow, I hit her in the head with it. I don't even remember doing it. She fell onto the bedroom floor and she just kept groaning. I walked away. I just left her there."

Carter looked down at his hands as he gently spun the gold wedding band he still wore on his ring finger. He paused for a moment to regain his composure.

"I went back a couple of hours later and saw that she was dead. I panicked. Tommy, you have to believe me when I say that I didn't mean for her to die. When I left her on the floor, she was still alive. It never occurred to me she would die.

"After I saw she was dead, I knew I had to do something, so I came up with the idea of staging it to look like a fall in the shower. You know the rest of the story from there."

"Carter, I can't believe this. I don't know what to say." Tommy was rubbing his forehead, as if he had a sudden headache.

"There isn't anything for you to say."

"Carter, why didn't you tell me this sooner? It wouldn't have changed the outcome. You still would have been convicted, but maybe of a lesser charge like manslaughter and probably a reduced sentence."

"That doesn't matter to me. I don't care about the charge or the sentence. But there's more. I need to tell you the entire story, but before I do, I want you to understand something. I truly loved Loretta, and I tried for years to hang onto that love, but it was like she was two different people. Lord knows I tried, but it just wasn't enough. I should have gotten her some professional help."

With a deep breath, Carter continued. "I don't know the specific details, but she told me once about an accident that happened when she was a child. She'd been playing with a little kid when he fell off the slide at some playground and died. At least, that's what she told everyone at the time, but she told me the truth. She had pushed him off that slide. He was standing on the top of the slide and she was on the ladder right behind him. She admitted to me he didn't move fast enough for her, so she pushed him. He lost his balance but instead of going down the slide, he fell more to the side, hit his head on a rock on the ground, and died.

"It doesn't sound like she intended for that kid to die." Tommy, his attorney's training kicking in, was trying to find some reasoning with the story. "She was just a little kid. She wouldn't have done that on purpose. It had to be an accident."

"She didn't kill him on purpose. That part is true, but I will never forget the look on her face when she told me that story. There was no remorse, no guilt, no shame, nothing. There was no emotion there whatsoever."

Carter had to pause for a moment to gain his composure. "And then there's the story of her grandmother."

"Her grandmother?" Tommy asked. "What about her grandmother?"

"When Loretta was about seventeen, her maternal grandmother got cancer. There was nothing they could do except make her comfortable, so they moved the grandmother into their family's home, with Loretta, her sister Kim, and their parents. They had someone stay in the room with her at all times and the family members each took turns watching over her. Her mother watched her all day, but then Loretta sat with her after school so her mother could get a bit of a break and fix dinner.

"Anyway, it got very bad towards the end and the grandmother was in a lot of pain, so they kept her doped up on morphine. One day, the grandmother couldn't take it any more. She begged Loretta to end her suffering. To make the pain go away."

"You can't be serious!" Tommy looked at Carter out of the corner of his eyes. He must have had an idea of what Carter was going to say.

Carter very slowly, almost imperceptibly, nodded his head. "That day, Loretta gave her grandmother a fatal dose of morphine. She died a few hours later."

"You're trying to make her into some kind of monster. If she did give the grandmother an overdose of morphine, I see it more as a mercy killing. She obviously loved her grandmother and didn't want her to suffer any longer. She was doing what the grandmother asked her to do."

Carter looked hard into Tommy's eyes. "If it was anybody else, I would agree with you. But Loretta kept referring to her as the 'bitchy old lady,' or 'the pain in the ass grandmother'. There was no love there. The grandmother was nothing more than an inconvenience to Loretta. She even said that taking care of the grandmother cut into her study time. Loretta was smart, but she never had good study skills. As a result, she had to work very, very hard to get good grades. Once she learned something, she was golden. But the learning part was the hard part for Loretta. I knew that from our college days.

"If you still don't believe what I'm telling you, you can check with her boyfriend, Bernie. About a month before she died, he called me. It was the only time I've ever talked to him. He came to her funeral services, of course, but I didn't speak with him. Anyway, like I said, he had called to tell me she had tried to hit him a couple of times. She never actually hit him, but he said that she raised her hand like she was going to."

Tommy asked, "Why would he call you? That doesn't make sense that her boyfriend would call you, being her husband, if he was having problems with your wife."

"Actually, I asked him that same question. He said he was very worried about her and he'd never seen that side of her before. Bernie admitted that they'd been friends for a few years at that point, although he referred to them as friends, without alluding to a romantic relationship. He just wanted to let me know she was having emotional problems because he cared about her that much. You can ask him yourself, Tommy. He owns the Lehrman and Sons jewelry store in Gaithersburg. Feel free to give him a call.

"There's just one more thing. I've already said that Loretta never hit the kids, but there was one day that she tried. Steven was about four years old, maybe five. He was always such a happy little guy and enjoyed being the big brother to Danny."

Carter smiled at the memory. "I don't think Margaret had even been born yet. One day, he was being a brat, which was actually pretty rare for Steven. I don't even remember why he acted that way, but at any rate, he got mouthy with Loretta and was giving her some back-talk. She raised her hand as if she was going to smack him. I grabbed her wrist, and I stopped her. I told her, if she ever laid a hand on him, I would take Steven and Danny and get the hell out of there. She knew I meant it, too. Hitting me was one thing, but I would never let her do to the kids what she did to me. As far as I know, she never tried it again.

"Maybe that's why I let her take it out on me. I would rather she hit me than to have her hit the kids. Lord knows, I might not have been the greatest father or husband in the world, but I tried. I worked hard, and I gave them everything they ever wanted. Everything they ever needed. They didn't want for anything.

"I'll admit, I hit her once, too, but then I realized I was doing to her what she was doing to me. That one time was the only time I ever hit her. And even though I cheated on her, I always loved Loretta and I never stopped loving her."

"Yeah, well, you sure have a funny way of showing it, Carter." Quietly, Tommy returned the phone to the cradle, gave Carter one last look, and left. It would be the only time he ever visited Carter in prison.

The next day, Carter was shackled at his wrists and ankles and loaded into a transport van. He was driven fifty miles away, to the prison where he would spend the rest of his days. He was born into money, had everything he ever wanted, and took all of it for granted. The privileged life of tailored suits and gourmet meals was gone. For the rest of his life, he would be in orange prison clothes and eating institutional food off of paper trays. The one thing he would have is plenty of time to think about the life he took and his own lost life.

About the Author

LeeAnne James grew up in central New York and received her college degree in Journalism. She is the author of *Murder at Gatewood*, a 2019 Central New York Book Awards Fiction finalist, and *Bunny Byrd, Amateur Detective*, a Kindle Vella book. When she's not working as an administrative clerk for the local police department, she loves to read and, of course, write. Her hobbies include cooking, baking, watching movies and enjoying time with her family and friends. She lives in central New York with her husband, son, rescue dog, rescue parakeets and goldfish.

Note From the Author

Word-of-mouth is crucial for any author to succeed. If you enjoyed *Justice for Loretta*, please leave a review online—anywhere you are able. Even if it's just a sentence or two. It would make all the difference and would be very much appreciated.

Thanks!
LeeAnne James

We hope you enjoyed reading this title from:

BLACK ❀ ROSE
writing™

www.blackrosewriting.com

Subscribe to our mailing list—*The Rosevine*—and receive **FREE** books, daily deals, and stay current with news about upcoming releases and our hottest authors.

Scan the QR code below to sign up.

Already a subscriber? Please accept a sincere thank you for being a fan of Black Rose Writing authors.

View other Black Rose Writing titles at www.blackrosewriting.com/books and use promo code **PRINT** to receive a **20% discount** when purchasing.

CPSIA information can be obtained
at www.ICGtesting.com
Printed in the USA
BVHW071107190422
634465BV00004B/13

9 781684 339976